FRANCIS CARSAC

THE CITY AMONG THE STARS

Translated by
Judith Sullivan and M. Schiff

This is a **FLAME TREE PRESS** book

Text copyright © 2020 Francis Carsac
Translation copyright © 2020 Judith Sullivan and M. Schiff

FLAME TREE PRESS
6 Melbray Mews, London, SW6 3NS, UK
flametreepress.com

Distribution and warehouse:
Baker & Taylor Publisher Services (BTPS)
30 Amberwood Parkway, Ashland, OH 44805
btpubservices.com

Thanks to the Flame Tree Press team, including:
Taylor Bentley, Frances Bodiam, Federica Ciaravella, Don D'Auria,
Chris Herbert, Josie Karani, Molly Rosevear, Mike Spender,
Cat Taylor, Maria Tissot, Nick Wells, Gillian Whitaker.

The cover is created by Flame Tree Studio with
thanks to Nik Keevil and Shutterstock.com.
The font families used are Avenir and Bembo.

Flame Tree Press is an imprint of Flame Tree Publishing Ltd
flametreepublishing.com

A copy of the CIP data for this book is available from the British Library
and the Library of Congress.

HB ISBN: 978-1-78758-424-2
PB ISBN: 978-1-78758-422-8
ebook ISBN: 978-1-78758-425-9

Printed and bound in Great Britain by Clays Ltd, Elcograf S.p.A.

FRANCIS CARSAC

THE CITY AMONG THE STARS

Translated by
Judith Sullivan and M. Schiff

FLAME TREE PRESS
London & New York

PART ONE

CHAPTER ONE

Sabotage

Tankar plunged, spiraling through space among the stars. Around, above and under him was an infinite array of impassive, unreachable stars. He turned and watched the Milky Way whoosh by like ice on fire. Each rotation of his body brought a glimpse of a gas cloud that was all that remained of his scout ship.

The maneuvers he learned at the Cadet Academy helped him control the speed of each turn. Slowly, the galaxy's bank of light appeared to rock back and forth; he was just like a toy top nearing the end of its gyration. Billions of kilometers from any life form – human or otherwise – Tankar Holroy was terrifyingly alone. His heart clutched in despair, not from fear of imminent death, but from the certainty that he'd failed in his mission. He would never deliver his message to the Admiral of the 7th Fleet on Formalhaut IV. His failure meant the rebels would win and the Empire....

His short-term, immediate fate wasn't his primary concern. Fury at the debacle roiled inside him, his anger more bitter because sabotage, rather than another soldier's wits, was to blame. He wasn't concerned by the thought of dying. After all, he'd put his life on the line the day he pledged his oath to the Emperor.

2 • FRANCIS CARSAC

From that day on, his life had not been his own, and every breath came at the pleasure of the Emperor.

The urgency of his mission meant Tankar had not had time to check the hypertrons. Who would have suspected sabotage on a starship belonging to the Emperor's personal security detail? The rot of treason had spread to whoever had created a death chamber on Tankar's ship.

He had no way of sending any message home. Hyperspace communication was in its infancy, and anything in use travelled at 15 light-years, max. No one had yet found a way to increase payload. The devices guzzled power and were only outfitted on massive cruisers, none of which Fleet 7 had yet.

He thought of the entitled scientists, experts burrowed in their labs. They were without loyalty. Seven had been executed for treason the day before Tankar set off on his mission. This time, the rebellion had been carefully plotted and given time to mature. Not like the impromptu uprisings that had overthrown Emperors Ktius IV and Ktius V and even the great Antheor III. Privately, Tankar had contempt for the current Emperor Ktius, a weak man who would have walked back all the recent reforms had it not been for the opposition of the Stellar Guard.

The morning the uprising reached his base, the shuddering barracks woke Tankar even before the deafening blast of the explosion shattered the air. He stared open-mouthed at the swirling column of fire where the Kileor arsenal once stood. He dressed like a shot to the sorrowful sound of shrieking alarms, and, five minutes later, he was standing at his place near the gangway to the starship. Tablet in hand, he scribbled down the name of the last man to board. And then, for the next two months, he and his men struggled against an enemy that constantly eluded capture. An enemy that refused hand-to-hand combat, that struck from behind and whose terrifying rebel starships always outpaced the

Stellar Guard's swiftest cruisers. Tankar fought on Mars, Venus, Earth, and he had been part of the raid on Abel, the third Proxima Centauri planet. The revolution stopped there.

Earth territories that were once Western Europe and North America had fallen. The rebels also claimed broad swathes of Asia, half of Mars, both Venusian poles, and every satellite belonging to both Jupiter and Saturn. Slowly, inexorably, Guard forces beat their retreat and inevitably left the capital city Imperia at risk. The Emperor at last reluctantly called on the External Great Fleet and its squadron not far from Fomalhaut. One, two, ten messengers were dispatched. None got through, and so the Admiral called on Tankar.

For five years running, Tankar won the Great Stellar Race from Earth to Rigel III and back. He had earned his first trophy as a cadet. If anyone could break through rebel lines and reach the 7th Fleet, he was the man. He had been given a sealed copy of the message and the fastest scout ship in the flotilla. He set off early one morning in the haze of a nasty chemical bomb and entered hyperspace just above the atmosphere. He did not mind taking the mission on solo. Most Stellar Guards lived ascetic, almost monastic lives.

No one seemed to be tailing him until an alarm shattered Tankar awake on the third day. The hyper radar screen was clean, but a quick check of the display board got his attention. The second hypertron was out of synch, and he needed to reduce speed, enter normal space and recalibrate. Guard training included advance hyperspace theory and Hytron practice. He knew he was up to the job. But mistakes come in pairs. After Tankar made the fix and was poised to leave his screens tucked as per regulation, a tiny asteroid sliced through his antennae. If he waited to get to Fomalhaut IV, it might result in missed signals. And the rule was to proceed only when any and all repairs were complete. 'A good officer never returns with a faulty starship he could have repaired himself.' So he put on his suit and walked out onto the hull.

Afterward – well, there had been one minor explosion, most likely chemical – he hovered in space far from the scout ship, which did not really matter as his chip implant would have allowed him to return. It was standard operating procedure to destroy after desertion. There was a tiny bomb tucked in the middle of three Hytrons that could destroy the central support mechanism and cause the hyperspatial axes to converge. Blasting wide open the gates of hell.

Tankar had about 10 minutes to rocket to safety. His poorly set jet-pack sent him wobbling away from the ship before the brilliant light of the explosion reached him. Three tons of matter was trying to occupy the exact same space at the same time. Ultradense rays shot down, and Tankar could only hope that his suit and the vessel debris were enough to shield him, although it did not matter; he would be a dead man soon enough.

Now he was nose-diving through the stars. No way to measure speed. The gas cloud did not help as he had no idea how fast it had been moving.

He could spend eternity tumbling through space, a shriveled mummy locked in his spacesuit. Or he could attract the gravity field of a nearby star and end up pulverized. In any event, he would perish without delivering the message to the 7th Fleet. Death was meaningless. People died from wounds, explosions, radiation, accidents or old age. He was 24 and strong. And yet, he would die soon. The odds against being rescued were huge but not impossible. Captain Ramsay was scooped up by a nearby ship exiting hyperspace after 16 hours adrift. Tankar knew his chances weren't as good as the captain's.

I'm going to die, he thought. It did not scare him. The thought fascinated him. He had seen so many people die in so many different ways. Comrades standing beside him on a starship gangway. Enemies found on debarkation calcified and shredded.

There was one night when he was guarding the palace basement and had seen the interrogation of Alton, the physicist, tried as a traitor. Tankar shook his head in an attempt to forget the memory of that death. He still had a grudge against the Admiral for including him with the three cadets standing guard that night. It was not as if the Empire did not have enough executioners and yes-men.

A methodical man, trained in space and its danger, Tankar quickly inventoried his resources. Enough air for 24 hours, 10 days' supply of easy-to-digest nutritional concentrate and electrical charge to last a month.

"So I'll suffocate," he muttered to himself. "Maybe at the end, I'll shut down the power and freeze rather than rot in the suit. Or just unscrew my helmet." No, that would be suicide, absolutely banned by the Guard's code of honor. Officers fight until the end.

Out of habit he made a distress radio call. Signal reach was minimal and he was pretty sure no friendly starship was wandering in this vector. As to enemies, they were too few and far between to be found this far from a planet.

There was no reply to his call. He put it on automatic SOS system, then tuned in to the imperial channel. He could hear nothing more than the usual static, the thrumming of the nebulae. Nothing else but the whistling of air pockets. He waited. He was moving in slow motion now and could have stopped rotating. He did not mind so much; in fact, movement gave him a panoramic view. He checked his digital timepiece and was stunned to see he'd only been gyrating for one small hour. Sixty short minutes. Another 23 units of time and he would be dead or dying. His breathing was growing shallower, his ears were buzzing, and his mouth opened in a vain search for more air. He hoped he had earned a place in the heavens reserved for true warriors.

Tankar had never been a student of metaphysics; few members of the Guard were. 'Obey the Chief and your Emperor, follow orders, fight with courage, remain loyal to the end and you will have nothing to fear.' He had been such a man but, in this cold moment of reckoning, doubt niggled at him.

The commoner religion was different; in their code, warrior virtues alone did not grant redemption. One also had to love one's neighbor and never commit murder. Tankar failed to see how people reconciled this final commandment with blood-soaked rebellion. The Empire approved the code of nonviolence for commoners, but not for the Guards. 'Thou shalt not kill!' And yet, he remembered the gruesome sight of police crucified outside the temple. The texts of the religious also read, 'Live by the sword, die by the sword.'

How did you establish and maintain the stability of the Empire without bloodshed? And if the Supreme Power was the same power invoked by the priests, how could anyone take issue with Tankar for being who he was? How could he be any different? He had been commandeered and groomed from birth to enter the ranks of the Guards. He had little recollection of his parents. His mother might have been blond with very long hair. His father was just a gigantic, shadowy silhouette.

From the time of his admission into the Academy he had only ever lived with other cadets, and later with the Guards. He spent his time in study, physical training and never-ending maneuvers. At first, his maneuvers were on Earth; then they took place in space and on some hellhole planets. For R&R the Guards visited Eugenics Centers where they were presented with commoner girls. They were all forbidden from talking to the terrified, drugged and hate-filled women. Early on, Tankar looked forward to these evenings. But over time he began to feel revulsion, sensing the men were as debased by the activity as the girls. He still remembered his friend Hekor's last words, "How long is the Empire going to treat us like breeding stallions?"

Tankar had not seen Hekor since the Center. That same day, Hekor was transferred to march duty where he died for the glory of the Emperor. He would have died anyway in some skirmish or other with the H'rons or the Tulms or some other non-human enemy.

Tankar's readout told him he had another five hours of air. He understood he was growing dizzy and disoriented. His thoughts circled through long-buried images in his mind: his fury at age 11 when a bigger cadet beat him up and he had cried bitter tears: not because of the pain, but because real warriors do not cry. The spring day when he smiled at a young commoner woman who sneered back at him. The corpse of a dog in the doorway of a derelict house....

He was in free fall now, his oxygen tank whistling. He was overwhelmed by his failure. Could his failure be the final end of the Empire? He should have checked the Hytrons, dammit, all good officers did. But then again, he'd been ordered to leave on the spot. He did not have time.

No, he could not have prevented the sabotage.

The air inside his suit was heavy and the sound of his busted valve was growing faint. After some quick math, Tankar realized that within an hour he would be finished. And so, he waited. After a time, the buzzing in his ears returned. The static sound briefly intensified then faded away. He thought he saw something very bright zipping between two faraway stars. He stared stupidly at the fast-growing point of light, now turning into an oval shape as it drew closer.

Finally, almost of its own will, his training kicked in and he saw a ship; no make or model he recognized. It seemed huge. It could not be part of the Empire's fleet. Maybe it belonged to rebels or some alien race. Not that it mattered. The worst outcome would be his murder as soon as he boarded. But, should he be taken prisoner, he might someday escape and return to the Guards where he belonged. With the little bit of strength remaining to him, Tankar launched the distress-mode apparatus and heard his own SOS piped across all bands.

Red rockets burst across a blackened sky and Tankar plunged headfirst into the night.

CHAPTER TWO

The People of the Stars

Tankar blinked and woke up to find himself staring at a brilliant white ceiling. Turning his head, he saw stark, unadorned white walls and a small metal table, all of which looked exactly like those found in an officers' infirmary on board any of the Empire's starcruisers. But he wasn't on board a cruiser. The bed he lay on was softer than any he had ever known, and the thin blanket that covered him was too luxurious for a lieutenant in the Emperor's Stellar Guard.

He found an alarm behind him on the head of the bed and rang it: the solid wall across from him slid open and a man of average height, with dark skin and curly black hair, entered the room.

"Oh, good. You're awake. The Teknor will see you now."

Brusquely the man pulled off the opulent cover without another word and pointed to a set of clothes resembling his own draped across the only chair in the room. Tankar got up, changed into the short tunic and harem pants, and joined the man waiting outside on a vast gangway that extended to the left and to the right as far as Tankar could see. He and his guide walked quickly for a long while. Tankar didn't get tired, realizing that it was because the gravitational pull within the spaceship was far weaker than that on Earth. The two men slid down an anti-grav shaft, which impressed Tankar – a device like that on Earth could only be found in the Emperor's palace.

They landed on a much wider moving walkway which allowed them to proceed even more swiftly and effortlessly. "Just how big is this spaceship?" Tankar asked.

"About five kilometers," his guide said, slowing and turning to him.

Tankar stopped in his tracks, but the moving walkway kept moving him forward. *Five kilometers?* he thought. Impossible! How many millions of tons did it weigh? The largest imperial cruiser measured only four hundred meters. He calculated that he and his guide walked the first gangway for about 10 minutes and now the moving walkway was speeding them along faster in the same direction. Tankar silently thanked the powers of the Supreme Being that this monstrous vessel was controlled by humans.

They passed many other people along the way: some tall, others short; some blond, others dark-haired. All were well-built, young and healthy. The personal style of each individual varied widely from elegantly complex to starkly simple. Some wore very little, including one young woman who was dressed in nothing but a loincloth. Tankar stared quickly then looked away. In the Empire, only a slave would expose herself like that, and a lieutenant in the Emperor's Stellar Guard would never ogle a slave.

Finally, after going across three walkways, the two men reached their destination, and Tankar crossed the threshold of an open door into an enormous room as his nameless guard vanished. Bitterly, Tankar remembered the tiny, cluttered space of his own command post aboard his destroyer. He surveyed the vast interior and saw that three of the walls were lined with shelves crammed with audio and bound books. On the fourth wall was a split screen displaying six panels. A large table carved from precious wood and covered in gilt sat in the center of the room. The floor was spread with rugs and furs. The Supreme Admiral's post was a dump compared to this space, Tankar thought with a grimace.

A man no more than 40 years old sat across from Tankar, staring at him, elbows on the polished table. Tankar stared back. The man was very tall, at least as tall as himself, with brown crew-cut hair, thick eyebrows shadowing piercing black eyes, an aquiline nose and thin lips set in a bemused smile. His tan sleeveless tunic revealed powerful sunburned shoulders. Instinctively, Tankar stood at attention and saluted the man.

"At ease!" he barked. Tankar relaxed.

"So you're an emissary from Earth." The man spoke fluent interspatial. "Being in such a remote part of the galaxy, we haven't seen one of you guys in a long time. You're lucky, young man, that I tune in to planetary transmissions for the fun of it. I heard your SOS and alerted the people on watch who saw your rockets and retrieved you."

Tankar watched as the man perused some papers on the desk in front of him and realized they were the contents of his portfolio that contained the sealed envelope with the directive to the 7th Fleet. A flash of anger crossed his face, followed by a blush of humiliation. His failure was now complete. Not only would the orders not reach their intended readers, but they'd likely fallen into enemy hands. Only a ritual public suicide could erase such a failure of duty. Unless....

The man rifled through the portfolio, pulled out an ID and read the information aloud: "Holroy, Tankar. Born May 12th in Empire year 1800 in Nyark, Earth. Rank: Lieutenant in the Stellar Guard. 3rd Destroy Corp." The man looked up. "How old are you?"

"It's easy to figure out...." Tankar began.

"Do you really think we count in imperial years? If I wanted to, I could check a history book, but if you expect me to know all of the planetary eras off the top of your head you have another think coming...." His face wrinkled in contempt.

"I'm 24," Tankar answered.

"Twenty-four Earth years. You're a very young man. What were you doing in space? Where did you come from and where were you going?"

"My starship was sabotaged. Hypertron convergence. I left from Earth, but I'm not allowed to state my destination."

"War?"

"No. Rebellion."

"And your mission was to deliver this message?"

The Teknor shoved the envelope toward Tankar. "Take it back. This doesn't interest us. I haven't looked at it. Planetary problems don't concern us unless there's a risk to us of hostilities."

"Planetaries?" Tankar did not understand the term.

"Anyone who lives on a planet surface, human or not."

"Don't you live on a planet?"

"We are the people of the stars," the Teknor explained. "Nomads. We trade with planetaries, sometimes we land on their worlds to hunt, to replenish supplies, or for fun. But space is our domain. We were all born here, or most of us in any event. But you'll have plenty of time to discover all of this since you'll be with us for a time – maybe even forever."

"But my mission...."

"Forget about it," the Teknor interrupted. "As I said, planetary matters don't interest us. One day you may be allowed to set foot on a planet on which we land and stay there. Unlike most of my compatriots, I'm keen to know more about humanity. Call it sociological, cultural, or historical interest." He paused to study Tankar further. "So tell me, what's the current political situation in this sector? As a *Tilsin* Teknor it's important for me to know."

Tankar remained silent.

"You're at war," the Teknor continued, "and so long as we have nothing to fear from your forces, I have no desire to get caught up in any fighting. Speak freely. Whoever your enemies might be, we have nothing in common with them."

Tankar hesitated.

The Teknor sighed. "If, out of some misguided loyalty, you don't wish to answer our questions, we have ways to force your hand. Our means are not cruel or harmful. A few minutes under the psychoscope and we'll find out everything we want to know."

Tankar swallowed hard. Among the Stellar Guards rumors abounded of a political-police device that could read a man's thoughts without his knowledge or permission. "So be it," he relented. "You're on the outskirts of the Empire. When I left, rebellion had spread throughout the Solar System and, aside from Alpha Centauri, we've had no news from outside planets."

"You don't have hyperspatial com devices?" the Teknor asked quickly. "Hmm, just as I suspected. A pity. So, it would seem Earth is the center of an empire, as it was in the past? How is it structured?"

"The Emperor is at the top," Tankar explained, "followed by his prime minister, then the Great Council. The noble class, then the knights, merchants, technicians and, lastly, the commoners."

"Hereditary nobility?"

"Is there any other kind?" Tankar asked with surprise.

"It's better for the state when there are other kinds. Where did you rank within the system?"

"Knight class. Lieutenant in the Stellar Guard."

"All right. Thank you." The Teknor stood up. "Now I must attend to several highly pressing matters. In return for our saving you, I'm asking you to draft a report on the makeup of the Empire. Please include details on military infrastructure, and please be thorough." After seeing the look on Tankar's face, he continued, "This is not treasonous. Your empire isn't threatening us, and, to be honest, we're not that interested. Remember: whatever happens, we have ways of finding out what we need to know."

"What will my status be on board?"

"The same as any other planetary who's crossed our path. You may not go through any doors with a barred red circle, but, apart from that, you're free to go where you will. We'll provide you with lodging and sufficient funds for clothing and food. My advice? Get yourself as soon as possible to the university library and read Mokor's *History of Interstellar Civilization*. Like most of our books, it's in interspatial. This should help you adapt and avoid any faux pas." With a final thin-lipped smile, the Teknor concluded, "Our society is far different from your own."

"What should I call you?" Tankar asked.

"I am Tan Ekator, a *Tilsin* Teknor."

"And if I refuse to comply?"

"As I said, we have our ways, which we only use as a last resort. We loathe the whole idea of intruding on a human conscience. Go to Compartment 63, 19th Street, Bridge 7 in Sector 1. Someone there will look after you. Goodbye, Holroy."

Tankar reverted to military protocol and saluted the Teknor before turning on his heel. In a mirror he caught a reflection of the smiling Teknor. Mildly hurt that he appeared to be a source of amusement to the man in charge, Tankar left the room to find his guide waiting on the gangway.

"Follow me," the man directed.

The next room was reassuring because it reminded Tankar of the supervisor's office at the barracks. Twenty-odd men and one woman worked away behind low tables. *Secretaries*, he thought. Obviously a starship as big as this one would require volumes of administrative personnel.

One of the bureaucrats called him over. "Holroy, Tankar? Here's your card with all the information you might need. You were an officer? We might be able to find a job for you.

Meanwhile, you have no definitive position or responsibility. I remind you that you may not enter any compartment with a barred red circle on the door. The consequence for that action leads to one punishment: space!"

"Where can I find the university library?" Tankar asked.

The scribe looked at Tankar in a combination of amazement and dismay. "What are you planning to do there?" he demanded.

"Your commander advised me to read the history of this place."

"Ummm, just a minute." The scribe picked up a phone, spoke a few words, then listened to an answer that seemed to surprise and displease him. "Odd, that…this is the first time…hey, Killian! Find another card, a Model-A for this guy."

"Model-A? For a planetary?"

"Tan Ekator's order. I checked."

A few minutes later, Tankar was handed a new pass. "Here's your Model-A card and a map of the *Tilsin*," the scribe explained. "The ban against entering doors with red barred circles remains in effect, but you may go anywhere else." In an undertone he muttered, "A Model-A card for a planetary? What's next?"

Tankar left the office and returned to the gangway, but his guide had disappeared. He was on his own, left to his own devices, so he took a seat on a bench and looked over his card and checked out the map. On one side, the writing was in a foreign language; on the other, the lettering was in interspatial. The document assigned him an apartment: Cell 189, 21st Street, Bridge 10, Sector 3, and a 'nonmandatory' cafeteria: Room 19, 17th Street, Bridge 8, Sector 3. He also was given funds amounting to 152 stellars per month, however much that might be, however much that might buy.

The map was intricate and complex, not surprising on a starship five kilometers in length! The vessel boasted 50 bridges divided into four sectors numbered one to four clockwise with one in front on the left. In some areas, there were places described as gardens or parks. In the areas between the bridges, there were concentric gangways, and, between them, a system of either radial or parallel streets that cut through the blocks.

Tankar pinpointed his location without much difficulty. He had memorized the numbers the Teknor had rattled off. He had no idea of the time, but he was famished, so, map in hand, he set off to find the cafeteria. He got lost almost immediately.

He used the anti-grav shaft but missed Bridge 8 and landed on Bridge 11 at an intersection. Annoyed with himself, he went upstairs, failed to get his bearings, and knew he really was lost. All the doors around him were closed, and he saw no passersby until, finally, he saw a young woman, a tall and slender brunette with dark skin. Tankar approached her.

"Excuse me. Can you tell me where to go? I'm lost." He spoke in interspatial.

She gave him a strange look. "Are you a planetary?"

"Yes." He nodded. "I was picked up a short time ago."

"Where do you need to go?"

"To the cafeteria I was assigned, if it's open for service."

"Service?" the young woman asked in surprise. "You mean, on your planet you can only eat at specific times?"

"Indeed," Tankar replied. When he saw her furrow her brow, he added, "They aren't absolutes. There's some wiggle room, at least for civilians."

"I see." Clearly, she did not. "Do you have money?"

"My card tells me my stipend is 152 stellars per month. Is that a lot? How long are your months?"

"It seems nobody's told you anything," the young woman sighed. "A planetary! Well, one month corresponds to 30 days of 24 hours duration. 152 stellars is a respectable sum, about what I get. So you have a Model-A card?"

"Yes."

"Strange for a planetary. Usually, you only get a B-card and 92 stellars." The young woman looked Tankar up and down. "You're one lucky fellow. First order of business: go to the bank and get your money. Do you know anything about our currency?" She did not wait for a response. "No, of course not. A stellar represents 10 planars and those are 10 satellars each. A meal usually costs 30 satellars to about one stellar."

"And where will I find a bank?" Tankar asked.

"Hall 5, along this street. Come with me."

In the bank, Tankar could tell that the tellers were taken aback by his Model-A card, but at least they did not comment. A few moments later, he was on the street with a wallet full of strange bills. He followed the young woman, who led him to a large dining room with almost no diners. "Here you go," she announced.

Tankar reached out to take her arm. "Please stay!"

"Why would I do that?" she asked.

"I have so many things to ask you. Would you please join me for lunch?"

The young woman stepped away with a look of revulsion on her face. "Kindness has its limits!" Pride wounded, Tankar watched in silence as she walked away.

CHAPTER THREE

The City in Space

The cafeteria was standard, just like every cafeteria he had ever visited before on Earth or on another planet. The almost military layout of the long tables, most of them empty, was familiar. The walls were decorated with horizontal pictures of planets Tankar did not recognize. A long counter was placed at the far end of the room spread with food selections in glass cages and attended by three servers. The comfort and familiarity of the layout gave Tankar the confidence to approach and pick up a tray.

"New guy, which city?" asked a smiling waiter.

"Imperia."

"Never heard of it. Must've been built after the most recent assembly." The waiter persisted. "Which clan? I would've thought you were a Finn. No? Sveri? Russki? Norwegian? Ah, I have it!" he exclaimed. "You must be an Angle or a Usian."

"No," Tankar replied. "I'm from Earth."

The waiter's friendliness evaporated as his face shut down. "A planetary. Then you don't belong here. There's a canteen just for Model-B cards."

"But I have a Model-A card!" Tankar handed it over and said, "Look!"

The waiter squinted at it in disbelief, then handed it back. "Guess it's true. So planetaries speak interspatial these days?"

"Speak it?" Tankar asked incredulously. "We invented the language during the reign of Kilos II the Glorious!"

The man's face turned to stone, and the nearest of his colleagues walked over. "Kilos the Glorious? Ha! More like Kilos the dog, the murderer!"

"How dare you insult the founder of the Empire?" Tankar demanded.

"Your empire is a long ways away, maggot. The sooner you forget it, the better off you'll be."

The third waiter interrupted. "Leave him be, Jorg. He doesn't know anything. Planetaries are all like that in the beginning. They're so arrogant it doesn't matter if they've come from the Earth Empire or the Confederation or a free planet." He addressed Tankar, "Listen up. You wanna eat? Choose, pay, eat, and then F off!"

Tanker held back. After all, he owed his life to these people, even though they saw him as a refugee. He would have to be patient, do his best to gain an understanding of this new world, and try to adapt. He would have to wait things out.

As a man of frugal tastes – gourmandizing was discouraged among the Guard – he looked at the food and randomly chose a slice of grilled meat, a green jelly, an oddly shaped piece of fruit, paid his 40 satellars and sat down at an empty table. The food was vastly superior to anything he had eaten before. At the table next to him two young men and a young woman were finishing their meal. The men were dressed soberly in short tight tunics cinched at the waist. The woman, a pretty brunette with coppery highlights in her hair, wore a longer, bright red tunic.

Her voice was loud, as if she did not care who heard her. "Rumor has it that Tan Ekator gave this scumbag a Model-A card. Just wait and see what happens after the Great Council meets on this!"

One of the men shrugged and replied, "He has the right to do it, Orena. Nothing in the charter says he can't. All you can do is vote against him, if you're still on the *Tilsin* two years from now."

"The right?" the woman queried. "The right? My ass! That's all you ever say, Ollemi. Our Teknor insults us, and all you can say is he has the right? You disgust me, and the same goes for you, Daras!" She directed the last comment at the other man sharing her table. Then she turned toward Tankar. "What do you think, brother? Do you think that anywhere other than on this stinkhole, Stellarans would let such an outrageous step go unpunished?"

Tankar did not speak at once, torn between embarrassment and fury at being disrespected. The woman prodded him again. "Where are you from? I've never seen you before...did you just get off the boat?"

He remained mute.

"So have the Mpfifis got your tongue? Or don't you have an opinion?"

Tankar shrugged and stood up. He knew that it would serve no purpose to engage in a quarrel that did not concern him, even though it was expressly about him. The woman, Orena, leaped up and stood right in front of him, her face flushing red with fury. "You're not going to sidestep this one so easily! When I ask a question, I expect a reply."

Ollemi intervened. "Orena, that's enough. Stellaran law...."

She turned her head to glare at her friend. "Oh, Rktel to the law. You quote it so often you forget the spirit of the thing!"

Tankar gently tried to push his way past her. In a second, she slapped him across the cheek. Until the slap, he had been patient in spite of the woman's humiliating slander, but the slap had him seeing red, more from rage than pain. His left hand reached for his missing fulgurator while instinctively he struck back with his right.

The woman first rolled onto the table and then onto the floor as plastic plates and cups rained down on her head. Tankar stood, ready for a fight, expecting the two men to attack.

"Are you completely insane, brother? You know a man doesn't hit a woman," reminded Ollemi.

"But she...."

"Orena is a piece of work, I grant you that. But the law is the law, and you know she will expect her due."

"Her due?" Tankar asked, having no idea what that meant.

"Your customs might be different from ours. Here, we leave you two in the Great Park. She'll have 10 bullets to your one, and you'll have one arm tied behind your back."

Another man broke into the circle of rubberneckers who now surrounded them and stood face-to-face with Tankar. "Enough already, you piece of work. Get out of here, now!"

The circle closed in, and one voice after another spoke up. "A planetary?"

"Yeah. That's the guy who got the Model-A card."

"Kick him into space!"

"No! Send him to the experiment cages!"

"Straight to the converter, I say!"

"Let Orena claim her due; she never misses."

"Yeah. She should aim right for his guts!"

A head poked out from between the men's legs. The head had short, tousled coppery hair, a quickly blackening eye and a bloody nose. "You move fast, planetary," Orena muttered. "Leave him alone, guys. I insulted him without knowing he was there, and I got what I deserved," she admitted. "At least he has the balls to act on his instincts!" She made a face and spat blood. "But, man, you hit too hard. In the end, I probably won't claim my due. Nope. It'd give these idiots too much pleasure. They'd enjoy our killing each other without having the balls to join in." She stood up. "Come with me!"

Orena took Tankar's arm and pulled him toward her. "Come

on! I want to talk privately." She led him to a small park where she sat him next to her on a bench.

"This'll teach me to look around before I open my big mouth," she said dreamily. "But I have questions for you, and the first is: why did the Teknor give you a Model-A card?"

"The Teknor?"

"Tan Ekator."

"Oh."

"He's only a technician, hence the name. At least that's the case in principle. For a city-state to work, someone has to direct and coordinate, but that's where his job ends."

Tankar shook his head. "I don't know about that," he confessed. "I just saw him for a few minutes about two hours ago."

"What did he say?" Orena demanded.

"Nothing that would interest you. He advised me to consult a book by a guy named Mokor at the university library."

Orena sighed. "I'm not surprised. The conservos think Mokor's book is the ultimate. We, the advantists, don't think much of it; it's not objective and gives the Pilgrims too much credit."

"If you keep talking in riddles like that, I think I will have to give Mokor a read," Tankar retorted. "I need to find my way around this place, and the sooner the better!"

"I can help with that," Orena offered. "I took pretty in-depth history lessons. What do you want to know?"

"Everything!"

"That a pretty tall order, don't you think? I can try and summarize the major points. But, be warned: don't be surprised if what I say about the early stuff doesn't correspond to what you learned on Earth." She paused to ask, "What was your line of work?"

"Lieutenant in the Emperor's Stellar Guard."

Orena whistled softly. "I better watch what I say! Let's get started. So, under the reign of Kilos II the assassin...."

"The Glorious!"

"If you keep interrupting...." she warned. "So...under the reign of the glorious assassin Kilos II, life became unbearable for every intelligent, freethinking person. Almost immediately after his coronation he issued edicts limiting research, cutting back on the rights of technicians, and setting aside all the important jobs for knights and nobleman. And that was just the beginning. Many universities closed, the professors deported or sent to the mines."

Tankar struggled to understand. "What was their act of treason?"

"You only commit treason if you defy an order you once agreed to carry out," Orena explained. "You do know how the Klutenide dynasty started out, right? By murder and usurpation? Nobody on Earth or in the outlying lands accepted their legitimacy; the people just submitted. But the Emperors secured the allegiance of military and civilian technicians by handing out massive favors. Those were the real traitors, in my book." She paused to stare at Tankar before resuming. "Rebellion was out of the question. Flight was the only option for those who wanted to remain free, and it wasn't easy. Two generations suffered horrors in silence but kept alive the flame of knowledge, stockpiling the right documents. Some of them were found, tortured, and killed."

She shrugged. "Why should I spell out the details? You'll read all about it in the books. Mokor may exaggerate their role in the events, but escape wouldn't have been possible without the help of the Pilgrims."

"The Pilgrims?" Tankar asked.

"At the time of the constitutional Empire under Antheor the 1st, three hundred years before Kilos II, a new religion was founded by Meneon the Prophet, a priest of ancient Christianity, and...."

Tankar interrupted again. "I've heard of Christians. There still are some in the Empire, but only among the commoners."

Orena gave him a look that clearly said: stop interrupting me! "So, as I was saying, Meneon had a revelation. He said that since God allowed humans to conquer space, it must be part of the divine plan. The human race's time on Earth was nothing more than a trial destined to eliminate original sin –" Orena grimaced at Tankar, "– maybe you know what that is, because I have no idea – one day man would find God in some corner of space, and a new era would begin.

"Of course, I'm summarizing and probably leaving things out. Anyway. Meneon quickly spawned disciples. This new religion appealed primarily to astronauts and well-off merchants who must have seen the doctrine as a comfort in their crushing loneliness. While the Menians, his followers, were few in number, they were powerful. The early emperors were not the stupid, bloodthirsty monsters that their descendants would become. They protected worship and gave converts perks and rights, especially the right to arm and fortify their monasteries, as well as the right to offer asylum.

"A few Menian priests joined each interstellar expedition, and most of them were good technicians. But, with the coronation of Kilos II, everything changed. He wouldn't tolerate the independent-mindedness of the monks, or of artists or scientists. Little by little, he sliced away their perks. The monasteries remained powerful, so the succeeding emperors stopped short of direct persecution. That wasn't from lack of desire, as the monks were unflinchingly hostile, in part for moral reasons, but their primary issue was that the starships in circulation belonged either to the Stellar Guard or to the merchant marine, and the monks were forbidden to travel that way.

"And so the monks forged an alliance with the technicians.

The monks would provide refuge in the monasteries and help build clandestine starships; eventually, monks and techs would all leave together to escape the emperors' tyranny and to find a free planet.

"They succeeded, and 432 Earth years ago the exodus took place. 745 starships took flight and transported 131,000 technicians, sages, artists, writers, and free men and women as well as 12,000 Menian laypeople and monks. The Emperor's Stellar Guard was so blindsided that only one starship was damaged."

Tankar cringed at the news the Stellar Guard had failed in its duty. Orena continued the history of the People of the Stars.

"Those men and women, our ancestors, found an unblemished planet near a star from the Swan Constellation. They established themselves and developed their new civilization over the next decade. But just as the first cities began to bloom, imperial starships showed up. After a short battle, my people were again forced to flee. Twenty-five years later, imperial forces showed up once more.

"After that, our ancestors decided to run far away, and, along the way, they found the first city-state floating aimlessly in space. We've never discovered who established it. It wasn't our enemies, the Mpfifis, though they do live and travel on similar craft. The city was intact but abandoned. All the equipment was in working order, but there was no indication as to who might have built it.

"The size of the gangways, of the rooms and doors, did suggest the previous inhabitants were not very different from us except that their lighting systems hinted that their eyes were especially sensitive to purple. We've analyzed traces of radioactive metal and concluded they'd been around for five hundred thousand years."

She turned to Tankar. "If you're interested, you can see the film someday." Then she continued, "The space city was enormous, and we were able to adapt the engines for ourselves.

The weaponry was far better than anything we had known or developed here or in the Empire. I've never seen that first ship," she admitted, "but it's still in service and is called *Encounter*. Many refugees established themselves there, and others followed.

"The initial plan was to use this empty city as a stepping stone to a livable planet as far away as possible because life onboard is so much more comfortable than onboard a standard starship. The seekers struggled to find a livable planet, but, over time, they got used to being nomads. When they did find the hospitable planet, they opted to use it as a base for building more city-states.

"As the population increased, new city-states were built; we have about a hundred in all now. They all meander through the cosmos and around our planet, which we call Avenir. That's where we have our home bases and factories, but we only live there when absolutely necessary. We've been in touch with some intelligent non-human races, and even some human-inhabited planets. Those planets have been luckier than we were, because the Empire knew nothing about them. The Teknor told us in the lunchtime news that the Empire is crumbling as we speak...."

Tankar struggled to comprehend their nomadic way of life. "And you can live this way, without roots?"

"Not only can we, we wouldn't want to live any other way!" exclaimed Orena. "As you may have guessed, we don't like planetaries, people who were born and live on planets. You all hook on to little balls and only leave them for a quick hop into oh-so-scary space. We are royalty; we get to travel whenever and wherever we like, from star to star. Soon we will be able to move from galaxy to galaxy."

"You've visited other galaxies?" Tankar was stunned.

"Why not?"

"But it's so far," he insisted. "Even traveling through hyperspace."

"We don't really care about travel time. We've come a long

way since our ancestors fled Earth, and our city-states are self-sufficient. Those first settlers were highly intelligent, and, in our society, almost everyone works in research in some form or another, even the Pilgrims who hitched a ride. It's been like this for four hundred years. You know, the two city-states that left to explore the Andromeda Nebula have yet to return."

Trying to get his facts straight, Tankar asked, "How is your society structured?"

"This will probably seem as murky to you as understanding your hierarchy would be to us. It might be easier if you understand that all of our ancestors were sages and technicians. They were all humans who simultaneously admired order, efficiency and independence." Orena considered Tankar. "Have you never been part of a scientific team?" she asked, curious.

Tankar recalled a six-month internship he had spent in the technical mastery center. He remembered a stimulating atmosphere that was at once calm and relaxed. And the discipline was as rigorous as in any branch of the Guards.

"So our ancestors were scientists," Orena picked up. "Add to that the dreadful tyranny of several centuries, and you'll see why we Stellarans don't want political bosses and prefer to be overseen by Teknors."

"Isn't it all pretty much the same as Earth?" Tankar asked.

"Oh, no!" Orena cried. "The Teknor's authority is limited to technical matters: how the city-states operate, defense against an attack, general commercial exchanges with planetaries, and, in a way, the overall game plan."

"But who handles internal security?"

"We do, of course, who else?"

"Well…what happens if a mechanic says he doesn't want to work on or repair an assigned motor, for instance?"

"First of all, that never happens, or almost never. The mechanics aren't stupid: if they ignore the motors they'll pay the price too."

"Okay, but what if someone wants a raise or threatens to strike?"

Orena looked puzzled. "He or she can't get a raise. All Stellarans get the same salary."

"Then why were you all so hot and bothered about my Model-A card?" Tankar demanded.

Orena stiffened and her body language became defensive as her voice darkened. "Because planetaries who live off a city-state should never get an A-card."

Tankar paused for a moment, thought, then asked, "If everybody earns the same, how do you reward initiative?"

Orena relaxed and explained. "The salaried work we do is for the greater good of our society and only takes about two hours per day. The rest of the day we can create things, and that can boost our income. For instance, I write fantasy novels set on planets. That's why I studied historical cosmology. Other people sculpt, or paint, or invent, or do research, all kinds of things. They can trade either within the city or with a different city-state or even with planets."

"What about the admin jobs?"

Orena nodded. "Those jobs are considered work for the greater social good of all."

"Do you have soldiers?"

"Yes and no." Orena could see that Tankar did not understand, so she tried to explain. "We have no professional soldiers, but many of us have studied the martial arts. We've had to because of the Mpfifis." Suddenly she understood his reaction. "Oh, I see; you were thinking of enlisting. Sorry, we have no army and, even if we did, as a planetary you wouldn't be allowed to join."

Bitterly he said, "And that's still my worst, my unforgivable sin." He grew melancholy and reflective. "I'm beginning to understand how commoners feel about the nobility, even the Guards. Any child can become a Guard if he is skilled enough. But here, to you and everyone else on this starship, I'll never be anything more than a parasite."

A bit embarrassed, Orena suggested, "Nothing can stop you from doing something creative."

"Creative? I don't think so. I was trained to destroy. Create? On my own? What would I create?" He spat out the last word. "Scientific research could be a noble thing, but scientists in the Empire never exceeded travel beyond 150 light-years, and you guys have visited other galaxies. What chance do I have of discovering something you've not found in four centuries? I'm young, and I'm strong, and the only job I know, the only one I've ever had, is soldiering. You would have done better to leave me adrift in my spacesuit. Everyone would be happier, including me."

Orena stood in front of Tankar trembling in frustration. "Have you planetaries sunk so low you've lost the capacity to adapt? When I first saw you a short time ago fighting us all I thought, 'This is one planetary parasite who acts like a grown man!' Could I have been wrong? Damn guards with their rules about hand-to-hand combat. With so many cowards it's no wonder your Empire is on its last legs." She stood before him, shaking with rage.

"I fought on my own!" he exploded. "I had a goal, and now I have nothing. I failed in my mission and now find myself living on your handouts with no hope of ever becoming a real man again. I have another question: what happens if your city-state is destroyed and all of your friends are gone?"

"I'd go to another city-state and keep moving. Why would this mishmash of steel plates called the *Tilsin* matter to me? I was born on the *Robur* and spent a few years on the *Suomi* and on the *Frank*. I also have lived on the *Uso*, the *Anglic* and the *Nippo*, and

I felt at home on all of them. I loved my companions, and I would have sought revenge if they'd been killed. But good companions can be found anywhere, no? I don't understand your question."

"And I don't get your perspective. Is frequent city-state hopping standard practice with you all?"

"For many of us, yes. At each conjunction, people move around; some come, some go. It's harder for specialists who need to do direct swaps, but there are always volunteers."

"That might make sense for a soldier like me who has no possessions, but for you guys? What about housing? Your stuff?"

"Lodging is always available. As to our possessions, they come with us, or we get new ones."

Tankar paused, deep in thought, then, "I'm afraid I'm going to struggle to adapt to a life here. Have any other planetaries spent time in your city-states?"

"Very few."

"What happened to them?"

"Some assimilated just fine. Others died. And a few became so anxious that they went back to their Earth. My father was one of them." She paused and looked off into the distance. "That's why I hate planetaries so much…and vice-versa."

Surprised, Tankar asked, "Your father was a planetary, and you hate us?"

"What's strange about that?" Orena demanded. "He spent 20 years here, was adopted into our world and then deserted us. He betrayed us."

"Yeah, I know the drill…you can only betray what you've accepted."

"Of course!"

"I accepted the Empire. Should I allow myself to learn how to be part of the world here, will that make me a traitor?"

"It's not the same thing, Tankar! Were you ever given a choice? Could you have done anything else?"

He thought for a moment and said, "No...I guess not. Guards are recruited very young. I was only three when they took me from my family. My father...."

Again, the shadow of his father's phantom figure crossed his mind's eye. But it was a shadow lacking nuance, missing specific, identifying traits.

"I barely remember my parents," he said, feeling suddenly and unexpectedly anxious. "I don't even know their names. My last name, Holroy, is unlikely to be my own, but it's serviceable. My mother...I can't recall...except she was blond...and smiled at me a lot. But what's the point of bringing up the past? I could've run into them on the street and I wouldn't have recognized them. I don't know what class they belonged to. I may have killed them during the spring uprising." Choking back unfamiliar emotions, he admitted, "I don't like rummaging through the past."

"And you call that civilization? You would lay down your life for that?"

"What else would I die for? I don't know anything else...or at least I didn't before I met you." Tankar stood up and began to pace.

"I was taken away from my family at the age of three! What does a toddler know of such things? Nothing. I was a piece of clay to be molded at will. In primary school, I learned to read, write and count, but I wasn't taught like other kids. I was taught an iron discipline from day one, and, in middle school? Long civics lessons."

He recited sarcastically, just like the good schoolboy he had been: "At the top of the Empire is the Emperor who reigns and governs for the collective good. His personage is sacred and none may look him in the eye. He is the embodiment on Earth of the divine. His word is the word of God. Right beneath him are the nobility...."

He paused. "You know, I still believe all of it, or at least most of it. Up until now, any other life would have struck me as crazy and finite. And yet, here you all are, you the descendants of the traitor-scientists. I'm beginning to think you could destroy the Empire, if you wanted to."

He turned back to Orena. "In any event, when I turned 13, I was sent straight to the barracks. Super-technical lessons in math, physics, chemistry, biology were drilled into us. We learned how to maintain our starships, how to survive and do battle in foreign or hostile settings. Awakened at five every morning, in bed at eight thirty no matter the time of year. And boy, were we in good shape! We all could run, jump, climb, swim in freezing-cold or near-boiling water, throw a grenade or a javelin, shoot a rifle or a pistol and handle a fulgurator. We learned to handle cannons in cold so bitter our hands stuck to the steel. Our hands would bleed, but we weren't allowed to dirty our training uniforms.

"Oh! And the discipline," he added. "The inhuman punishments. We were whipped, deprived of food and drink and, worst of all, sleep. I went through all of that, for the great glory of the Empire. And you're trying to convince me it was all for nothing? How could I believe that? I'm a Guard and will be one for the Emp—. Oops, I did it again, didn't I? And don't forget the combat training with and without weapons."

He stared down at his clenched fists and unfurled them. "I can kill a man with these as easily as I could a chicken. Killing is what I do best. Even if you were to take me in, me, I'd never fit in. Too much is different."

"Less than you might think, maybe. There are worse places in the cosmos – say in Mpfifi-space."

"Who are they?"

"The Others. Non-humans. Like us, they live in nomad cities. They attack us, kill us all, and destroy everything. Sometimes we win, but more often...." She listed a litany of vessel names. "*Kanton, Uta, Espana, Dresden, Rio, Paris II, Norge II*. All lost. Once, we arrived at the *Roma* in time to save some survivors. I was on the *Suomi*."

Tankar asked, "*Suomi, Roma, Espana* all sound like Earthly place names to me. Is that right?"

"Yes, you're right. In the past, we borrowed names from the base planet. *Tilsin* is the newest of our space cities, and it was settled by people from other starships: the *Frank*, the *Usa*, the *Suomi* and the *Norge I*."

Tankar checked his digital time display, and cracked a smile. It was still on Earth time. "What's the time here?"

"16:32. We divide time into 24 chunks, just like on the old planet."

"Handy for me." He looked into Orena's eyes. "I really would like to thank you for all the info and, um...." He hesitated, feeling awkward. "I'm so sorry I hit you! My fist struck out automatically, and I failed to restrain it. On Earth, no one, not even one of noble or royal rank, would've spoken to me as you did."

Orena unpocketed a small mirror and looked at her reflection. "Oh, it's no big deal. No broken teeth, which would've meant expensive dentures. My nose is still slightly swollen, but it'll be okay tomorrow. Would you like to take a tour of the city now?"

"I don't want to impose. I have a map...." He picked it up from the bench to show it to her.

"I put in my two hours at the hydroponic grounds this morning. I'm free."

"As somebody who despises planetaries...."

"There are different types of planetaries. The ones I've met to date have little cultural understanding and less backbone. You're not like them. Plus, I find you amusing."

He started to get upset but decided to laugh it off. "So be it. Let's go."

They fell into step as they crossed the park to an unconstructed gangway that they followed to find a six-street star-shaped crossroad.

"Let's take the first on the right. I can't guide you everywhere; I haven't seen it all myself. But once you've gotten an overview at Observation Post 32, you'll have a sense of the general layout."

The street seemed to go on forever, backlit by dreary fluorescent tubes. The sole distinguishing feature on each metal door was its number.

"This is a residential area. Isn't it hideous? Inside, however, the apartments are very different. In the shopping districts, the stores are cheerful. You can buy stuff from many different planets, including Earth."

"What?!" Tankar exclaimed. "How is that even possible?"

"Smugglers from the free worlds beyond the sphere of influence of your Empire sometimes lay over at your outposts."

Tankar recalled overhearing a conversation between two senior officers. The men had spoken of starships so fast that nothing in the Empire could catch them.

He and Orena went down an anti-gravity shaft to another walkway where they hopped a transport wagon to the outer edge of the *Tilsin*. They finally arrived at a door that opened onto a wide railed gangplank.

"Beltway 7," the young woman answered before Tankar could ask the question. "This area is part of the *Tilsin*'s defense system, and it transports both people and materiel over that bridge anywhere on the chassis. The signals are steady, so we can proceed. Never cross if they're flashing," she instructed.

They saw a porch and crossed it to greet the guard in charge.

"Names. Cards?"

"Orena Valoch. Hydroponist and novelist."

"Tankar Holroy." He hesitated before Orena added, "Planetary".

The man raised his eyebrows. Orena explained further. "Model-A card, on the Teknor's orders."

"Fine. Proceed."

"The observation posts are the city-state's eyes, and they are always staffed, but, in peacetime, people can visit."

When they arrived at the actual post, it was a largish room with a gray screen covering an entire wall. Five technicians sat before it comfortably ensconced in ergochairs, backs to the screen.

Orena spoke to the youngest tech, who looked to Tankar to be of Mongolian descent.

"Hi, Pei." She addressed the other men. "Hello, brothers. I'd like you to meet Tankar Holroy of the Earth Empire's Stellar Guard."

"A planetary. Are you out of your mind, Orena?" one of the men demanded.

"Model-A card, Teknor's orders."

"I suppose Tan knows what he's doing. Hey…." Pei stumbled then said, "Mister Holroy."

"The actual title is Lieutenant but it's not important. Rather than discussing rank, I'd really like to know how the observation posts work. Why is the screen dark?"

Pei half smiled. "Have you earthling Guards really found a way to study hyperspace as you fly through it? We'll emerge shortly."

Tankar scanned the room for an empty seat or a guardrail. Transit in and out of hyperspace was tricky enough on a terrestrial starship.

"What do you need?"

"Somewhere to sit or something to hang on to."

"Ha! You guys must still use Cursin hytrons. We dropped those a long time ago. Don't worry, you won't feel anything." Another tech grinned, "If you had half a brain, you'd have guessed. Since you've been aboard the *Tilsin*, we've emerged twice."

"Okay, guys, just shut up!" Orena said. "It's not Holroy's fault that he's from a land of savages. Why don't you show him your screen since we've just emerged? You're some security guys; you didn't even see the emergency light blinking."

Embarrassed, the men turned their attention to the control panel as the screen lit up. The stars teemed, and Tankar cried out in surprise and wonder.

"Is that the galaxy's center?" He recalled his cosmography lessons as a young cadet and the huge mock-up of the Milky Way hanging in the Academy's foyer. In the past, he had often stood there daydreaming in front of the spacescape, contemplating the tiny purple area on the outer edge that marked out the total Empire.

"No. It's a globular heap."

Fascinated, Tankar looked all around. To the right a nebula of gas like a flickering curtain veiled a whole segment of the sky while, on the left, a large opaque scarf appeared looking like an abyss toward which their star city was plunging rapidly.

One of the men stood up and spoke into the phone. "We're approaching a planetary system the Teknor wants to investigate." The man leaned over a device in front of him as Tankar approached to look into another viewer. Shiny bands pulsed on the screen.

"Do you have this in your fleet?"

"Nothing like it. What is it?" Tankar whispered.

"It analyzes unusual weather conditions. Every time an object enters or leaves hyperspace, it captures the Lursac waves and analyzes the movement. Here, have a look."

The top band was rigid. A string of numbers rolled out on the display.

"Distance, 300,000 kilometers. Incline plus 30. Right ascent 122. This might indicate another race or our people; we might never know."

Tankar was about to ask whether there was a way of tracing the thing in hyperspace but thought better of it. Nothing in the mechanism seemed to resemble a tracer.

An alarm bell rang. Pei said, "Ah. We're about to dive back in. This was a short stop. Must not be much of interest in this system."

Orena spoke. "It's 6 p.m, Tankar. I intend to take you to dinner, so we must go. Bye, all!"

"See you this evening, Orena?" Pei asked.

"Not tonight."

Pei's face darkened. "I see."

"We're both free agents, Pei."

After they left, Orena was uncharacteristically silent, leaving Tankar to his own thoughts. They arrived at Orena's flat some time later.

To Tankar, accustomed to monastic Guard cells, Orena's flat was small but lavishly furnished. On Earth, only someone noble or royal would own sofas covered in rare fabric. Have a polished natural-wood table and leather-bound books. Some paintings, mostly planetary landscapes full of light, hung on the walls like open windows. Tankar stopped, compelled by one of a reddish desert almost covered in purple mist where, at a distance, might have been hills.

"Mars?" he asked.

"No, just some random planet."

"Did you paint these?"

"Me? No, of course not."

"So you bought them? The Emperor would give thousands of dollars to own one of those such works."

"It's not likely he'll ever get a chance to see them. They were painted by Pei, you know the young guy we met at the observation post?"

"Right. Yes. Tell me: why did he look so angry when we left? Because I'm a planetary?"

She smiled. "That's part of it. But his main problem is that you'd be having dinner with me instead of him."

"So that's it. You're all an odd bunch."

This time Orena laughed out loud. "You think so? I need to leave you for a bit to get dinner ready."

While he waited, Tankar scanned her bookcase and found that most of the volumes were about history. Several were in interspatial, others in various languages he didn't understand except for one in English and another in French. The English one was *A Brief History of Space* by A. C. Clarke, London 1976. How was that even possible given it was only 1884 in Empire years? The book must be several millennia old, published during the first civilizations before the Great Catastrophe. The other book he noticed was called *Aperçus sur la Colonisation de Mars* [*Perspectives on the Colonization of Mars*] by Jean Vérancourt, dated Paris, 1995. Not much more recent. He thumbed through both volumes and thought of borrowing them. He was intrigued by the revelation that, long before the Empire, men had launched into the cosmos, albeit only within Earth's solar system.

Orena laughed from the kitchen. "Food's on, noble Guard!"

He turned so abruptly he nearly dropped the book. Orena had changed from the red tunic she had been wearing since he met her in the cafeteria and was wearing a long diaphanous dress from material so silky and thin he had never seen anything like it even at the imperial court.

"And this evening's menu," she spoke, oblivious to his embarrassment. "Betelgeuse consommé, roasted lakir from Sarnak, Aldebaran turmak shoot salad, hydroponic fruit and Téléphor-II wine."

Tankar smiled. "That doesn't tell me much. I have no idea what those delicious-sounding foods might taste like."

"The lakir is a small animal. Turnak is a vegetable. As to Téléphor, it's actually a very old human colony, one of the first from before the Empire. I hope you'll enjoy the wine."

"I've never tasted wine. Among the Stellar Guards we drank water or, on especially hard days, liquor."

Delighted, Orena said, "Then it's about time! Come with me."

The table was set with sparkling crystal and silver. He sat across from Orena. "I need to ask you a question, Orena, maybe a stupid one and surely a crass one. But I need to know so I can better come to understand this world. Are you rich? Are you a member of the upper class?"

"How many times do I need to tell you we have no social classes here? Am I wealthy? Well, my books do sell pretty well. But why would you ask that question?"

"These luxurious fabrics, these collectible books, the silver, the crystal."

"Oh, you poor barbarian." She sighed. "Okay. My dress was expensive. The rest is within the reach of anyone with a Model-A card. We have silver forks because they're pretty, crystal glasses because they're as easy to craft as glass ones. The linens in our homes are lovely because the Vélinzi sell them to us in exchange for the weight of the iron they sorely need. That's the secret to commerce, Tankar, not just here on the *Tilsin* or on our other city-states but throughout the Empire too, I'm pretty sure. You bring merchandise to the place where it's in short supply from a place you can get it cheap. As to the paintings? Once again, they were a gift to me from Pei. You know, the comm tech from the observation post. He's also a painter."

"…and your friend."

"If he weren't, he would hardly have given me five of his paintings, would he? He usually sells them for five hundred stellars each."

"The Emperor would pay a hundred times that."

For a moment, Tankar imagined he was back on Earth with 10 or so of the paintings. He could have sold them and been able to afford the initiation fees to join the noble class. And his harsh soldiering life would have been over. His future children would have no fear of hard laws and unfair administrators. He might even reconnect with his family. But no. He shook his head and returned to reality. That couldn't, wouldn't ever happen.

"Aren't you drinking, Tankar? Don't you like the Téléphor wine?" Orena asked.

"Oh, I do. Everything's superb, Orena, it's just that it all feels so unreal. Four days ago, the war minister handed me secret fleet orders. Just yesterday, I tumbled into the void and thought I would die in space. This morning, I woke up fully expecting to be treated like a prisoner of war. I thought I'd spend my days hopelessly rotting in some dreary metallic cell. And tonight, I'm having dinner with a beautiful woman. It seems as though I'm simultaneously a wealthy man and a pariah.

"For the first time in my life I'm free. But I'm stranded in a foreign land that tolerates and nourishes me as if I were some kind of a parasite. And the person serving me this wonderful meal is the woman who routinely shows nothing but contempt for all planetaries as well as being the woman I punched in the face. I don't get it. And I can't feel that I'm absolutely safe, not yet."

Orena listened attentively as Tankar went on.

"There's a game the political police play on Earth. They swear to a prisoner that he's a free man. Then, as he walks out the camp's gate, they execute him by shooting him in the back. There have been legitimately released prisoners who refused to leave until hunger and despair compelled them to risk everything."

Then, abruptly rising from his chair, he asked, "Are you playing a similar game with me? If you are, it's not worthy of you. I'm a soldier, and if I'm to be killed, please deal with me honestly."

"Don't you dare to compare Stellarans to the scum of the Earth, Tankar. We have our shortcomings, vices even. We aren't saints; we're not even Pilgrims. But if there's one thing we would never do, that is lock a man up whose only crime was to be different. You mustn't expect much friendship from the People of the Stars. To most of us, you're planetary vermin, and that's all you'll ever be. Some will try to kill you, but in that case it'll be personal and in-your-face. In our world, assassination merits one punishment only: exile into empty space without a spacesuit." She sighed before adding, "Some day you might assimilate, just as my father did. I hope you'll be able to learn while you're here, as my father did. I hope you'll gain even more from your experience, and that, unlike him, you'll not go back to your Earth."

"Could it be your father is the reason I'm here?" Tankar asked.

"Partly." Orena nodded. "I saw how lonely you were, and I remembered the six long years it took him to adapt. And, as I said, you amuse me." Changing her tone, she added, "Enough of this! Do you like music?"

"Yes. I even play the flute," he admitted, blushing with embarrassment. "Guards are encouraged to undertake any activity that will add spice to cruiser life."

"I've got some excellent recordings of pieces you're unlikely to have heard. They're by composers who predate the spatial era, and they were discovered in old colonies like Téléphor or Germania. Have you heard Beethoven?"

"No."

She slipped a thin magnetic band into a small module. "You'll like this. It's his Concerto no. 5, said to be composed for an emperor. A prehistoric emperor, or almost."

Music flooded the room, and the two of them listened in rapt silence. When it was over, Tankar took his time to emerge from the waking dream created by a man long dead. "That was magnificent, Orena," he said in hushed tones. "Our modern composers can't touch the brilliance of such an old master, save maybe Merlin. But it's getting late. I need to go. I don't even know where my lodgings are!"

"You mean you haven't figured that out yet? The apartment will be empty. You need to buy furnishings. You can't go there now." She smiled mischievously. "But if you agree to stay the night, I can assure you nobody here will take offence...."

CHAPTER FOUR

Alone

Orena was gone in the morning. He dressed quickly and found a note. *Tankar, I'm off to work. See you around, Orena.*

Tankar found the short, impersonal message slightly humiliating. He shrugged. *Other cultures, other customs,* he thought. After a moment, he decided, *I know very little about them, so I can't judge.* It was eight thirty. He was not feeling hungry, so he explored, wandering through the small apartment. Orena's office was in a room he had not yet seen. There he found an unfamiliar processor, and, next to it, piled-up pages of an incomplete manuscript. The top page, in interspatial, would have been a challenge for him to read as the processor used very different symbols from the ones he knew.

So, they haven't managed to directly transcribe human speech. He got the general gist: the complicated story seemed to take place on the planet Kaffir, which he had never heard of and which Orena might well have made up. The hero was in a tight spot between a cliff he could not scale and a troop of kalabin soldiers on drorek-back, whoever or whatever they were.

I'll have to track down Orena's books, he thought, *first because they'll give me insight, but also because they might give me a better sense of this society.* He remembered a conversation he had overheard one night as he stood watch at the palace, as immobile as the pillar behind him. A court ball was taking place inside. Two noblemen had stopped near his post. He recognized the younger man as Bel Caron, a historian and a cousin of the Emperor.

"That's a mistake, my good friend, a serious mistake!" Bel Caron exclaimed. "There's far more truth in novels than you might think, especially if you're hoping to find out about society itself and not just looking for historical fact. Believe me, some of these older works tell us much more about pre-Empire society than history books do. And I don't mean the official history, which is just propaganda for the ignorant commoners."

"Shh." His associate nodded toward Tankar.

The historian turned around. "Oh, him. A Guard. Only two possibilities. Either he's intelligent, and he's been aware for some time, or he's stupid, and he'll have no idea what I'm talking about."

The two men then walked away, chattering as they did.

I must have been stupid, Tankar thought. *I believed the official history books that told us the only thing in space was chaos and non-humans, the latter waiting for the Empire to weaken. With humanity gone, all that would remain would be other independent worlds and massive nomad cities...which are, at least, civilized.*

He placed the page on the top of Orena's manuscript, walked out into the street and let the apartment's magnetic door shut behind him. He found a nearby visitors' center, where he learned that, contrary to what Orena said, his apartment was closer than either of them thought. He had suspected as much. He went to the apartment to find that the layout was identical to Orena's.

His next stop was General Store 17 where he could pick up the requisite furnishings.

He bought a narrow bed, a table, two chairs, some bookcases, and equipment for a mini-kitchen. The whole thing came to a hundred stellars, so he paid half then and there with the rest due in four months. He was given a mandatory communication device for free. He took the rest of the morning to move in and, once finished, went to the canteen where he first met Orena.

The waiter recognized him. "Back so soon, planetary? You were really lucky that Orena didn't claim her due. She's an excellent shot."

"So am I. It's my job."

"You know she's already killed three men?"

Tankar bit back the retort that he had killed several dozen himself and ordered two dishes for lunch.

"Come on, swamp rat; don't look so annoyed. We're not all bad guys on the *Tilsin*. You must have done something special to merit an A-card." The man leaned forward, smiling broadly. "Anyone bothers you, come right to me. I may be able to help."

Tankar froze at this friendly offer from someone he would have considered untouchable back on Earth, but not for long. After all, he did not know this man's status. In this weird civilization, maybe the server was an eminent personage outside of his work hours. "Where?"

"Not here, no. During the day I can be found at the lab on Bridge 7, 12th Street, Room 122. After 7 p.m I can be found at Apartment 57. Both locations are in Sector 3."

"In the lab?"

"I'm a chemist. Just ask for Pol Petersen."

Tankar daydreamed as he ate. Aside from the Teknor and the young woman at the bank, only two people had spoken to him. But they had been friendly, and, in Orena's case, very friendly.

When he finished eating, Tankar set off to explore. The map indicated it would be a quicker tour than he initially thought based on the size of the *Tilsin*. Most of the sectors were laid out symmetrically. From the beginning, one place caught his attention – in each sector, and on three of the bridges, were rooms labeled 'machine rooms'.

He headed for the nearest one and got lost only once before he found it. But then he faced the unpleasant surprise of a barred red circle on the door. "Off limits for me," he muttered. "I should've expected that. Even on our cruisers only the mechanics and officers have access to the machines." Deep in thought, he retraced his steps and quickly realized that anything he might have liked to see lay behind a door with a barred red circle.

But that left the libraries. The university library was dead center of the city bordered by a park on each side. Tankar walked through a mass of shouting children playing just like their Earth counterparts. He entered the library's front hall and saw two doors. The first was labeled *Lending* in interspatial and other languages. The second was labeled *Reading Room*, and he walked in.

He found himself in a small room where a young woman sat behind a desk. Tankar stopped dead in his tracks. Compared to this girl, Orena appeared plain. Even Countess Iria, the woman the soldiers referred to as the Impossible Dream, seemed pale and charmless in comparison. The woman had red hair full of natural copper highlights, huge green eyes, a patrician nose and a slightly wide mouth.

She stood up and smiled. "What do you need, brother?"

He smiled a bit hesitantly. "I'd like to read some history books."

"That's not a problem. Which ones?"

"I don't really know."

"Okay. Where do you want to start? Telkar, Jacobson, Ribeau, Hinihara? Salminen, perhaps?"

"Someone mentioned Mokor."

"Mokor? He's not the one people usually start with. His work is tricky. Which do you want: *The Great Migration*? *History of the People of the Stars*? *Essay on the Meaning of Galactic History*?"

"Which would you recommend?"

"The first one." She paused, tilting her head. "Which clan do you come from?"

This is it, he thought. "None," he said.

"You're a planetary? This is no place for you, then." Her tone of voice quickly shifted from casually friendly to overtly hostile.

"The Teknor sent me."

"Oh! You're that planetary! I haven't the faintest idea what my uncle's thinking these days. The one time somebody asks for my grandfather's work it's an Earther." With a look of utter contempt on her face, she handed him a sheet of paper.

"Fill this out. Give me your card. Hmmph, just as I thought, an A-card for an earthling. Take it back, go through this door to Room D, Carrel 14. Do you know how to use a reader?" She registered the look of surprise on Tankar's face and continued, "You don't think we're going to let you handle the original, do you?" As he turned away she added, "And next time, try to come when I'm not on shift."

The reader was a microfilm projector, slightly more technologically advanced than what he was used to. He sat down and dove right into *History of the People of the Stars*.

Overall, the dense work confirmed what Orena already had sketched out for him, but that in no way made things any easier for him to read…or understand. The book was packed with precious detail; the first to strike him was the change to the names of the *Tilsin* residents. Some were Earth-style names, such as Petersen, Valoch, Ribeau, Hanihara. With his background within the cosmopolitan Guard corps, Tankar easily traced the geographic origins: former Scandinavia, former central Europe, France, and Japan. Other names such as Tan Ekator, Mokor and more he had spotted on Orena's bookshelves – Oripsipor, Telmukinka – seemed odd.

At the time of the great migration, Starship 3 passengers cut all ties with the mother planet. Those born aboard the ships and christened in space picked artificial names. Mokor wrote that even today people used those names, having forgotten the names of their ancestors. The residents of number three tended to intermarry amongst themselves. That was not enough to create genetic risks, but the changes were noticeable. The tendency to change, to evolve, went hand-in-hand with a strong anti-planet bias.

Tankar smiled to himself as he thought, *I'm guessing the lovely librarian has some name like Erioretura Kalkakubitatum.* He skimmed the bit about the history of the Star People's beginning with a view to coming back to it later. He had all the time in the world for that. The contemporary section was the subject of most vital interest to him.

The People of the Stars had had no contact with the rest of humankind for a long time. As they hopped among different uninhabited planets they widened their footprint in the cosmos. Three times they encountered non-human races, but no war ensued. By then, the city-states had already given up the Cursin hyperspatial apparatus – *the only one we've known or used to date,* he thought with bitterness – in favor of the system developed by the unknown residents of the abandoned city now known as *Encounter.*

And then one day, the *Roma* entered into contact with the first of the pre-Empire colonies. On the eve of the first cataclysm – *what the Empire calls the War of Unification,* Tankar thought – several brave groups had used infra-photic starships and hibernation in the hope of conquering the galaxy. They had almost carried out their crazy enterprise, the kind of effort that proved the old Guard dictum that the more desperate an adventure might seem, the greater its chances of success. Widely dispersed as they were, they developed unusual social structures, different from those of both Stellarans and Earthlings. Most often these groups remained within a single solar system, although there never was much love lost among the groups. The Stellarans established trading ties with these half siblings and played a general role as inter-civilization arbiters.

Nomad groups themselves splintered into two political schools of thought. The conservatives considered that the status quo was satisfactory while the advantists anticipated a day when civilizations would erupt into space and compete with the Stellarans. Because of that concern, the advantists advocated for placing everyone in quarantine and banning all interstellar flight.

Orena claims to be an advantist, and that makes her especially anti-planetary. I really must amuse her. On the other hand, the Teknor said he was conservative, yet he is one of the purists who dropped the former Earth names. This conflict is just as twisted as palace intrigue!

Tankar skipped to the final chapter, which ended on an upbeat note. Whatever their views on the subject, neither of the parties considered seizing power by force. There was no short-term risk of war breaking out. *I'll have to read the* Essay on the Meaning of Galactic History, he thought to himself. The afternoon had sped by, and it was already 7 p.m. He left the library and noted the spiky redhead was gone, replaced by a petite blond, who was also getting ready to leave.

"What are the open hours?" he asked.

"The library is always open," she replied, "except for the lending service, which just shut. Oh...you're the planetary?" she confirmed.

"News travels fast. See you tomorrow, perhaps." He was nearly the only person in the big dining room. Petersen was not there, replaced by a tall brunette who served Tankar in silence. After his meal, Tankar retired to his monastic apartment to order his thoughts and impressions.

After an act of sabotage my starship explodes. I'm picked up by a nomad city inhabited by the traitor-scientists who escaped the Empire under Kilos II. These people profess utter contempt for planetaries, especially for those from the Empire. Nobody misses a chance to let me know that. A young woman insults me, I lose my cool and knock her down. From that moment, she becomes my mentor, has me over for dinner...and for dessert! She's a novelist and hydroponist; like her peers, she has two jobs: one is socially relevant and takes about two hours per day, the other one is discretionary. The server who insulted me in the canteen is now offering to help me. He's a chemist. Some guy called Pei, a communications technician, is, from what I can tell, one of the greatest painters in the galaxy.

These Stellarans are very civilized, more so than us, but they also have this stubborn streak, and it makes me wonder how their society manages to function so smoothly. Unless they're hiding something from me, that is. Another thing is that their chief gave me an A-card, the standard one for citizens, even though I crossed their path by chance, and I hail from the much-loathed Empire. And it seems that everyone sees some hidden meaning in my arrival. I don't get it.

Oh, hell! I'm not a sociologist or a philosopher. What possible difference does it make to me what the foundations of their society are? What does matter to me is that I get back to base and justify what I've done.

The base seemed so far away then. Longing caused him to fold in on himself. Tankar missed his tidy life where he had almost no decisions to make, and everything was taken care of by commanders. The life in which routine flowed from the first call of the morning to the last call of the evening.

Nobody can live for 21 years in the same rhythm without it defining his entire being. He missed his friends too, young guys just like himself. He missed his eighteen-meter torpedo and his 10 crewmates who'd become a combat unit as swift and as dangerous as a cobra. Who was at the helm of the *Scorpion* now?

he wondered. Hug Brain? Hayawaka? They even might have picked little Jan Laprade, a guy who hated being teased about his stature, and who'd defied the rules and taken on Thorsen the giant, killing him with his sword. Laprade had backed the right horse and moved straight up the ranks to become a second lieutenant. Tankar hoped the short guy had been given the job. In his care, the *Scorpion* would continue to sting. It was certainly stinging at that very moment, or it was a cloud of metal ash blowing in the winds of the cosmos.

Tankar slept badly that night. Increasingly foolish plans of escape ran riot through his mind and kept him awake. He thought of using the launch he had spotted at Bridge 1, Corridor 6; he even imagined assassinating the Teknor and destroying the city. Then the communicator alarm woke him. The screen remained blank but a disembodied voice ordered him to meet the Teknor after lunch.

He made breakfast and managed to use his new kitchen equipment. Then he returned to the library, where the receptionist on duty was an older brunette. With a look of distaste, she directed him to Carrel 17. He finished his speed-read of Mokor's *History*, only focusing in depth on the chapter about the Mpfifis.

The Mpfifis were a non-human race encountered for the first time about 30 years ago when a launch from the city *Suomi* landed on an unknown G1 star planet. In a lakeside area, the Stellarans had seen traces of debris left behind from a recent visit by other beings: metal boxes, charred earth, a broken weapon and a grave. The weapon was not of a type used by humans, and the grave had been opened. The decomposing body was that of a young man with some humanoid traits. Two days after those finds, a pyramid-shaped starship leaped from nowhere and spit out a volley of projectiles, then vanished. Its hull pierced in 17 places; the *Suomi* lost 127 crew members.

This encounter took place shortly before one of the meetings at which a hundred city-state starships gathered together in the sky above the home planet, Avenir. One hundred and one vessels had been expected, but the *Kanton* never arrived.

Ten years passed with no further encounters. Then the *Uta* tragedy took place. The starship was at the edge of hyperspace near Déneb when the *Uta* was approached by a much larger ship. Suddenly, the enemy rushed through the target's corridors. The battle was ferocious if brief, but the 10 hours it lasted were not wasted. One heroic technician recorded from beginning to end everything he could about the enemy, including their weapons and their rules of war. He managed to put the recordings into a communications torpedo that landed on Avenir and the Stellarans found it during the next starship reunion. All that information and data collected since then comprised Trig Sorensen's book, *The Mpfifis*. In the interim, five other starships had been lost with a handful of survivors rescued by chance at the last minute. Mokor did not divulge technical details as it appeared all his readers would have been familiar with the Mpfifis. For further detail, the reader was referred back to Sorensen.

Tankar returned to the front office. The older woman was gone and now a younger woman was there in her stead.

At her curious glance, he said, "Yes, I'm the planetary with an A-card. Can you give me the Sorensen work on the Mpfifis?"

She looked very surprised. "We don't have that here!"

"Where might I consult it?"

"At your own home, of course. You should have a copy; it's given to every man and woman over the age of 14."

"Nobody gave it to me."

"Go to any digital bookstore."

"How much will it cost?"

"It's free of course!" The young woman's voice was condescending. "Reading it is mandatory." She was losing patience.

"Thank you. One more thing, do you change shifts every two hours?"

"Yes."

"Everybody? Even the mechanics and the pilots and the Teknors?"

"Don't be stupid!" She rolled her eyes. "Mechanics and pilots change every five hours and Teknors don't change at all...at least not in between elections. Even a planetary can grasp that."

"You don't like planetaries?"

"Who does?" She shrugged. "They forced our ancestors into exile. It ended up being a good thing, but it wasn't well intentioned."

"For a society full of individualists, you sure put a lot of importance on collective responsibility. What do people from four hundred years ago have to do with me?"

"Has nothing really changed on Earth? I've been told the Empire is still standing."

"That's true." Tankar paused and then asked, "What's the name of the young woman who comes on at two o'clock?"

The woman behind the desk laughed out loud. "Anaena, the Teknor's niece? She got your attention, eh? But she's no good for you, she doesn't like Earth trash. She—" The young woman stopped and said no more. The conversation was over.

Tankar spent the hour before his lunch date sitting on an oak bench, thinking, looking around and trying to figure out how he was supposed to fit into this world. He was an unwanted refugee foreigner. Soldiers were not needed here.

Idly, he watched the children around him playing a fast-moving game he had not seen before. The kids kicked a ball in between two posts. At one point the ball rolled over to his bench. He tossed it back, and the child who caught it was about to thank him when another of the boys interrupted. "Igor, don't mess around with a rat like that guy." The first kid wiped the ball in disgust, as if it had fallen into a contaminated puddle, before returning it to his friends.

Tankar left the game and headed to the dining room where Petersen, the waiter, signaled Tankar to remain silent. Tankar ate alone at a table and noticed that not a single Stellaran sat near him. He lingered until 2 p.m. and headed to the Teknor's command post.

Tan Ekator welcomed him with a bemused smile. "So Tankar, what do you make of the *Tilsin?*"

"The craft, or the people on it?"

"Both."

"As for the spacecraft, I've not seen anything of much interest to me. As to the people, with two exceptions nobody has been friendly."

"One of the exceptions is a woman, I think."

"How you do know? Am I being spied on?"

"Do you think I have time for that?" the Teknor snapped. "I don't. But Teknors must know everything. We Stellarans are a group of individuals, and that means no one sticks their nose in other people's business without paying for it. It also means that each citizen is entitled to consider others as he or she wishes, so sometimes, tongues wag. We're not a very big city, at a population of twenty-five thousand."

"So I can't do anything without someone finding out?"

"Does it really matter to you? Don't get overly excited. Other than your fling with Orena, I have no idea what you've been up to these past few days. All I need you to know is that if you'd been up to anything significant, I'd know about it. Be careful with Orena, Tankar."

"Why? Is she dangerous?"

"Not in the way you mean it. She's just the most Stellaran

of us all. If you make the mistake of falling for her, you'll come to understand."

"I haven't seen her since yesterday."

"Oh, you'll see her again. And she has many positive qualities, even though she's an advantist. But I didn't ask you here to discuss Orena. Please give me a straight answer: when you were a Stellar Guard, had you ever found a way to follow a starship through hyperspace?"

"Do you think I'm going to answer that? It would constitute a betrayal of the Empire!" Tankar spat back.

The Teknor was growing weary. "I'm not asking you to commit treason, Lieutenant. I have a broader vision than you do. I studied history. It was a family thing, we all did. My father was Mokor."

"Was? Mokor is deceased...?"

"He died 10 months ago on the *Norge* II, killed by the Mpfifis, our common enemies. Have you read the *Essay on the Meaning of Galactic History*?"

"Not yet."

"Read it. Mokor believed your Empire had in it the seeds of a future galactic state, a peaceful confederation of the races. He saw it here, as well."

"The Empire is not pacifist! Only weaklings are pacifists!"

"You're just parroting what you've heard. In reality it takes great strength to be a pacifist; the weak use force because they know no other way. Your Empire is strong enough for peace to have reigned for almost two millennia, but weak enough to have made the peace possible using force alone. The end was predictable. But be patient for a few years, and you'll be able to return to Earth. You will find that either nothing will have changed other than the names of those in power, or the whole place will have descended into chaos. If the person is good, it won't matter if the chief has been elected or secured the post by divine right. If the person is bad, as your emperors have been for the last few centuries, he will, out of stupidity or cruelty, undermine his own position. Do you really believe that the exodus of the four thousand sages and scientists helped your planet?"

"The departure of the traitors, you mean?" sneered Tankar.

"Think for yourself! You're spouting state propaganda. Think. Who did the traitors betray – Earth? The human race? Or a demented emperor? The real traitors are people like you who abet tyrants out of inertia. I really need an answer to my earlier question because our real enemies are the Mpfifis. And they do hold the secret to tracking us in hyperspace and launching a surprise attack. Do you think they'll respect your planet? Ask the survivors of Téroé III."

"Téroé III?"

"Yes, that's a recent catastrophe, just a month back. The word hasn't spread. Had the *Napoli* not traveled less than two light-years from here, we wouldn't have known. Téroé III was a colony of Rapa, itself a pre-imperial Polynesian colony. About five million people lived there. When the *Napoli* came to the rescue, there were fewer than six hundred still alive. The Mpfifis massacred the others."

"And you think that our fragile civilization on Earth has the tech that you need?"

"Oh, we'll get it all right. Might be a month, a year, 10 years from now. Until now we've not needed it, so we didn't look."

"But for the past 30 years the Mpfifis have been attacking your cities…." Tankar wondered why they had waited so long.

"In the beginning, we thought they were just lucky. After all, the attacks weren't very frequent. Two city-state starships lost. Maybe it was just an amazing stroke of luck. But then the losses began to accumulate over an eighteen-month period, and we began to think that your Empire, at war with its own colonies, might have developed the technology."

"If you're right, why would I give it over to you?"

"Because, as we speak, an Mpfifi city-state starship might be tracking us through hyperspace. They might be preparing to melt into us even now, and the threshold between life and death might appear in a matter of hours."

"Teknor, the Empire does not have that secret."

"What a pity," the Teknor sighed. "I'd hoped.... You're telling me the truth?"

"Why would I lie?"

"Who can understand the mind of a planetary?" The Teknor shrugged. "Think carefully, Tankar. If you change your mind, if you have the secret, please hand it over. In the long run, we are, after all, the best protection for your Earth." The Teknor stood. "Now, please go to the bookstore at 806 of the street we're on and get an unabridged copy of Sorensen's book. Say I sent you. I want you to know everything there is to know about the Mpfifis."

Relieved, Tankar ran out of the room. He finally had the upper hand! Of course imperial cruisers had the science and technology to detect and track an enemy starship in hyperspace. Tracer theory was taught to all cadets. The units were delicate and their settings tended to shift.

Just for a second he was tempted to offer to build one for the Teknor. But he went to the bookstore. *I'll do it later, when they start being nicer to me.*

The door of 806 had a big sign that read *Historical Research Center*. A young man looked up from his desk and smiled warmly at him when Tankar walked in. "May I have Sorensen's book on the Mpfifis, unabridged?" he asked.

"It's not out yet."

"The Teknor sent me."

"Ah. Okay. Anaena, please come here!"

It was the same woman he met in the library. She was not happy to see him. "You again? What do you want this time?"

"He wants the unabridged Sorensen. Tan sent him."

Tankar interrupted. "Your uncle sent me."

She activated a communicator. "Hey, Tan. The Earth rat is telling us to give him a Sorensen." She listened. "Oh, okay. You, come here!" She pointed at Tankar and took him into a small book-lined room, shut the door and turned around, her face ablaze with fury.

"Who said you could check up on me? Who said the Teknor is my uncle? It's none of your business, planetary."

"You told me yourself when you took my card the other day."

"That's not true. You…you're spying on me. You've got some nerve. You're nothing to me, and you'll never be anything to me."

"I think there's clearly some confusion," Tankar snapped back. "I'm not interested in you that way. Why would I care about a redheaded shrew?"

"You. You and Orena. That advantist bitch."

"Why do you care? I don't exist in your world."

Anaena abruptly regained her composure, retrieved a copy of the book and threw it at him. "Here's your damn Sorensen. Now get out, parasite." He stared at her mockingly, his arms folded across his chest.

"Stop baiting me. I won't hit you because that would give you 10 bullets to shoot me with leaving me with only one, with one arm tied behind my back!" Tankar was dead serious.

"You're even more annoying than I thought. Go!"

He went straight to his apartment and settled down to read, everything else forgotten.

The Mpfifis were a type of humanoid. They had two legs and

two arms with six-fingered hands. Each very long finger had five joints. Mpfifi heads had two eyes but no external nose or ears. Their brains were encased in a tough silicon casing. An adult male stood about six-and-a-half feet high and had greenish skin freckled with little silicone pins. The women were smaller, thinner, and their reddish-brown skin was smooth.

They breathed in normal atmosphere but were capable of going without air for several hours if they didn't overexert. An organ next to their heart served as an oxygen tank. They had greater physical strength than most humans and were just as intelligent, but they moved more slowly.

Almost nothing was known about their social structures. Their city-states were often bigger than the Stellarans' and appeared more densely populated. Nobody knew where they first came from. They were fearsome warriors, seemingly immune to suffering and death. Their weapons were powerful: in hand-to-hand combat they had a weapon similar to a fulgurator. They also masterfully wielded curved sabers, pistols and grenades. For distance fighting, they had guns with explosive bullets, mortars, cannons and rockets.

At first, the goals of their attacks were unclear. Some captured city-state starships unsuccessfully tried to negotiate. The worst outcome, Sorensen wrote, would be to discover the Mpfifis were an advance military force acting on behalf of a massive, expanding empire. Some postulated the Mpfifis were out-of-galaxy invaders from the Andromeda Nebula.

The book was thorough and rich in technical detail on the Mpfifis' weaponry and tactics. The final chapters were fascinating. The Mpfifis were fearsome adversaries, masterful strategists and skilled hand-to-hand warriors. The author analyzed in detail each documented battle against the human race. After a while Tankar pulled out his pad, pencil and starship map to put his own knowledge to the test.

Every battle started with the sudden appearance of an enemy starship. This was followed by a volley of nonatomic explosive projectiles before the enemy broke through into the star city.

Looking through the names of attacked city-state starships, Tankar saw gaps in Orena's knowledge. There'd been at least 30 such invasions, and some of the nomad cities managed to repel the enemy before, or even after, they boarded. In his professional guise as a Stellar Guard, Tankar picked apart both offensive and defensive tactics. In three cases out of five recent defeats, the Stellarans might have contained the attackers until help could come. In another case, they could have won the battle.

It was easy to spot the weakness in the nomads' defense strategy. While brave, indeed, the Stellarans lacked combat training. They did not lack discipline, but they were too slow in execution of their strategic plans, which in any case were not as strong as that of the Mpfifis. The Stellarans failed to take advantage of their knowledge of the city's layout and quickest communication routes.

"If I tried to talk to the Teknor about this, he probably wouldn't listen. Why should I bother?"

Tankar put the book down. Should he eat in or at the canteen? His room was cold and dreary. Loneliness had begun to weigh on him, and it was a loneliness he had never felt in the Guards. He decided to go to the canteen and face the hostility head-on.

CHAPTER FIVE

The Duel

Petersen was there, eating at a table rather than standing behind the counter. He smiled, but when Tankar walked up, he stood and said, "I'm sorry, planetary, but it's best we not be seen together. Not yet."

"Oh, that's okay. I'm getting used to it."

Tankar sat at a remote table and started to eat, but a friendly "Hello, Tankar!" had him turn around. Orena and Pei and a third guy, big and tall, walked in. Tankar waved, and Orena sat down next to him, bringing in the other two.

One protested, "No way, Orena. Not with the Earth rat."

"You forgot I'm a free woman, brother?"

"Come on, Orena. Don't be an idiot. You're living in a fantasy world."

"Our fling wasn't meant to last, Pei. I'm no more accountable to you than you are to me. When it comes to my fantasy world, that's my business. Worried?"

"Come on, guys. You're not gonna fight over an Earther?!"

"Not the issue, Hank. I resent Pei treating me like he owns me. That kind of thinking is planetary. Who knows? Maybe Earth is past it too. Tankar?" Orena leaned over toward Tankar, smiling.

"I've not much experience, Orena, but I think some people think that way, at least among the commoners. Don't argue with your friends on my account," he added. "I'm certainly not worth it and will always be only Earth trash to them."

"Earth trash or not, I'm having dinner with you tonight. And those two morons can go hang elsewhere."

"Fine, goodbye, Orena. Come on, Hank. Leave her to her gigolo. They deserve each other."

Tankar did not know what was going on but, from the shocked look on Orena's face, he guessed she had been seriously insulted. He stood and grabbed Pei by the neck. "I don't know what you just said, but you're going to take it back right now."

Pei's friend moved closer and looked Tankar right in the eyes. "Gigolo!" Tankar slapped him. Instantly, Pei's friend jumped Tankar's back. Tankar shook him off in no time, and Pei's friend crashed onto a table. Both men stood and shouted, "We're claiming our due. Did you see this, brothers?"

Petersen spoke up. "We saw it, and we also heard your insult."

"You're not going to defend him, are you?" Pei asked. "The *Tilsin* will be clean again when this one's corpse rolls into space!" He pointed at Tankar.

"I don't think a duel will be necessary, and, in any event, Orena needs to second the motion since you also inexcusably insulted her. Scram, or you'll insult me as well, and I'll claim my due," Petersen calmly replied.

He turned to Tankar. "So, planetary, you sure don't do things by halves. Two at once. Will you take his side, Orena?"

"Me? No way. But if they do him in, I'll reclaim my due. I'm not worried," she added with a look at Tankar. "I won't need to."

"What does all this mean?" Tankar asked.

"You hit them, so you'll have to fight them."

"What was I supposed to do? Let them insult me?"

"What you should've done is launch a preemptive strike and

threaten a duel; then you would've faced Pei only. Now you face them both."

"Fine." Tankar stood resigned. "When, where and how?"

"Tomorrow, after lunch in Park 12. Since the blows came in response to insults, you'll be able to select your weapon. Your choice. You can't choose a fulgurator; they make too much of a mess."

Tankar shrugged. "I could use a javelin as easily as a cannon. That was my job. But my disadvantage, and that's a big one, is that I don't know the site."

"We'll go inspect it tomorrow morning. I'll wait for you at 9 a.m. at Gate 3."

Once Petersen left, Tankar turned to Orena. "You'd have been much better off not talking to me."

"Why? Are you afraid?" she prodded.

"Do you believe that my life here is so wonderful that losing it concerns me?" He finally asked, "What's a gigolo?"

"There's no such word in interspatial."

"Go on."

"I'd prefer not to translate," Orena admitted with a blush. "Ask Petersen."

"You Stellarans are a strange people. Are these duels common?"

"Pretty much. We're a hot-blooded people. I've been in three."

"That's right! I heard you killed three men."

"Why shouldn't I?" Orena demanded.

"Because you're a woman," Tankar reasoned.

"Women don't fight in the Empire?" Orena wondered.

"Very rarely."

"What do women do when someone insults them?"

"Their father or husband defends their honor, of course."

"Ah, I see. In your world a woman is either on her own and defenseless or in a long-term relationship."

"Exactly."

"Not a place where I belong," she confessed, reaching out to take his arm. "Come along."

"Where?"

"To my place, of course."

"No, Orena. Tonight I need to sleep."

Orena shrugged. "Sweet dreams, then. Tomorrow morning go to the battle provost and choose your weapon. I suggest a mark three carbine. As you have two opponents, you'll be entitled to 10 bullets."

Tankar slept well, ate a hearty breakfast, and walked over to Park 12. Petersen was there. "Not too worried?" his friend asked.

"Not particularly. Putting my life on the line was my profession. Waste of time and effort to fight over something so trivial."

"You're not so proud. Gigolo!"

"What does that mean? Orena didn't want to explain."

"I get that. I'm surprised you don't know it as it's an old Earth term. It's a slander no Stellaran would forgive." Petersen explained before describing what would happen later.

They stopped in front of a clear level field banked by bushes. "Here. This is where the provost will place you. Your opponents will be at the other end of the park, one on the right and the other on the left. At the signal, you'll walk toward each other. From then on anything goes, except weapons other than those provided. A judge in that cabin up there –" he pointed, "– will count your shots. Any hint of cheating means death by expulsion into space."

"Have you fought here?"

"Only once. Come on! We have just three hours for you to get the lay of the land. Your opponents know the terrain well... especially Hank."

At noon Tankar went to the provost's and selected a short,

high-caliber carbine. Its initial speed was very high, and it greatly resembled the guns used by the Empire fusiliers. Petersen joined him at the cafeteria where they saw Orena. Much to Tankar's surprise, several of the customers waved to him.

"They'll all be there later. As will I, of course," Petersen said.

"So it's going to draw a crowd?"

"Life here can be extremely dull, Tankar."

People are the same everywhere, Tankar mused. On Earth, the emperors organized circus games similar to prehistoric ones, which he'd heard other people talk about. So even Stellarans, surely the most sophisticated civilization in this part of the galaxy....

For the first time someone other than the Teknor or Orena referred to him by name rather than the snippy 'planetary'... or worse. He sat with his two friends, eating little and drinking water instead of beer. A passerby asked if he expected to survive. Tankar smiled. "Why not? Orena, why is everyone being so nice to me?"

"You're taking on two guys at once. That doesn't happen often, and they're all hoping you succeed in defending yourself."

"The show must go on, huh?"

"It's more than that," Orena insisted. "We appreciate bravery, especially when it's foolhardy. Hank is not a popular guy."

"I'm not foolhardy, Orena. I'd never have provoked those guys if I'd had a choice. Then again, I've done battle under far worse conditions."

"Watch out for Hank," Petersen warned. "He's the more dangerous. Pei isn't a very good shot."

"Not to worry. I think it's getting to be time."

Tankar presented himself at the gate to Park 12. A motley crew of men and women were waiting. He held his head high and walked past them, holding the carbine in his right hand. The provost was waiting, as were his two opponents and the judge.

"In accordance with the law of the People, you will now do battle to erase the insults. Names!"

"Pei Kwang, technician."

"Hank Harrison, pilot."

"Tankar Holroy—"

Someone interrupted, shouting, "Planetary!"

"Lieutenant in the Stellar Guard of His Majesty Emperor Ktius VII." He spoke calmly.

"Even though one man dueling against two is unusual, nothing in the law prohibits it. Each of you will have five cartridges per opponent. You, Holroy, will have 10. As soon as the rocket's smoke rises, the duel may commence. Only the deaths of one side or the other will end the fight. You may use the weapon of your choice in the manner of your choice. Here's your ammunition. Take your positions!"

Tankar remained immobile. He already was in position. The judge took the elevator to the little cabin suspended over the park that would be his lookout post for the alleyways and grove below.

The crowd pulled back behind a makeshift barrier. To the sound of applause, Pei and Hank ran to their positions. A shout cut through the noise. "Kill him, Stellarans! Kill him!"

Tankar swiveled to see the Teknor's redheaded niece in the front row, her head rising up above the rest of the crowd. Hank saluted her.

Gradually the hubbub died down. Tankar checked that his weapon was ready to fire with nine bullets in the magazine and one in the barrel. He walked slowly toward the grove, his actual starting point, and waited, eyes toward the sky.

As always before a battle, Tankar felt calm. This idiotic show was nothing compared with the dangers he had faced in the past. The only thing he missed having was a brother-in-arms. He felt alone among these hostile people except for two individuals he still wasn't sure about. Was he just a plaything for Orena? Did the friendly chemist have a hidden agenda?

The smoke bomb went off with a bang and shot straight up to the vaulted ceiling. It almost reached the metal roof and disappeared before it deployed its parachute, which dropped and fluttered toward him. He had two options. One – hide and wait; or two – approach the two men directly. He opted for the second: more to his taste. He slid to the left, mindful not to brush against the leaves; their movement would betray him. Then he crawled in a straight line toward a stream that ran in a closed circuit. All the while, he listened intently and peered through the foliage until he reached a long diagonal alleyway.

They've not reached here yet. The stream runs between the two walls, so they'll have to come this way. I'll wait.

Cloaked in thick grass, Tankar remained stationary for a long while, gun cocked, scanning both sides. About a hundred meters away he heard rustling in the grove and focused his senses on that point. Something white moved. Checking his surroundings every five seconds, Tankar aimed at the grove. In a flash, a head appeared then vanished like a turtle pulling back into its shell.

He knew it: Pei! Tankar calculated the clear space at a distance of 15 meters, figured the artificial gravity at 0.9 grams, and guessed at Pei's physical abilities. With no momentum it would take the man two seconds at least to cross. His bullets had an average velocity of 800 mm per second, so it would be tight but doable. He aimed for the far edge of the grove.

Pei surfaced. At the last instant, just as he was about to shoot, Tankar changed his aim. He could not kill this man who disappeared through the brush. *Did I miss?* he wondered. He did not think so. As a Guard, he had been a champion archer, top-ranked in all firearms categories, and he had hit much trickier targets than Pei. He crawled away at speed with a smoke cloud to his rear.

Pwiououn!

The bullet passed to his right, way too high. He scanned the area and noticed a blue balloon dissolving in the air. He fired three times in a fan formation and kept on crawling.

Unless Pei was badly hurt or the other guy had shot at him, Tankar had only six bullets left to their four, but he knew that Hank could not use Pei's weapon; it was against the rules.

He walked toward the place where he thought Pei had fallen but kept the alleyway in his sights. As he approached he was surprised to see a figure suddenly standing before him, weapon cocked, no more than 20 meters away. Tankar quickly rolled onto his side and heard a projectile dig into the ground near him. Gravel popped all around him as he shot without aiming and rolled behind a stand of trees. In between the trunks he spotted Hank racing away at a diagonal, but the branches obstructed his aim. He leaped away in the other direction and saw a spray of pebbles just as he dove into the tall grass.

Five bullets to three. Thankfully, Pei was no better than an amateur. Tankar continued to crawl, careful not to brush up against the bushes that provided cover. He thought that Hank wasn't much of a shooter either, even if he was good on the approach. *How did he manage to blind me to everything?* he wondered.

To his right, he saw a little ravine only a half meter deep. *This is why it's good to know the lay of the land. If one man can do it, another can too. But does Hank know the terrain well enough to spot this ditch? I'll give it a go!*

He returned to the alley where the trench veered into a pipe too narrow for him to pass through. He took out a handkerchief, silently ripped it to shreds and made himself a rope that he hooked on to a slender tree. He then gently pulled the rope from below and the tree shook slightly. Nothing. He waited, pulling now and again on the rope. The minutes ticked by.

An explosion close by made him jump. He lifted his head and shot into the smoke without aiming. A resounding scream pierced the silence. He rose on his elbows and felt a pain in his shoulder. He heard the shot a moment later.

Stupid man. Triple idiot. How did I get taken in by that? Gooey, warm blood flowed down his left arm. He moved his shoulder and winced in pain.

Nothing broken. Just a flesh wound, he thought as he crawled quickly, expecting Hank and his gun to show up at any minute. A few meters on he stopped, turned around and listened. All he heard was a light swishing sound. He moved forward making sure his wounded arm did not stiffen. He reached the edge of the park near the see-through wall. Two impassive Stellarans watched him. One pointed to the widening red spot on Tankar's jacket. He smiled at the two men and kept moving.

He stopped again at the diagonal alleyway and paused to think for a moment. Hank had one bullet left to his own four. If he could force Hank to fire, the enemy would be at his mercy. Cautiously Tankar removed his jacket, prodded his wound, a long stripe down his deltoids. It was still bleeding, and he had no way of bandaging it without freezing his arm.

He looked down the alleyway to his right. Nothing moved. He dug his toes into the earth and locked them in place then jumped up and down and disappeared into the grass. Unfortunately, he heard no shots. Nobody could have hit him from that spot. Had Hank shot, he would have missed.

Tankar followed the wall all the way back to his starting point. Behind the see-through barrier Anaena looked at him with contempt. He shrugged, winced in pain and lay down behind a thicket that had a landscaped hole cut through the center. He would wait.

He spun around by instinct. The woman behind him waved

her arms and pointed at his hiding place. She stopped when she realized he was staring at her and casually walked away.

That little bitch! She's giving away my location. Cold, terrible anger rose within him. So the Stellarans were loyal only to one another. He suddenly thought that Orena had provoked this dispute, and now others would finish the job. If Anaena were signaling to Hank, he couldn't be far.

Tankar left his watch post and crawled with great effort. His muscles were cold, and a searing pain hit his shoulder. Another 30 meters and he heard the sound of a bush rustling. Going hell for leather, Tankar stood, then leaped up and spun around just as a shot was fired. As he fell he lunged toward the figure in the branches and fired. He stood up shakily and walked, weapon cocked, toward the bush. The thick heap on the ground confirmed that there was no doubt about it: it was Hank, dead from a bullet to the skull.

"That was lucky. But I didn't need luck; I've still got three bullets." Tankar had spoken out loud.

Fearlessly, he walked to where Pei had fallen. His digital readout showed less than two hours had elapsed since the duel had begun even though it felt like weeks. He easily found Pei hunched into a ball, groaning, his gun at his side. Tankar lowered his own gun and, in a fit of rage, ejected the cartridge. He leaned down to examine the wounded man and mumbled to himself, "If they don't come for him soon, he's lost. More's the pity; he's a really good painter."

Tankar turned toward the gate. Several Stellarans stood in a circle around Hank's corpse. He could not see Orena or Petersen, but the redhead was there, pale as death. He picked up the man's body by the neck of his jacket and dragged it toward Anaena. An assistant tried to help, but Tankar gave him a ferocious look, so the man backed away. In a final effort, Tankar dumped the corpse at the redhead's feet.

"Here's your mate." Tankar was intentionally vulgar. She

blanched even more. "Now I understand the loyalty among you people."

She glared at him, her eyes sparkling, and he couldn't help himself admiring her. *She's as beautiful as a panther*, he thought. "Will you denounce me?" she asked.

"What would happen if I did?"

Despite her self-control, her voice cracked as she answered. "I'd be cast into space."

"You? The Teknor's niece?"

"You don't know Tan."

He felt sorry for her. "I won't speak of it. After all, your actions helped me more than they helped him."

"And you expect gratitude?" she hissed. "I didn't like you before; now I hate you."

"So what?" He shrugged and winced. "Doesn't bother me." Tankar turned on his heel and walked toward the exit. Orena, Petersen, the provost and few other locals waited there.

"This is wonderful, Tankar! You got them both," Petersen the chemist said, smiling broadly.

"No, just the one. I merely wounded Pei, but he won't be worth much if you don't collect him ASAP."

The provost asked, "Why didn't you finish him off? Custom usually—"

Then Tankar exploded. "May you and your customs go to hell! I don't care about them; they don't matter to me. One of your females set me up to fight two men at once. Well, I killed one man, but I won't kill another. You finish it if you wish. Leave me alone."

"Careful, Tankar," Orena warned. "I didn't set you up at all, and please don't call me a female."

"Really? You sure acted like a female with me and the other guys. And you tried to have Pei and Hank kill me."

"Me? I would've challenged them both if they'd killed you!"

"That's true, Tankar," Petersen said. "I don't think Orena is to blame. Hank told everybody he would challenge you and kill you, or cast you into the void as a coward if you refused to fight. Orena barely knew him. Hank was likely the one who got to Pei, a good guy but jealous as a caveman."

Tankar was suddenly exhausted. "What does it all matter in the end? Your feelings and the way you think are beyond me. Please just leave me alone."

He went home to his apartment. He sat down heavily, exhausted by the tension and the blood loss. He had not locked the door so Orena just walked in. "What do you want this time? I asked to be left in peace."

"I want to look after you. Let me see the wound."

"Why don't you go to Pei? He needs help more than I do."

"He's in the hospital. They're trying to save him."

"That's good news."

"Why did you spare him? He would've killed you without flinching. And he's just a technician; you're a soldier."

Tankar smiled sadly. "Maybe that's why. I've killed so often that I've grown tired of bloodshed. I never enjoyed it. I didn't choose the profession. Would I have killed Pei for one slight? What he said was a lot less troubling than some of the whispering I overheard on Earth. And some of it I deserved. Also, I like his work, his landscapes. He's had a chance to develop his gifts, and I haven't."

"What would you have wanted to do?"

"Me?" He paused to think. "Pure math, maybe, and…. What does it matter?" He slumped down farther in his chair.

Gently, she bathed his scar. "You were very lucky. A few centimeters to the right and the bone would have been crushed, but it won't be a problem. A few days R&R with some antibiotics

I'll leave here, and you won't even have to go to the hospital. It's done."

"Orena, is it really true that you didn't set those two poor fellows against me on purpose? Did you want to see the back of one of us?"

"Why would I have done that, Tankar? Your one night with me didn't give Pei the right to want to kill you. I'm not his possession, and he knows that. Some of his views are outdated. I'm as free as he is. Hank and I weren't even friends. But to those guys, you're a planetary, not much more worthwhile than a cockroach. Their spite probably came from thinking I'd debased myself spending time with you. Instead of asking me about it, they wanted to act and to destroy the cause of my supposed dishonor."

"If this circus starts up again, I might as well kill myself. It'll be faster."

"Now, everything has changed. By challenging you to a duel, they unwittingly began the process of accepting you. You're sort of Stellaran now."

"Okay. I'll never fully understand that." He looked up at her. "What am I to you, Orena? A new plaything?"

She thought for a moment. "In the beginning, maybe. But remember that my father was a planetary. To me you're a guy like any other guy. A stranger. Let's drop all the complicated stuff. I'm going to cook for you."

She vanished into the kitchen, then returned with a furious look on her face. "This is all you have? I'm going to have to outfit your apartment for you. How will you be able to host when I come to visit?"

She puttered around, poked her head out the door occasionally and said a few words. Tankar felt his doubts ebbing away. After all, he had only been on the *Tilsin* for a few days, and some of the events that had occurred that he did not understand may have happened for a reason.

"Dinner!"

Orena had worked wonders with his meager supplies. Dinner was delicious. "You must be exhausted. Lie down. I'm going to stay here to check for fever. I'll set up a camp bed."

The vague remnants of his puritan sensibilities led him to protest meekly, but he gave in quickly, happy to have a friend, whatever that meant, however long it lasted. He fell asleep peacefully.

PART TWO

CHAPTER ONE

The Pilgrims

When Tankar woke up, he was surprised to find the pain was gone. Bits of his flesh were red, but they were not festering. Orena still slept, so he made breakfast and then he softly called her name.

"Awake so soon? How do you feel?"

"Wonderful! What did you put on the wound? We have nothing that effective on Earth."

"Biogenol. It's an antibiotic, and it helps with scarring," she explained. "In a few days, you'll be good as new."

"Come, let's have breakfast."

She muttered about the mess in the kitchenette but complimented him on his cabor tea that Stellarans drank instead of coffee.

"I need to get to work," she said. "I took an early shift today so I can be free later."

"What exactly do you do?" Tankar asked.

"I'm a sub-biologist at hydroponic farm 35."

"I really don't understand your system. Two hours isn't much."

"Almost everything is automated. Under some other system, many people would end up having no work at all."

"What do people do the rest of the time?"

"Giving the collective two hours per day makes everybody feel useful. It's just different from what you're used to, Tankar."

"I thought you were all individualists, keen on freedom."

"Those two things aren't mutually exclusive, you know."

"Hmmm. I see. Don't forget I'm a pariah, a leech."

"Some day, maybe, that too will change."

"I doubt it. Do you enjoy your line of work?"

"Oh, yes."

"So why not keep going after your shifts end?"

"I have in the past. But I don't really have green thumbs." She headed out. "See you soon, Tankar!"

"This evening?"

"Maybe."

After she left, he realized he was starting to like this strange woman, so very different from the girls he had known on Earth. He put the dishes away and ran the dusting and cleaning equipment. *Tankar Holroy, lieutenant in the Guards and model housewife!*

The day stretched ahead, and he had no plans. He had no books of his own and was not sure where to get any. That led him to think about Anaena. "That little bitch," he said out loud. "She'd have had me killed if I hadn't spotted her."

But he did not regret not turning the woman in. The high moral standards of the Guards precluded telling tales. Back in Imperia, a well-known thief, with the reluctant help from Tankar's peers, had hidden in the mess basement for three months. If he had been a political criminal, they would have turned him in as there was little love lost between the Guards and the Popol political enforcers. Having protected Anaena was a victory of sorts, in this quiet war she was waging against him. She now owed him, and it must really rankle her!

He checked his map and decided to go to the library at a time she would be on shift. He thought of calling Petersen in his lab, but, when he reached Bridge 8, he looked closely at a wide area he had earlier taken to be a park. The interior was the typical *Tilsin* maze of streets, squares, and gardens, but there were no signs, except some posters reading *Pilgrim Territory*. He remembered what he had read about the Pilgrims and suspected the area would be off limits.

Traveling the mobile walkways, he reached Gravitational Slide 127 that would take him to his goal, proud for once that he had not gotten lost. The slide led to a vast hall, full of atmosphere-replenishing plants. At the far end a door bore an ornate sign he recognized: the Menian ankh-styled cross he'd seen on some monasteries on Earth. The door was locked, and he accepted that he would have to turn back. Then from the corner of his eye, he spotted movement and stopped. A peephole slid open and behind it was a bearded face.

"What do you want, brother?"

"You're a Pilgrim, sir?"

"Yes, I am."

"I'm a foreigner, a planetary, an earthling."

"All men are our brothers."

"I've only been here for a short while. I landed by accident."

"Come in, brother. The patriarch will be glad to get news from the mother planet." The door swung open, and Tankar entered Pilgrim territory.

The bearded man said, "You were lucky I heard your knock, brother. I was just passing by. When our brethren from outside wish to come call, they use the communicator in advance."

"I didn't know that."

"It does not matter, but if you ever wish to come back…you know how to find us."

If the streets of the city-state were as austere as a barracks, the Pilgrims' cloister, in its stark simplicity, recalled a monastery. The two men walked through a park where children played under the care of women in somber outfits. While Stellaran women wore outfits of precious fabrics and bright colors that often covered very little skin, these women were all in severe, dark, almost floor-length dresses.

"I mainly see children. How many people live here?"

"One thousand, six hundred thirty, brother. But aside from the guardians and men on duty, most of the adults are in temple. Today marks the birthday of our founder, the blessed Menno Simons. You will get to meet our saint patriarch, Holonas the Wise."

"But I'm not of your faith."

"We will not ask anything of you that might undermine your own faith. We will ask you only what has happened on Earth since we left. And we will pray for the Lord to give you light."

Tankar refrained from shrugging. He did not wish to offend anyone. The two men approached another door featuring a huge cross festooned with rubies. The closer they got, the better Tankar could hear a hum-like sound that eventually became a hymn sung by multiple voices. The Pilgrim opened a side door and the majestic sound of the hymn greeted him.

"Come in, brother."

He entered to find a long, high vault built like the hull of a ship. In the back, behind the altar, a cloudy spiral shone in the half darkness and, at its center, a red ankh sparkled. Rows and rows of people knelt in silent prayer.

A man stood at the altar and raised his arm in a sign of blessing. The Pilgrim bowed his head and Tankar followed suit. The man began to speak and Tankar realized he was the patriarch.

At first busily orienting himself, he did not listen to the words in interspatial. The minister was a tall silhouette against the background of stars. The temple was bare, lacking adornment save the image of a nebula behind the altar. Tankar recalled visiting churches on Earth out of curiosity. He had left in a flash feeling out of place in his uniform, a dark sacrilege in a place of light. Save for one occasion in a church in a village partly destroyed after a battle on Fomalhaut IV, he never before had observed so many people in such a deeply contemplative state.

Snippets from the sermon gradually penetrated his consciousness. The minister referred to the story of faith founder Menno Simons during the blessed time when monasteries had provided refuge. He spoke also of the persecution that followed.

"Brothers, we must never forget that we owe our survival to the Stellaran scientist-ancestors of our neighbors. More than that, they ushered in our right to follow in the steps of the Master. Yes, they have not seen the True Light, but we must humbly admit that we have not always led them to the Truth. We have no right to look down on them. They exist as natural beings, good and bad, without benefit of divine enlightenment. This may be our doing. Their sins are less important in the eyes of God than our lack of faith."

He continued, "Those of us whose job it is to guide you cannot caution you enough against the dangers of their dream of a man-centered universe. The universe is too great for man alone, brothers. Humans hop from star to star and proudly and wrongly claim ownership. At some point, the universe must take revenge on the wretched master and crush him.

"In the gloom of their labs, humans labor to prolong their lifespans, and they've seen surprising success. But death claims each man without exception. We know death is but a new phase and a new birth into a better world. As an idea made flesh, we represent just one leg of the journey that will end when God decides. And on that day, we will see him in all his glory.

"The day will come, my brothers, though we know not when."

Looking away from his congregation and up at the cross, the Patriarch continued, "Oh Lord, we have sought your presence in this galaxy. We have so hoped for a signal, for the sign that says this tribulation has ended, that heaven on earth will come again. We bit into the fruit of the Tree of Knowledge before we were truly ready. We have struggled to expiate our sins. Century upon century of battles, plagues, thousands of deaths, too many of them innocents. Oh Lord, will you one day grant us forgiveness? Will you unfasten the veil of galaxies that hides your true face? Will we once again see the shining Arch of Alliance in the cosmos above?"

He paused. The Pilgrims, hunched over, continued meditating for a while. More spiritually moved than he would ever admit, Tankar remained standing behind a pillar as his guide knelt at his side. Slowly the spiral in front of the altar paled and the lights flickered. When the Pilgrims stood, the guide also stood and spoke, "Come, brother."

They walked along the nave against the tide of Pilgrims on their way out. They entered a small bare room to the left of the altar. A very tall, gray-bearded, elderly man was putting his vestments into a wooden trunk. He turned around, and his deep-set gray eyes under thick eyebrows met Tankar's gaze.

"Father, may I present a man from Earth."

The old man's face was joyful. "A man from Earth! When did you travel here?"

"Just a few days ago." Tankar hesitated, unsure how to address the priest.

"Call me Holonas, my son, as you are not one of us. What is your name?"

"Tankar Holroy, Sir Holonas."

"I am not a nobleman," Holonas smiled. "So just a few days ago, you were on the mother planet. Do you know if any of our brethren have survived?"

"Yes, we still have five monasteries."

"Thriving ones?"

"Not so much as before. The Empire is displeased with your support for the traitor-scientists."

"So our brothers are persecuted?"

"Not precisely," Tankar explained, "but they can't bring in new followers, and their numbers are slowly dwindling. But they do have some sway with some nobles and Guards. The commoners have little liking, and some Christians take issue with your lot as heretics."

"Are Christians powerful?"

"Again, among the commoners, yes. I suspect they fomented the rebellion that was raging when I left Earth."

"Rebellion? More bloodshed, more death," the old man sighed. "I must know of these things. Would you like to join me for a simple supper? Do come…come."

The streets were busy, and the cheerful mood of the men and women contrasted with their severe dress.

"This is a whole new world," Tankar wondered aloud.

"Indeed. Our contact with Stellarans is limited. They do not come to us, and we rarely leave our enclave. We do not share their customs, so we only join forces when danger looms. Of course, we contribute to everyday life on the *Tilsin*. We have labs and factories, watch posts and one machine room. I remain in close touch with the Teknor and some of our sages communicate with their counterparts. That is about it."

"Don't you ever get cabin fever?"

The old man smiled. "At times. When the city-state stops somewhere, we take our launches so we can stretch our legs on actual soil." The two men stopped. "Please come into my home."

The home was simple but cozy, and Tankar was surprised to see one older and one younger woman present. "Please meet my sister Ellena and my niece Iolia. Sadly, her parents were killed in an accident last year."

Like the other women in the enclave, Iolia wore a simple brown shift. She was petite, her dark brown hair pulled into a bun. She had a clean forehead, a slender nose and a lovely mouth. But she looked at the ground rather than at the visitor.

"Ellena, our guest hails from Earth." Tankar bowed at the older woman whose lined face hinted at great earlier beauty.

The simple meal that soon followed was delicious and eaten in silence as Tankar followed what he took to be Pilgrim custom. When he lifted his gaze from his plate, he caught Iolia staring at him. Her eyes were huge, brown with flecks of gold. She smiled shyly and bent her head again. The meal closed with prayers, which made Tankar uneasy as he had no idea what to do.

"Well, now that we have regained our strength, please tell us all the news from Earth," Holonas began.

"There's a great deal of news, some of it disturbing, and I'm unsure if I—"

"Iolia may be young but she knows how difficult life can be. You may speak freely," Holonas assured him.

Tankar spoke at length, cautiously at first. But as his hosts' empathy became more apparent, he relaxed. He spoke of the changes residents of Earth had undergone since the Great Exodus. He spoke of power concentrated in the hands of emperors and noblemen, the reach of the political police, and the loss of individual freedoms.

For any unambitious person of noble birth, life within the Empire was not too dreadful, he explained. For others – laborers, farmers, civil service types or small business owners – life was difficult. And for any champion of individual freedoms, life was untenable.

Commoners were not wretched, if one considered only

material things; few went hungry or were deprived of a roof over their heads or of medical care. But these people were nothing in the big picture. Their lives did not matter. They easily could be lost to the whim of a nobleman or to a soldier's perceived slight.

"What about learned men and priests?"

"The state keeps scientists on a short leash. They dream only of bringing down the Empire, even though it feeds and protects them. As to Christian priests, they live like commoners. Those of your faith never leave their monasteries. The practitioners of the new faith are part of the upper classes, of course."

"And what is this new religion?"

"It's all very complicated. We had our own version in the Guards, with similar tenets."

"And what are those tenets?"

Tankar recited by rote: "There's a Supreme Being that created the world for his worshipers; His incarnation made flesh, the Emperor, must rule the Empire and extend his rule throughout the cosmos; the priests are his aides, and the army is his right hand; what the Emperor agrees to is right, and what goes against him is wrong and must be crushed; those who loyally serve the Emperor will have eternal life; all others shall be ejected into the void."

"And do you believe in all that?" Holonas queried.

"Why wouldn't I? At least...I think I believed it. Since fate dropped me here, I'm no longer so sure." He paused before wondering, "Is this nothing more than a test of my loyalty?"

Holonas did not reply. After thinking for a moment, Tankar went on. "However, when I left – I know it's treason even to think like this – but the Empire was nearing its end. The rebellion had gained the upper hand almost everywhere. How can God's emissary be vanquished? Is he not also the messenger for the divine? Then again, this may be just one more trial for me to suffer through."

"I think you are a bit naïve, Tankar Holroy, even more so than other men of your age. You speak like a man who has never wondered about these questions."

"Why would I have asked them? I wasn't paid to think. I did the job I'd been trained to do. I was a soldier and a good one at that. What else could matter to me?"

"It mattered enough that you knew you were among the fortunate ones, and that others around you suffered...."

"Of course I observed the disparity, but it didn't strike me as abnormal. Only now have I begun to wonder at it. As to my privileged status, I paid a steep price. Training to be a Stellar Guard is tough in ways you wouldn't believe. I'm not ashamed of my privileges; I earned them."

"What were they?"

"I received a tax-free salary, a pension at 40...if I lived that long, precedence over some noblemen when I wasn't on call and on all of them when I was on call. There were other perks, but I don't want to talk about them. On the downside were the inhuman training courses and the loss of family. I've not seen my parents since I was three years old, and I don't know if they're alive." He added without emotion, "I may even have killed them myself during a riot."

"You must have suffered so much!"

In shock, Tankar looked at the young woman who had spoken. "Suffering. I don't think so. Had I stayed with my family I might have become a laborer or a farmer. The Guards trained me and educated me. Without that background, my world would've been so much smaller, unless, of course, I had been born into a technician family. But I doubt that was the case as I've never heard of it happening."

"What will you do now?" Iolia asked softly.

"Who knows? For now, I'm a pariah, a planetary, an untouchable...."

The old man gently interrupted, "Why not stay with us?"

"Do you think I'd be better off here?" Tankar paused to consider that option. "In some ways, you think more like I do than those others, but that might just be the aspect you're choosing to present to me.... How do you defend your terrain? Would you really and truly accept me? While my former faith is wavering, I don't know if I can embrace yours."

"We would not ask you to. All you would need to do is to accept our habits and customs."

"I don't know if I can do even that."

"Well, why not come around now and again and see how you respond?" Holonas suggested. "You will always be welcome in the house of Holonas, Tankar Holroy." The old man held out his hand, but the soldier paused before shaking it.

"The first of our customs is that we always shake hands on departure. Goodbye."

Keen to comply, Tankar extended his hand to the young woman. She blushed, turned away, then turned back and shook his hand.

"That is not quite how we do it," the old man said pleasantly. "You should have waited for Iolia, but it is not a big problem."

Iolia's grip was firm and warm. He did not wish to let go but did, bowed and took his leave. As he left, he thought, "Now let's go taunt the she cat if she's still at the library."

The patriarch's kind treatment had emboldened Tankar as he realized that the enclave might well be a place of asylum for him. He had no doubt that tough social pressure existed within the enclave, but he thought he could adapt. There would be bitter times in such a refuge, but, even as strangers, the Pilgrims treated him with a respect that contrasted with the reception he had received from the Stellarans.

Just as he entered the library he found Anaena packing up to leave. She looked startled. "Oh, it's you. I told you not to come here while I'm on shift."

He sat down on a table, swinging his leg in an attempt to look nonchalant. "I'm free. My A-Card allows me to do all the same things as native Stellarans. One of those things is 24/7 access to the library. And when you're on shift, as you still are, you must serve me."

"And what services do you yourself provide?" Her voice dripped with contempt.

"None. That's the beauty of it all. Your people see me as a lesser being, so they haven't asked me to work. There are jobs I could do, and they're important ones. But as long as I'm an outcast...." He waved dismissively and sat up straight. "Now," he said, sarcastically, "would you be so kind as to give me some novels written by the lovely Orena Valoch? And don't try telling me you don't have any, because I've already checked."

She hissed and spat like an angry cat. "She could give them to you herself. If you wanted to read garbage like that you really didn't need to bother me."

"As it so happens, I need the atmosphere of a major library to fully appreciate literature," he said coolly. "I shall be here every day. I'm told Orena has written more than 20 novels, and I'm not a fast reader."

"Alcove 44. And my shift is over." She spat out the words as she headed for the door.

"See you tomorrow, redheaded angel!" Tankar called after her.

Orena was in his apartment when he returned. "How did you get in?" he asked.

"All apartments have two keys. When I left I took the one you left on the bookcase."

"You might've mentioned that," Tankar muttered. He had nothing to hide but resented the intrusion on principle. *I hope she doesn't imagine that she has claims on me just because we slept together,* he thought. Like most Empire men, he was used to obedient and deferential women, and he could not help thinking of Orena as an impudent courtesan. *Then again, fair is fair. I was perfectly happy, as recently as yesterday, to have someone to talk to. And while some of her habits shock me, I benefit from most of them.* He grinned. *I need to be less hypocritical and not judge her by my cultural yardstick.*

"I had an interesting day," he told her. "I had lunch with the Pilgrims' patriarch."

"Ah." She did not seem to care much.

"You never really see him, do you?"

"No. We've got nothing to say to them. Same for them, unless it's Bible-thumping."

"And his niece is lovely." He wanted to catch her reaction.

She burst out laughing. "You men are all the same! So the Teknor's niece isn't enough for you? You need to chase Pilgrim girls all wrapped up in gray dresses? I really doubt you'd get anywhere with her. They have an antediluvian approach to their so-called virtue. In Anaena's case, I don't know what's holding you back considering what you did for her."

"What's that?"

"Don't play the fool with me, Tankar. You could've had her cast into space for her felony, Teknor niece or no Teknor niece. Why you didn't is beyond me...unless you intend to use the favor."

He reached for Orena, to pick her up. "Don't insult me."

"Get over yourself, caveman. If you feel insulted, the park is over there." She nodded in the direction.

He put her down abruptly. "So, what is it? You guys spend all your free time fighting duels?"

She curled up on the sofa and smiled. "The proof's in the pudding. I'm not going to challenge you because of what you just did. I like you, Tankar. I'm intrigued by your oddness, your fits of anger, your strength and your intelligence. If you bide your time, you'll be accepted into our society. With the right mentor, you might do really well. It'll be interesting to watch."

"Like Dhulu the meropian and Thalila the brainmare?"

Orena looked pleasantly surprised. "You've read my book?"

"Today, at the library. I forced the redheaded minx, as you call her, to give me a copy. I had fun. Tell me – why does she dislike you so?"

"Pfft. I'm an advantist, and she's a conservative. And anyway, how many times have you met two attractive women who like each other?"

"Couldn't tell you as I've known so few women. The dynamic between men is different; we respect each other's strengths. That's how it is in the Guards, in any case." He paused and slowly smiled at her. "I learned a great deal about you reading your book."

"Ha, so you're a shrink now. I wouldn't always trust what you read. I need the books to sell, so I design them for the readers."

She jumped off the sofa. "You're boring me now. You're as chatty as a Teknor or a Pilgrim. I'm going to cook dinner."

He took her spot on the sofa. He was not in love with Orena, but he was grateful to her, and she was funny and had a nice body. There were more advantages than disadvantages. How it would all play out, he did not know, nor did he much care. He had no game plan. Returning to Earth was not an option, and he did not even know in which part of the universe the *Tilsin* was currently floating around. He would have to wait.

The days passed, one after the other. They turned into weeks and then months. Tankar spent much of his time reading a hodgepodge of novels, science and history. For some reason, every time he requested a book about the mechanics of the *Tilsin*, it was always on loan. Eventually, he gave up.

He went to the movies often and saw documentaries as well

as features. There were films about planets the *Tilsin* or other city-states had visited. One love story film prompted his second duel. A short one. Some greenhorn had defied him and lay on the ground hit by two bullets, but Tankar again refused to finish him off.

Some days he watched the solar systems go past as the *Tilsin* ambled through normal space. The city-state rarely stopped, and murmurs had arisen among Stellarans opposed to the Teknor. Some had gone so far as to call for the Great Council to convene and demand a stop.

Almost every evening Orena was waiting for him when he returned to his apartment, so she was present on the day Pei came to visit. Tankar had not seen him since the day of the duel when the ambulance took him away. He knew that Pei had survived and returned to work. As Pei came into the apartment, Orena briefly took a step back as Tankar stood up, ready for anything. While assassinations were frowned upon, they were not unheard of among the People of the Stars. But Pei smiled and held out his hands, palms open.

"I've come to thank you, Tankar, for sparing my life." Pei spoke slowly and with dignity. "For a long time, I judged your treatment of me as scornful, but when I found out you'd treated Carston the same way, I understood that it was either a learned behavior or your own generous spirit in action. Either way, I owe you a debt of gratitude as well as an apology. I freely admit that there is one planetary person who is equal to us."

"I had no reason to destroy you, a man I respect," Tankar replied. "Artists as skilled as you are rare within this galaxy. Your work would fetch handsome prices on Earth."

Pei bowed. "You are too kind. The real masters are Héron from the *Frank* and Rodriguez from the *Catalogna*. Their work is far better than mine. Have you visited our museum?"

"No," Tankar replied. "I didn't know you had one. I didn't see it on the map."

"Park 19. May I escort you there tomorrow morning at nine?"

"Thank you. That would be perfect."

Pei turned to Orena. "Are you happy?" Then he returned his attention to Tankar. "Is she still as skilled at cooking Sarnak lamir?" He walked out smiling.

Orena commented, "Poor old Pei, he likes me a lot. But, like you, he's from a different time and place. He can't accept that I'm a free woman."

"I do."

"That's because you don't love me...yet. I've been your life raft, your safe place. I don't really matter!"

"That's not true, Orena!" Tankar protested. "I have a great deal of affection for you."

"Nobody said you didn't. And I like it better that way. If you wanted to be exclusive, like Pei does, I'd leave you."

The museum had an impressive collection of paintings, sculptures and artifacts from different worlds. Tankar was especially intrigued by the historical and ethnographic displays. The current technology room was 'closed for repairs'.

Later the same day, the Teknor called Tankar in. Tan greeted him cheerfully, even warmly.

"First off, I'd like to thank you belatedly on Anaena's behalf. Some Stellarans would have used the opportunity to question my loyalties. I know my niece, and I know she'll find it difficult to thank you herself, but that's not the reason I called you in.

"The Mpfifis have struck again – three times in fact. The *Uta* and the *Provence II* both disintegrated after a final torpedo barrage. The *Bremen*'s escape was a matter of sheer luck. I plead with you, again, to share the method of identifying a starship in hyperspace."

"How many times must I say the Empire doesn't have one?"

The Teknor stood as he grew more heated. "How can you wage war then? How can you defend your planets? What's the point of a Stellar Guard that arrives after the damage already has been done?"

"We don't defend our planets; we destroy our enemies' planets."

"And your enemies don't pillage Earth or the Empire's other territories? I find that very odd." The Teknor paused and took his seat with a sigh. "As you wish, Tankar. I'm not upset at your lack of gratitude, but think about this: at this very moment, an Mpfifi city-state may be tracking us, and you'll die right along with the rest of us."

"Even without this tracer you think exists," Tankar argued, "you could defend yourselves. I've studied Sorensen's book, and you often have failed to make the best use of your assets."

"You may be right," the Teknor admitted. "Strategically speaking, we're amateurs. We learn new things every day but now the clock is ticking. Is there any chance you might share your thinking?"

"Do you have the book handy?" The two men sat down.

"Okay. Let's take the battle of the *Donetz*. This is how it was defended, but you should have done it this way." He scratched out a battle plan. The Teknor hung on his every word.

"I see what you mean." He nodded. "Had we done that we might have seen them off. Poor Malenkov." He continued, "As you know, we no longer have professional soldiers. In time, we'll pick up those skills, but, in the short term, we may pay a heavy price in terms of lives lost." Turning to Tankar he asked, "I would like to appoint you as an instructor. Do you accept?"

"No."

"Why not?"

"I'm nothing more than Earth trash."

"For the love of Rktel, how would you have treated one

of our people who arrived out of nowhere onto your precious Earth? Of course you're running up against prejudice. Of course it's unpleasant. But you won't gain acceptance by draping yourself in stubborn pride...nor will you be accepted by hanging out with Orena Valoch.

"I know that a chemist tried to befriend you, but you've never gone to see him. If you accept this job offer, our men will have to realize that even a planetary refugee can be a man. Will you accept?"

"No." Tankar stood.

"So be it." The Teknor sighed at the futility of it all, then looked up at the defiant young man. "More's the pity, Tankar. I hope you never come to regret your decision."

CHAPTER TWO

Anaena

Life went on at its humdrum pace for Tankar. Gradually, over time, some Stellarans chatted with him in the cafeteria and on the gangways. Anaena had accepted his frequent library visits. She handed him the requested books without a word, so he was surprised the day she spoke.

"You've now read the entire Valoch oeuvre. What novels do you want to read next?"

"I don't know, anything's fine."

"May I give you some advice?" she offered.

"If you wish." Tankar hesitated.

"I'd suggest *The Wind of Kormor* by Paul Valenstein. We consider it the best book ever written here on the *Tilsin*. Valenstein lived and wrote in the last century."

"Why are you so friendly all of a sudden?"

She curled into herself and answered without looking at him. "Let's just say that I now understand my debt to you."

"You owe me nothing at all, if you're referring to the first duel. You helped me more than you did my unfortunate opponent."

"No regrets there," Anaena admitted. "In any case, Hank was such a troublemaker he wouldn't have lived long. But still...I breached the rules of the game; what I did was inexcusable."

"So, why did you do it?"

"I loathed you," she said bluntly, meeting his look.

"But it's not my fault I'm on the *Tilsin*."

"And it's not my fault that your ancestors forced mine into exile."

"How am I responsible for the behavior of my ancestors? I don't think mine were even involved."

"We are the products of our worlds, Tankar," she said, using his name for the first time. "Stellarans hate and look down on all planetaries, and, worst of all to us, are the Empire planetaries. Do you realize you're the first of your kind we've rescued? And that happened because Tan is the Teknor. Could you in absolute honesty swear none of our habits strike you as laughable? Or awful? Can you swear that your main goal right now isn't to escape and return to Earth?"

"I wouldn't swear to that, no," he replied, shaking his head.

"You complain about how much we despise you. But what do you think of us? Do you think we can't tell? That we don't notice?"

He shook his head in denial. "I don't have contempt for your civilization. I admire how you've built these monstrous stellar-travel vessels even though I don't fully understand your way of life. And yes, you're right, I do dislike some of your customs, like the idiotic duels, which no true man should take part in. If the point is to show bravery, there are far better ways."

"You really don't understand, do you? We all take personal responsibility for our actions, and that's the basis of our freedom. I can insult anybody I like, but I have to be willing to pay the price. How do you resolve questions of honor on Earth?"

"Sometimes by duel," he admitted. "Soldiers do, in many cases. But a duel only takes place following a ruling of the duelers' peers. For the commoners, there are courts. For the nobles, the Emperor is the judge."

"I like our way better. Your book is in Niche 23. Happy reading."

Anaena tossed back her mane of shining coppery hair, then promptly resumed her previous stance, and Tankar wondered whether their chat was a singular event. He suspected their relationship had shifted in some still mysterious way. Her face was more open, and, a few times when she did not know he was looking, he spied a smile.

On that day he left the library at the same time as Anaena.

She spoke first. "Since I opened hostilities, maybe I am the one who offers a cease-fire. I'd like to ask you some questions about life on Earth. Would you like to have dinner with me? Don't get the wrong idea, please," she warned, "I'm not like Orena."

He hesitated briefly. The offer was tempting, but was she hiding the reason for her offer? She noticed his hesitancy and said, "Don't misunderstand me, we're a long way from being friends. I'm simply asking for a favor, and I can repay you by showing you a machine room."

"They're off limits to me."

"Not if I go with you, under Teknor's orders."

That decided him. "Okay. Where do I meet you?"

"My house, 144th Street, Apartment 530, Bridge 4, Sector 2. Seven p.m. I'm also a decent cook, as you'll see."

He sent Orena a comtext that he'd likely be home late. He was surprisingly happy, but he was not ready to admit it.

If Anaena is at least cordial to me, the others will have to accept me. I'll have a place in this city and stop being a do-nothing parasite. I'll teach the men the martial arts. I'll build a tracer or at least show them how. Wait! That thought stopped him in his tracks. *No, that's my ace in the hole; I'd better save it. But at last I'll be a man again.*

His reverie ended with a jolt. He'd arrived in an unknown street, virtually deserted at that time of day. It extended in one long line of identikit doors and unadorned partitions. *Where the hell am I?* The next crossing enlightened him. He was on Bridge

4, Sector 2, 144th Street. He checked his digital timepiece and realized he was 90 minutes early.

"I must be in a hurry," he muttered to himself.

He passed Door 530, then walked the whole street, wandered around, then retraced his steps, consulting his timepiece from time to time. He was five minutes late when he rang the bell.

Anaena's apartment was very different from Orena's and his own; bigger, it featured an anteroom with floor-to-ceiling shelf-lined walls. The shelving held old books and microfiche cases. Since the young woman had failed to come out and greet him, he nosed through the books. Most were about physics and other scientific disciplines excluding two entire rows devoted to books about the Mpfifis. When the curtain between the anteroom and the rest of the flat lifted and Anaena appeared, he could hardly believe his eyes.

Her red hair cascaded down her shoulders framing her golden face and shining malachite eyes. Her delicate green floor-length dress enhanced her curves and her little white feet were laced up in gold leather-strapped sandals.

"I remind you to watch it, Tankar," she warned. "This is not a proposition."

He stood at attention. "Am I not allowed to admire beauty without being accused of inappropriate intentions?"

She smiled. "Please come in. And let's observe the truce. This evening, like good adversaries after a tough fight, we shall be as friends."

The room was cozy despite the dark décor. It felt intimate despite the bright light from three old-style floor lamps. Tankar was very happy. He had never enjoyed, had, in fact, objected to Orena's preference for veiled light and corners bathed in the half-light of the vid-screens.

"Sit, please. Take a book if you wish. Our meal is almost ready."

He chose *The Mpfifi Threat* and sat down. He leafed through it without paying much attention but was quickly engrossed in the first chapter. It was a taut analysis of the available data on the enemy. The content was tighter and more nuanced than in Sorensen's so-called classic. One section on defending city-states seemed quite good. *Why were the principles not applied?* he wondered.

Anaena returned. "Are you enjoying that?"

"Very interesting. Especially the analysis of your defense weaknesses."

"I really like it too."

"Why don't you follow the advice in there? It's totally relevant."

"It was just published yesterday."

He looked at the publication date and the author's name: Anaena Ekator!

"You...."

"Yes, except for the chapter that you like so much; you wrote that!"

"What? What do you mean, I wrote it?"

"Don't you remember your last meeting with my uncle? He recorded everything, and I made good use of the material. Your name really should be on the cover with mine."

"So you're the one in charge of assessing the Mpfifi threat?"

She stood and adopted a mock serious stance. "May I introduce Anaena Ekator, chief of the anti-Mpfifi unit?"

"But I thought...."

"That I was just some redheaded feline, as our mutual friend Orena calls me? I'm an expert in alien culture and biology specializing in non-human races. Aside from the mortal danger they represent, the Mpfifis fascinate me as much as they terrify me. Shall we eat before the food gets cold?"

The dinner was simple but delicious without the type of

culinary flourishes that Orena mastered. Tankar praised the food, but Anaena owned, "I know my limitations. So rather than fight on a terrain where I know I'm going to lose, I prefer to work within my comfort zone."

"You're an odd type of girl, Anaena. How old are you?"

"Young enough to reply without taking umbrage. Do your years last 365 days, and days 24 hours like ours do?"

"Yes."

"So I'm 22 and a half."

"I'm 24."

"Not much of a difference, then," she said cheerfully. "Now it's for you to return the favor of dinner, as I said earlier. So, tell me about your Empire, your planet."

He spoke. First he rattled off technical material as if presenting at a conference. Gradually, in response to her subtle queries, his answers became more personal. He told her about his experiences, his now-dashed hope of one day commanding a fleet that would set foot on undiscovered worlds.

"You'll see more unknown worlds with us than you would've done for the Empire."

"Maybe...but as a passenger? That wasn't the idea." He sounded miffed.

"Or as one of us if you make the effort to assimilate."

"You think that might happen? You all never let me forget I'm an outsider."

"Who knows?"

"Tell me about yourself, please," he said. "It might be easier for me to understand your culture if I can get a handle on how a typical citizen thinks and wishes and fears."

"I don't have much to tell, really. Unlike most Stellarans, I've never left the city I was born on aside from a few planetary pit stops. I lived like many others until I turned 15, and my uncle became the Teknor. I became his personal assistant while I was in college. I studied alien culture because I wanted to. I became an archivist as my social-good job. That's it. We don't have all kinds of wild adventures like you did as a Guard."

Tankar looked at her furrowed brow. She was speaking in a very neutral, calm tone. Had he missed something, or was she actually envious? "You said most people have traveled more than you. Is that the normal course of things?"

"Oh, yes. We like variety, and, under other conditions, I might've swapped city-states too. But the *Tilsin* has a concentration of everything we know about the enemy, so my place is here. Without that.... After a couple of years you get to know everyone and always see the same old faces in the gangways. Don't overthink the way Orena behaves toward you. You're the new kid in town, and that newness dominates people's views of planetaries. She has those biases too, though maybe a bit less than the rest of us because of her father.

"The other thing is that it's good for a nomad-race as a whole to swap men and women so that the gene pool stays fresh. We saw what inbreeding did to the very few, isolated colonists of Tircis, after their starship dropped them on that tiny, arid island. They're barely human now." She paused. "Would you like to see some photos?"

She got up, slid open the door to a closet, and pulled out a projector. On the blank wall he saw a strange face, totally normal at first blush, but, looking closely, he saw the eyes stared straight ahead but were both too big and too pale. The ears were so small they seemed like an afterthought. The skull was pointy and sheer under a crown of yellow hair that resembled a light, down-filled quilt. Another slide revealed a whole man with the skinny legs of a stork or ibis, overlong arms and shoulders so narrow and flaccid it looked as if the arms grew out of the torso itself.

"And it's not just their physique either, Tankar. The changes to their brains meant communication with them was almost as tricky as with the Mpfifis."

"Do you have photos of them?"

"I can do even better than photos. I'm going to show you something, even if it's a bit of a pity to end such a pleasant evening on such a sinister note. When we recovered the *Roma*, we found some still-intact automatic cameras and film. I have copies." She fumbled through the closet and came out with a much bigger projector than the first and spools of film. "These are ours."

The screen revealed a section of a gangway like the ones on the *Tilsin* blocked by a barricade of stacked-up bodies and weaponry. Then an almost human shadow crossed the screen and a Mpfifi appeared in a corner. Tankar automatically leaned forward and noted the figure was not dreadful. He just felt a vague discomfort as if looking at a nasty cartoon.

The greenish skin covered in white needles seemed both flexible and tough while the face lacking ears and nose was stony, inexpressive. Gloomy eyes darted around the gangway. The figure moved toward the camera until its face filled the screen, and Tankar was able to see its breathing apparatus pulsing under its jaw. The Mpfifi vanished from the screen.

Other film fragments followed with battle scenes that Tankar found compelling. There also was footage of a last-men-standing council meeting in a room with shattered walls. The fracas around them made the conversation hard to hear.

"This is their document," Anaena explained. "The Mpfifis' eyes don't have the same light sensitivity as ours do, so the film may seem underexposed. We found the camera under an Mpfifi corpse, one we killed when we arrived. The only human survivors were eight women and about 50 children who'd hidden in a hold. When the Mpfifis saw us arrive on the *Suomi*, they fled without even trying to fight back and, without tracers, we were unable to pursue."

The film appeared to have been shot in an aggressive orange light. It lent a weird hue to the plants and made the whole atmosphere feel off in some undefinable way. The film illustrated the taking of the *Roma* from the invaders' perspective: their careful movement from gangway to gangway, from park to park. The battle had been ferocious, and the Mpfifis paid a high price for their victory. Twice the images swung around as if the cameraman dropped the equipment and another person's hand had saved it from crashing to the ground.

"Now I understand where you learned about their tactics," he murmured quietly.

As the battle drew to its end, the Mpfifis got sloppy about advancing. "Look closely, Tankar. You'll see why we hate them so much and fear them as well."

The camera focused on about 50 human captives, primarily women and children, their backs against a wall. One of the few men pulled into the foreground hands in the air. He spoke, though his voice was garbled by the recording device. His words were hard to understand, but his request was obvious from his hand movements. He was begging for mercy for the sorry herd of survivors. One Mpfifi came into camera range, raised his weapon and, in a burst of energy, burned the supplicant's feet. The man fell to the ground and, with apparent pleasure, the non-human slowly burned the man alive. His face remained impassive as he set fire to the human's hands, then his arms and legs and finally the torso with a final spurt of fire. Other non-humans then made their way through the ranks, and slowly they roasted the men, women and children. Sometimes they allowed the prisoners to flee a few meters and then burned away their legs. By the time

Anaena flicked the projector off, only three women were visible. Anaena wept.

"No. I can't watch anymore. The last woman was my mother, Tankar, do you get it? My mother? She was just visiting the *Roma*. We arrived a few hours after the carnage. If only we'd been able to follow the enemy through hyperspace, if we could've pinpointed their home planet, their empire! We have bombs powerful enough to send a kingdom out of its orbit, to zap it into oblivion. We'd so happily use those things. But we can't! We have nothing. Our physicists search and search and never come up with the answer."

And that's not going to happen anytime soon, Tankar thought, *since you abandoned the Cursin hyperspace apparatus*. In the Empire, the discovery had come about in part by accident, such an unlikely event that he doubted it could be reproduced. Should he give them the secret? Put them on the right track? He remained unsure.

Anaena spoke softly but with passion. "My uncle is convinced you have such tracers, Tankar. I agree with him that, without them, your Empire wouldn't be in the shape it is in, so big now that you no longer can visit all of the planets the Empire claims for itself. If you have this thing, please, please give it to us. You've seen what the Mpfifis can do. They've not yet started to attack the stronger planets, but they well may one day, and, on that day, Earth will not be immune. When you were drifting in your space suit, my uncle rescued you for that reason."

Her words wounded him. "And I guess that's why he gave me the A-card. No, Anaena, we don't possess the secret to the tracer. I've told you this over and over, and I'm tired of repeating myself!"

"I don't believe you," she spat. Then, regaining control of herself, "Yes, we've harmed you, I admit that. Once we rescued you we should have fully embraced you, but we just couldn't. There's been far too much bad blood between us and the Empire, even though, admittedly, no blood has been shed in a long time.

"Do you understand what I'm saying, Tankar? My uncle doesn't care about ancient history, but there are others who'd never have accepted you. Tan is a Teknor, but he's not an all-powerful emperor. His authority rests only on his technical skill, granted him by the Great Council. As for me...."

"You were the opposite of friendly. I'm not even reminding you of your attempt to have me killed. This evening, you've proven to be the sole Stellaran other than Orena to show me friendship. Tonight erases any debt you might have owed me.

"The Empire had no tracers," he lied, "but, a few days before the rebellion began, I attended a conference of military technicians, and they spoke of the possibility. I'm going to rifle through what I remember. Unfortunately, that day I wasn't really giving the talk all my attention. If I remember anything important, I will go see the physicists right away." He stood and said graciously, "Good evening...and thank you."

She walked him to the door. Tempted to lean over and kiss her, he was annoyed at his own desire and did not.

As he headed home, he mulled over the horrifying film and the conversation that had followed. Why had he made that half promise? Why the white lie? Would he give up his only tradeable item in exchange for small gestures of friendship? In fact, did she even feel friendship toward him? He'd find out soon enough.

Orena was waiting up for him and reading. "Good evening? How was the redheaded feline?"

He nodded his head yes.

"You're free," she said.

"It's not what you think. She pumped me for information about the Empire, Earth...."

"Yes, the habits of savages have always interested her. Especially their mating habits."

He lost his temper, and shouted at her. "She is nothing

to me. The only thing she wants from me is to say we have hyperspace tracers."

"Do you?"

"No!" He spat the word out.

"Me, I don't really care. Goodnight, Tankar."

"Aren't you staying?"

"No, not tonight. I don't deal in other women's castoffs."

"Not everyone has the same habits as you."

"You did when it suited you."

"Hell, Orena, I keep telling you that the girl is nothing to me; she's my enemy! You may be right that I've been a bit too stuffy, but I'm getting really fed up with you all. You don't even have the generosity to save a man from the void without a hidden agenda. You're not much more humane than the Mpfifis."

"What do you know about that?"

"Anaena told me. The Teknor rescued me because I'm from the Empire, and he thought we had the tracers."

"Son of a bitch! Now you see how low the Ekators sink."

"Honestly? I would've done the same in his shoes. Goodnight."

"No, I'm staying."

"I'm not a charity case."

"Can you see me giving to charity?"

★   ★   ★

Tankar saw Anaena several times more over the following days. She was cordial but distant. He remained convinced that her invitation was part of a plan to manipulate him that had failed. Then things changed yet again when he ran into her in the street.

"Come see me, Tankar. I still have a lot to learn about the Empire."

"I'm not so sure you really care."

"Don't. I promise that I won't mention the tracers again. You want to withhold the secret? That's your choice."

"So what are we going to talk about?"

"Everything and nothing, if you wish."

"Why the sudden interest in me?"

"Are you afraid of me?"

"No! Of course not. When should I come over?"

"Tomorrow night. I'll invite some intelligent people."

"To show them what a tame planetary looks like?"

"Don't be ridiculous. I'm doing it to break the cycle of loneliness you seem to be caught in."

Tankar had to admit that he spent a very enjoyable evening. There were six people in total, four men and two women. Anaena's female friend was a pretty brunette, and the three male Stellarans were lively and witty. Much wine was drunk and songs were sung. The others praised Tankar's singing of the 'Guard Heroes Song'. Eventually the four guests left and he was alone with Anaena.

"I'm nosy, and, like all women, I love a good story. Tell me about the first battle you fought."

"It's not very interesting, Anaena, believe me. All wars are pretty much the same."

"We've never really waged war from the *Tilsin*," she replied. "And our city-state versus city-state battles are heavy affairs with fortresses and the like. Nothing like your fast cruisers rushing around."

"Okay. If it's that important to you. I was just a cadet, fresh out of school when—"

"Not that stuff. Tell me about the first time you commanded a cruiser."

He smiled, both flattered and amused. "It wasn't a cruiser,

Anaena. Just a recon scout. Me and five other guys."

"Even better. It'll be more interesting. But you quickly got to the point of commanding a cruiser, yes?"

"I was on a torpedo boat when the uprising began. If you really want to know the whole story: I'd just taken over as commander of the *Saphir* when the Martian riots broke out. Mars is quite close to Earth, one of the closest in the solar system. It wasn't even really a police operation. The only major issue was that three cruisers that landed on Mars joined the mutiny and backed the rebels.

"Seventeen vessels, ten cruisers and seven scouts, took off. My job was to keep watch on the squadron's left flank. We bombarded Mars until they surrendered. When I say we, I mean the bulk of the flotilla. But I was following the enemy ships heading to Pluto. My scout was faster, and I was gaining on them when they plunged into hyperspace. It was my first trip as commander, so I didn't know what to do at first. Follow them or wait for backup? But then a quick look at the screen on the tr—"

He stopped midsentence and said, "Oh, shit!" He stared at her and sighed, "Your match, Anaena."

"What?"

"Don't play the innocent with me. Now you know we have tracers. This evening, this whole setup was intended to get me to admit to it. Your out-of-the-blue friendship should have warned me, but I'm as gullible as a cadet, so I bought it."

He mocked her speech patterns. "No, not that. Tell me all about your first battle where you commanded a cruiser." He shook his head. "I'm an idiot. One of the first things we learn in the barracks: call the adjutant 'lieutenant'...what's the risk? But you still don't have the secret, and you won't get it even if the Mpfifis burn me alive."

"Come on, Tankar, be reasonable. Should it become necessary, we always have the psychoscope. You remember that you and Tan talked about it? I hate the idea, and my uncle doesn't like it either, believe me or not."

"From Tan, I believe it, no problem. I think he's the sole man in this city-state worthy of the name. As to you, why would you look out for me?"

"Because I don't believe anyone has the right to invade another man's subconscious," she said in a dignified manner. "And because I've come to admire you."

"Riiiight. There's another one of your tricks."

"I'm a Stellaran, Tankar, and I can't lie: we're under threat. Slowly but surely, we're losing to the Mpfifis. I'll do anything in my power to get the secret out of you."

He looked at her smugly. "Anything? Really? Anything?"

She blushed, furious. "Yes, anything," she spat, "but I'll kill you afterward."

He shrugged. "I'm not going to ask you for anything. The day I decide to give up the tracers, I'll do it for free. But I'll have enjoyed being your friend."

"And you're so sure you don't already have my friendship? Do you really think I would have had you in my home twice—"

"You told me you'd do anything to get your hands on those blueprints."

"I did say that," she acknowledged. "It's true that we've eroded your trust, and that's a pity. I would've liked to help you fit in here. We need men like you on the *Tilsin*."

"If only you'd decided that one sooner."

"You're being childish, Tankar. You're acting like a kid who throws his toys on the floor because he doesn't get his way. How could you possibly expect immediate acceptance from a society that has a multitude of good reasons to hate the Empire? We had to study you; it took time."

"Maybe I'm impatient," Tankar admitted, then paused. "Let's make a deal."

"Yes?"

"I'll sketch out blueprints for a tracer. As I'm doing that, I'll give all of this more thought. When I complete them, I may hand the sketches to Tan, or I may not. In return, all I ask of you is friendship. Nothing more."

Anaena held out her hand. "Thank you, Tankar. I give you my word that, until you make up your mind, I won't ask you about the tracers again."

He went home, his heart feeling light. Orena was not in the apartment. He went to bed but could not fall asleep right away. Eventually he got out of bed and began to scribble.

In the morning, he bought a small strongbox and some drawing materials. He only left the house for meals and declined two invitations from Orena. He accepted a third after she burst into a fit of jealousy, preceded by her 'You're free' mantra.

He spent a few happy days absorbed by the interesting work that gave him the sense of being a man once again. The task was a daunting one. He knew the theory behind hyperspace tracers, of course, but was unsure how to apply theory to a blueprint. He wished he had his reference books. He realized there was a world of difference between maintaining and fixing a neutrinics-based machine and creating one from scratch. He had moments of despair but only once did he slip all the papers into a folder and consider bringing them to a physicist to complete. Then he went back to the job at hand with determination to see it through himself.

"This is my ace in the hole. I can't waste it," he said out loud. Had he in fact analyzed his approach, he would have realized he was unwilling to admit defeat.

Tankar reached completion except for building and fine-tuning a prototype. He did not have the tools. Partly out of bravado but in greater part for Anaena, he had decided to hand over the plans to the Teknor. He did not think he was in love with Anaena. He was used to living among fellows except for brief forays to the Center for Racial Perfection. Orena was meeting all of his emotional and physical needs, but he was enjoying the mental chess match with the Teknor's niece. He had been ahead just once in their relationship, when he had not turned her in after the duel. She had regained her edge by having him over for dinner twice. Now he would be vastly increasing her debt to him: once personally and once for her people, the Stellarans. He had no idea what would happen next, but he did not worry about it. Anaena had brought spark back into his life.

If I ever accept the teaching job the Teknor offered me, it would be fun to toy with the Stellarans and make them bend to Guard rules, he dreamed.

He smiled mischievously at his plan to hand over the blueprints to the Teknor as he headed to the library where he expected to see Anaena.

And then the *Tilsin*'s sirens rang out three times.

CHAPTER THREE

Encounter in Space

Tankar stood still. What was happening? For an instant he thought the Mpfifis might have struck, and he regretted dragging his feet, but the men and women passing by him did not seem anxious and, if they appeared to be rushing, it was the springy step of people on the way to a party. He stopped a young man. "What's going on?"

"We're going to greet the *Frank*. Didn't you know?"

Tankar continued hesitantly in the direction of the library. The door was shut. Stymied, he turned to follow the flow of humanity in the streets until he heard a clear voice calling his name. Anaena was smiling at him. "I was looking for you."

"And I for you."

"I've come with an invitation from Tan to ask if you'd like to witness the command post maneuvers?"

"So now I'm allowed into the restricted area?"

"Those rules are over. I told my uncle of your promise."

"I haven't actually promised to deliver the blueprints, Anaena...."

"He knows. Follow me."

They went through a door with a red circle and down a narrow corridor to a gravity slide that led to the city's nerve center. It was the central location for flight commands, shooting instructions and huge electronic computing modules. There were three secondary centers that were idle in normal conditions but now buzzing and clacking sounds came through the closed doors. They finally reached the command and control center itself.

The circular room had walls covered with screens and dashboards monitored by engineers. About 20 men sat around a doughnut-shaped low table surrounding an opening in the floor. Tan Ekator stood waiting for them. "Welcome, Tankar. Two hours ago we received a message that the *Frank* wished to set up a conjunction. I thought the operation might interest you, so I sent Ana to pick you up. Sit next to me." He waved to his left.

"I'm going to be pretty busy," the Teknor apologized, "so Ana will fill you in as needed."

Tankar sat at a section of the desk not filled with instruments. He leaned forward and had no trouble seeing the bottom of the opening around which the table was centered. It was split into six hexagonal shapes, each reflecting one segment of the sky – right, left, forward, back, top and bottom. In the zenith area, he saw a point of somewhat brilliant light moving across the starscape.

The young woman pointed. "That's the *Frank*. It'll approach from above. For 30 hours our two cities will adhere to each other and will communicate via five gravity slides. This is what we call a conjunction, and we do one every other year. This time's a bit different as the most recent conjunction happened just before your arrival."

The *Frank* descended rapidly, concealing more and more stars. On the screen the *Tilsin* seemed to be climbing, but Tankar could not help looking up and feeling some apprehension. The Teknor noticed. "Good, Tankar. You have the instincts of a skilled starship commander, and your brain rather than your heart is leading you to think the *Frank* is coming from below. Don't worry; it won't shatter the hull."

Tankar blushed. Anaena said softly, "Don't feel bad. We all had a similar reaction the first time. I've witnessed several conjunctions and, even now, I crawl into my shell, shoulders hunched up to my ears at the thought of millions of tons of starship settling on top of our city ship."

The Teknor motioned for them to be quiet. He stared attentively at the radar-telemeter screen. When the *Frank* appeared to have come too close for the on-screen directions to be of use, they moved to the gravitometer. Tan click-clacked on the keyboard, and Tankar understood he was remotely adjusting the *Frank*'s speed. A red light turned on. The Teknor leaned back in his seat and breathed out heavily.

"Done! In a few minutes my old friend Gadeau will be here. He's the Teknor on the *Frank*."

Indeed, fewer than 20 minutes later, a fifty-something thickset man with brown hair entered the command and control center, followed by three young Stellarans. He shook Tan's hand enthusiastically.

"Tan, you old pirate! Happy to see you again, you and the lovely Anaena. Sadly this isn't just a social call. Where can we talk privately?" He paused and remembered, "Please meet Clan Dillard, Jules Moreau and Wladimir Kowalski."

"Still with you, I see," the Teknor smiled. Then, with a small wave, "We can meet in my apartment."

"And who is this young man?" Gadeau asked.

"Tankar Holroy, from the Empire of Earth. Officer in the Stellar Guards."

"You've had the same thought I did."

"He was lost, and we scooped him up."

"Bring him along, then. What I have to say concerns him as well. Anaena, you must come as well; we need you."

And so Tankar paid his first visit to the Teknor's private quarters, which were much larger than others he'd seen. They had a large rectangular room with walls reflecting space. He felt as if he were in some tall tower with hundreds of windows overlooking the city. Yet he knew he was actually in the center of the city. Low-slung seats encircled another doughnut table cluttered with materiel. Tan waved at the chairs.

"Sit, please. Gad, are you still partial to wine from Téléphor?"

"Brr. If there's no Novagallia wine, it'll do."

Tan pushed a button and within seconds a man and a trolley laden with glasses and bottles of golden liquid appeared. Anaena smiled and spoke softly to Tankar. "This is the sixth time I've sat in on a meeting between Tan and his friend. They have the exact same exchange each time."

The waiter filled everyone's glass and took his leave.

"To the People of the Stars! May we live free and strong forever!"

The Stellarans clinked glasses. Tankar held back wondering what the People of the Stars' happiness really meant to him. Anaena poised her glass for a toast so he joined the ritual.

"That being said," the Teknor said, "what is so urgent that you rushed to see us? You know you were lucky that your message was received? I tweaked the agreed route, and I didn't switch the times of our emergence from hyperspace."

"You shouldn't have. What if the Mpfifis…. In any event, this is what has happened. It's not good, Tan, the Mpfifis are now targeting the stronger planets!"

"Damn it! Where? When? How?"

"Falhoé IV about a month ago."

"Were they pushed back?"

"Yes, but the price was steep. Three hundred million victims."

"And their losses?"

"Three cities decimated."

"That's not much. I would have thought Falhoé would have better defended itself."

"That's the surprising thing, Tan. The enemy arrived via

hyperspace less than a hundred thousand kilometers from the planet."

"New weaponry?"

"Not that I know of. But they did use fusion bombs. The battle lasted two days, not a minute more, and an entire continent is in ruins. Then they left."

"How many cities?"

"Twenty-two that we found. We were supposed to make a stop on Falhoé, as we always do. We arrived three days after the invasion and were almost killed ourselves. The residents there shoot first, ask questions later."

"This is bad news. Very bad, indeed, if it means that the Mpfifis believe they have the upper hand and are in the second stage of empire expanding."

"Do they have one? Or are they nomads like we are?"

"Those two cultures are not necessarily mutually exclusive. Don't you think we would've developed an empire if we'd wanted to?"

"Maybe, Tan. What I do know is we need to change tack vis-à-vis the Earthlings. They are, after all, humans like us, and we would do well to ally with them. When I saw that young man, I thought you'd beaten me to the punch. What do you think, Officer? Is the Earth Empire...."

Tankar stood. "For all I know, the Empire may no longer be standing. When I left, the rebellion was gaining the upper hand. I have no idea how it ended. But I doubt the forces of the Empire, or those that succeed them, will be strong enough to make a difference...for decades, at least."

"That's too bad. I must admit I had been counting on the Empire to help out. Better the devil you know, etcetera and so forth. The Empire had the only well-organized and super-strong army. You guys were always at war with someone, so you must have developed new weaponry. Maybe you could lend some technical support?"

Tankar inhaled deeply. He'd reached a Rubicon. He spoke directly to Tan Ekator. "You do know that since Anaena wheedled the information from me – I'm not mad at her, she played it masterfully – you know that we have hyperspace tracers. So I have reconstructed a blueprint for one such model."

The Stellarans rose as one. The Teknor asked, "How long would it take you to build one?"

"That all depends on how quickly your physicists can accomplish the task with the technology on board. A month or two, perhaps."

"That fast, really?"

"Maybe longer. I won't have a clear picture until I've talked to your tech people."

"Is the blueprint ready?"

"Almost. I'll be honest; I planned to barter for the tracer."

"In exchange for what?"

"Sending me back to Earth or allowing me to stay on another Empire colony, but I've changed my mind. If the Mpfifis are attacking the planets, then Gadeau is right. Now is the time for all human armies to rise up and unite as one before it's too late. I'll hand over the completed sketches in a few days. In fact, it would be best for me to get back to them now, if you don't mind."

Tankar stood, bowed to the company and took his leave. He'd barely reached the gangway when Anaena ran up to him. "Thank you so much, Tankar."

He looked at her radiant expression. He smiled bitterly. "Happy now? You've won."

Remnants of her earlier hostility flashed in her green eyes. "Oh, just stop thinking in military terms, soldier. Yes, okay, I won. I succeeded in persuading a stubborn soldier to embrace reason.

Why must you spoil everything? Why turn it into something negative?" She shrugged. "It doesn't matter. Thank you, again." She spun around and vanished in a whirlwind of copper hair.

He took the shortest route home. The streets teemed with a motley crowd in which he saw many new faces. Laughter, music and songs blasted through open doors. He crossed Park 6, which rang with shouting and running children. He smiled.

I guess each conjunction is like a party for the Stellarans. And double the fun when it's unexpected.

He put groceries in his refrigerated device. He had no intention of leaving his apartment until he was ready to deliver perfect blueprints. By about 6 p.m., he had finished except for one element that he thought might take another two hours' work. He stood and selected a random can of food and put the oven on to heat it. The announcer bell rang. "Orena really could have let me be tonight," he muttered.

But it was Anaena at the door, accompanied by two women he had not met before. "Tankar, may I present Helen Pirron and Clotilde Martin, two old friends who arrived on the *Frank*."

He bowed. "Please come in."

"No, no," she protested. "We've come to pick you up. Nobody on the *Tilsin* should be alone tonight. We're having a party for everyone from the *Frank* except for those on guard duty...."

"What if the Mpfifis come now?"

"They'd never attack two city-states at the same time. Also, we're way out of their field of operation."

He looked into his tiny kitchen, his pathetic provisions, his cluttered work surface. "What about the blueprints?"

"Tomorrow."

He shrugged and grinned. "Okay, I'm coming with you." He turned the oven off and put his papers into the strongbox. Then, hesitantly, he asked, "Would you...would you mind if, just for tonight, I wear my Guard uniform?"

"Not at all!"

"That would be wonderful," said Clotilde, who was as brunette as Helen was blond.

"Give me a moment, then."

He took his uniform from the closet and put it on quickly. Although it felt strange at first when he checked himself in the mirror, he recognized himself, a tall man with cold gray eyes. He mimicked a salute. *So happy to see you again, Lieutenant Holroy. How have you been?* He walked back to the main room. "Here I am. Where to?"

"Dinner first!"

The streets outside his apartment were still unusually busy, and, at first, Tankar moved self-consciously. He stood out in the formal uniform among Stellarans in their loose, multicolored outfits. Eventually, he relaxed. The looks of passersby betrayed no more surprise than they would have at the sight of one young man squiring three young women.

He did not recognize the interior of the restaurant. Potted plants covered the walls; brightly colored garlands floated from the ceiling and lit the center with different shades. An orchestra he couldn't see played soft music. Stellarans were there drinking, eating and laughing. There were no waiters on duty as a huge buffet groaned under the weight of dishes and bottles. Two young men stood up and waved at Anaena.

She made the introductions. "Jan Pomerand from the *Frank*, Luig Tardini from the *Tilsin*, Lieutenat Tankar Holroy of Earth's Stellar Guards."

The other guys did not need an introduction. "Luig, go get some food and drink. I happen to know Tankar has a soft spot for Sarnak lamir. Tiliir filet of beef for me, please. We're a tad late."

The meal was very good and the wine plentiful and, for Tankar, provided an entirely new experience. The Stellarans had abandoned any reservations they had about their Earth visitor. He discovered why when another one of them came up to him and whispered, "Thanks for the tracers."

As to Anaena, she was transformed. She glowed with happiness; no longer was she the efficient and surly librarian or the head of the anti-Mpfifi division. Tankar was used to the birdbrained ladies of the Empire courts and the ignorant commoner women. He had never in his life met a woman with all the grace of a noblewoman combined with a profound intelligence. He relaxed and let himself be carried along by the general euphoria around him. The atmosphere was so very different from the brutal partying he'd experienced during his time as a cadet when they had visited dives near the astroports or the all-male mess-hall events among buddies.

At the far end of the room, a man waved to Anaena, and she apologized before excusing herself to go see him. Their conversation was brief, and she nodded her head yes a few times. Tankar felt a flash of jealousy. Was she agreeing to go on a date with that guy? But she was back in a flash.

"That's the problem with being the head of a unit. People can't leave you alone even at a party."

By the time they had finished their meal the room was only half-full, and those who remained were streaming out. Pomerand checked his watch.

"We won't get seats, Anaena."

"Yes, we will, I reserved for six. But you're right, we need to make a move."

"Where are we going?" Tankar asked.

"Park 18 to see a show. You'll like it, I think."

Around the central common dotted with bushes here and

there, stands had been erected, and Stellarans from both city-states piled on top of them. The crowd was colorful as it flowed in and around the projector lights. Anaena led her friends to the center of one of the stands.

"We're going to see some dancing," she told Tankar. "It's an interpretive dance called *The Future of Men* by Silja Salminen of the *Frank*."

The lights flicked off suddenly. Just one projector swept across the square, cutting through the shadows of the shrubs. Something slid behind a tree and passed underneath the light: a slowly moving hunched figure.

"First figure. *The Human Conscience Awakens at the Onset of the Fourth Century*," said Anaena.

The stooped form kept on walking with awkward grace like a clumsy animal. The shape began to inflate and, in the center of the lawn, a semi-clad young woman with long flowing brown hair appeared magnified four times.

"That's so great! How do you create that effect?" Tankar asked.

"I'll explain later," Anaena whispered. "Look."

The young woman was dancing mimicking a pithecanthrope… or other prehuman being, he wasn't sure. She emerged from the forest, tapping on the savannah as if afraid of the void or the view to infinity. She embodied Courage and Flight, with Fear hiding behind the friendly trees. A man leaped down from the branches and, hand in hand, the two walked toward the rising sun.

Then the grass was empty again.

The tableau continued, shifting and evolving. The first Homo Sapiens camped in front of their caves, safe from fire; the glory of antiquity built on slavery; the slow procession toward well-being and liberty. Then, under a red light, atomic war appeared as the nameless nightmare that predated yet spawned the Empire.

"Don't take the next tableau personally, Tankar," Anaena warned.

Crude light from a projector crushed the young woman who was tied to a post, her hands and feet shackled. A monster watched over her, whip in hand. Anaena snickered. "A thousand pardons, please, Tankar, but this deformed being represents the Empire. You got that, right?"

He smiled, happy enough to ignore the insult.

Two new characters appeared on the stage. There was a hunched old man with a compass in his hand and a book under one arm. The second figure was a monk carrying an incense holder emitting thick smoke. He was swinging it under the monster's nostrils. Delighted, the monster lost its focus on the woman and missed seeing the monk build a wall of smoke in front of the captive.

"Science and Religion come to the aid of Humanity," Anaena whispered.

Then Tankar stifled a laugh. From the points on its compass, Science could unlock the toughest of chains.

"Yes, I know," she said. "It's pretty ridiculous, but that's not what matters. Watch the actual dancing."

The chains fell to the ground, and the young woman ascended to the starlit sky. Her feet left the ground as she swam upward with unimaginable grace. Below her the impotent monster frothed at the mouth. Slowly, Humanity, her loose hair floating in the wind, plucked at the stars as if picking flowers.

"Aside from the admittedly flawed background arguments, how did you find the show?"

"It was lovely. This young woman, on Earth, would have every nobleman at her feet."

"Join us on the *Frank*, Tankar, and you can see her anytime," Clotilde said.

"No, thanks," he muttered through a thin-lipped smile. "It was difficult enough to get used to the *Tilsin*. I'm staying here."

In another park, couples danced different steps from those he knew on Earth. They moved in the lower gravity, and this allowed the dancers to slide as he had never seen before. In spite of his protests, Tankar let first Clotilde, then Helen, and finally Anaena lead him to the dance floor where he stayed. As they spun around, he held her fragile muscular body close, and it was as if he had never known a world other than the *Tilsin*, and he had no wish to discover any other.

And so Tankar's night continued, moving from pleasure to pleasure, surrounded by agreeable, cheerful people. They attended other shows and drank in different bars. At around 5 a.m., Anaena said, "It's time to go home. We do have to work tomorrow. Thank you for joining us."

He wanted to respond and tell her how thankful he was, but his brain was fogged by all the drinking and his pasty tongue could only allow him to utter platitudes.

"Drop my hand, come on." She was smiling. "See you later, Tankar, Lieutenant of the Empire's Stellar Guard."

And so he stood alone among strangers, declined a few invitations, and went home. He found a cylindrical tube and a note on the table. He looked at the letter first

Tankar, I prefer to leave before you abandon me for that she cat. I saw Pei this evening, and we've decided to stay together. I'm not angry. I wish you luck and hope that you occasionally think of me and my efforts to ease you into life aboard the Tilsin. *Pei and I are going to live on the* Frank. *I hope to see you as a friend at the next conjunction. I liked you very much, you Earthly barbarian, and I think I could've loved you. See you again somewhere in space.*

He opened the tube, which contained several lovely paintings by Pei. There also was a note, which read, *I know what I'm doing isn't in the best of manners, but I can't resist Orena. As a memento from someone who once tried to kill you and whom you saved, please accept this modest gift. Fondly, Pei.*

Good luck to the both of you, as well. He spoke to the walls.

He went to the bedroom, exhausted. He sensed that something was not right. It was the strongbox. It had been forced open and the bolt sawed off. He rushed to look inside and saw the box was empty. The tracer blueprints were gone.

CHAPTER FOUR

Iolia

Tankar stood frozen in shock, not moving for a long moment. So Anaena had double-crossed him. Again. He could not doubt it; everything was so clear. Knowing that his plans were almost complete, she had lured him out of the apartment and, during dinner, had instructed the cafeteria worker to break in and steal the plans while, all along, he naïvely had been enjoying her company. Due to his nature and training, he had nothing but contempt and hatred for betrayal and, because he had believed in her empathy, he had dared to hope for even more. Disgusted, he spat on the ground.

That manipulative bitch. I'm still just a planetary parasite, less than nothing to her. She certainly had her act down pat.

A flash of hope struck him: what if she were not responsible? Why would she steal the blueprints knowing he would hand them over the following day? He would go see her a little later, and all would be revealed. He paused again. No. Everything was perfectly clear already. The reason was obvious: if he handed over the blueprints he would be a hero in the eyes of many. She would not be able to keep him isolated anymore, a pariah.

He paced, drunk with rage and shame. How could he, a lieutenant of the Stellar Guard, have allowed her to toy with him? He looked for harsh enough words to describe her — *treacherous and manipulative bitch.* The rules of the Guards were wise: women were to be used for pleasure and to incubate future Guards.

Now he was driven by one wish and one wish only: revenge. He would love to batter her lovely lips with his fists, smash her lying mouth, but even that was not enough. Did he want to kill her? Should he challenge her to a duel? He was not sure that he, as a man, could do that. In any event, one bullet for her 10 made for terrible odds.... He did not care about dying, but to allow her to emerge triumphant? No. He paced around his apartment. He needed to wreck the *Tilsin*.

For that he would need time, and he was not sure he had it. His usefulness to the Stellarans was spent. The blueprints were gone. Not quite completed, but any physicist would be able to work it out within days. Then they would be happy to get rid of him.

He instinctively reached for his belt. Empty. He had not been given his weapons back when they returned his uniform. Assassins already might be on his trail. He smiled bitterly; at least he would die in uniform as he should. However, in a world like the *Tilsin* there had to be a hiding places, a refuge....

A refuge? Words he had heard recently came back to him. One of the articles in the convention between the Menians and the Stellarans gave the Pilgrims the right of refuge. He had to reach their compound quickly. He looked around for something that might serve as a weapon. All he had was his compass. He laughed mirthlessly, thinking back to the dance hours earlier... the compass that frees captive humanity.

He put together a pack of provisions as he had no idea whether he would be in hiding for hours or days. He inched open the front door. The street was empty. He gave his apartment one last look and wistfully eyed Pei's paintings. Art held no interest for potential dead men.

He encountered almost no Stellarans on his way to the Pilgrims' compound. The main door of the Menians' area was shut. He should have alerted the Pilgrims, but he hadn't dared in the event his communications might be monitored. He hid behind a metal pillar awaiting daybreak.

Tankar didn't recognize the man who answered the door. "Hello, brother. How may I help you?"

"I wish to talk to Holonas the Sage."

"That will not be easy, brother. Have you made an appointment?"

"He told me to come anytime."

"That is fine, brother. I shall take you to him."

The old Patriarch welcomed him with delight. "You are back then, brother Holroy. I am happy to see you. What would you like from us?"

"Refuge."

The word smacked the air like the snap of a whip. Tankar had debated and wondered whether it might not have been better to trick his way into asylum, but trickery was not in his nature. In any event, the Pilgrims would find out the truth soon enough.

The old man sat speechless for a time. "Aside from a duel, have you killed another human being?"

"No."

"What are you afraid of?"

"That I'll be killed, or rather hunted down like an animal."

"Please sit. Stellarans are not in the habit of killing for no reason."

"It wouldn't be for no reason from their perspective. The reason would be to rid the city of my presence."

"You look exhausted, son. Sleep now, and, when you're rested, you can tell me the whole story. Have no fear. If it is refuge you seek, you have found it."

Cumulated fatigue weighed heavily on Tankar. He was led to a bedroom where he collapsed into a deep sleep. He slept for a very long time and awoke rested, still trying to erase the previous day's events from his mind. He heard a young voice singing a hymn that was both grave and joyful. He walked out and spotted a young brunette sewing. He had never seen anyone sew on the *Tilsin*, and her swift, skillful motions intrigued him. He approached. The young woman turned around and beamed. "Brother Holroy, I am so happy to see you. My uncle mentioned we had company but didn't say your name. Are you going to stay a bit longer this time?"

"Your uncle's not here?"

"He is not, but he will be back soon. Are you hungry? Thirsty?"

"Pretty thirsty, yes, thank you."

She brought a tall glass of cold water. "Please say you will stay a bit longer this time. I would so like you to tell me about life on Earth. I have not seen many planets aside from Avenir. As for the others, my uncle always claims they are too dangerous for a young woman."

She looked straight at him, animated and cheerful. Her brown eyes locked on to him expressing neither shame nor daring. As he stared into them, he remembered another pair of eyes, brilliant green reflecting laughter and great intelligence. To himself he thought, *Yet another mass of female protoplasm who's not yet caught on to the art of trickery.*

At last he spoke, "This stay might be longer, indeed, if your uncle allows it."

"Why would he not?"

"I can't say. It might be a risk for him."

The words had barely escaped his lips that he regretted them. Why should he arouse her suspicions? Instinct told him he was not in danger from this naïve young girl. How old was she... sixteen? Seventeen?

At that moment, the Patriarch entered the room. "Holroy! You are awake, I see." Turning to his niece he said, "I hope you did not pester our guest with questions, Iolia."

"I just woke up. And she wasn't pestering me!"

"Come with me to my office, son. I should, of course, listen to your confession in temple, but you are not of our faith." The office was just a small book-lined room. The old man sat and motioned to Tankar to take a stool. "Speak to me, son."

Tankar told him about the humiliation he had suffered on the *Tilsin*. All of his pent-up frustrations flowed out of him. He told the Patriarch about his rescue, the duels, his lonely home life with Orena as his sole companion, and then the warped friendship with Anaena. He spoke of her subterfuge that had led him to reveal the tracer information, and her subsequent betrayal as well as the fear that betrayal had sparked in him. Holonas listened in silence.

"That surprises me about Anaena," he said at last. "She is violent, but she is loyal."

"You know her?"

"Do you think I run this compound and maintain no contact with the Teknor? Of course I know him, and I like him. If Anaena shared our faith, her presence would honor our little group. True, she is fanatically devoted to the *Tilsin*. That intense feeling may well have led her to try anything to secure your blueprints."

"I was due to hand them over today!"

"You should have given them up much sooner, Tankar. She may have thought you were playing her and that you would charge a good deal for what you should have given away freely out of human compassion."

"Human compassion? How much of that was given to me, the planetary refugee?"

"I know all about that," Holonas sighed. "The Stellarans are not ones to forgive slights from years, decades, even centuries before. You should have risen above that. I do not believe that you genuinely are in danger, but there are no guarantees with our friends from the outside, so we shall grant you asylum. Your card applies here for as long as you have it. If it were to be taken away, we will look into it. What kind of work would you like to do? Everybody here is employed."

"Do you have a physics lab?"

"Of course."

"I would like to start again, to perfect the tracers; that would make me appear useful to the Stellarans and would protect my life were I to return to them."

"Once again, I do not think you are in danger. I will pay a visit to Tan Ekator and try to shed some light on the situation. While we find you a place to live, you can stay here with us. My niece is extremely keen to ask you questions. I will see you soon, Tankar Holroy."

The common room was deserted. Tankar sat down to reflect. Things were not really that bad. He had been granted asylum and would work in a laboratory where he could plot his revenge under the guise of perfecting the tracers. One thing troubled him: along with the Stellarans and himself, he might annihilate these kind Pilgrims who had done him no ill. He wanted to save them.

What he had in mind was not an atomic explosion; it would be too quick, and it would require difficult-to-procure materiel. Destroying the motors somewhere in space would be better. He could do that far from inhabited areas by sabotaging all spacecrafts, except the ones belonging to the Pilgrims. No, that would not do. The Pilgrims would try to save the others. He had to come up with a better idea. He had plenty of time to think it all over.

The Patriarch came back to see him a few hours later. "Tan has sworn to me that they had no part in the theft of the blueprints. He was counting on those documents. The *Frank* has left, and its Teknor now deems you nothing more than a bluffing parasite. You do best to stay here with us; the people of the *Tilsin* are very upset with you. Your life may in fact be in danger. You were right. Make the tracer and take it to them as a display of good faith.

Tankar laughed. "I'm the one who needs to show good faith? That's a joke."

"I have a letter for you from Anaena."

"I don't want it."

"Do not judge before you listen to what she has to say; calm down!"

"I don't wish to see it!"

"Your call. When you are ready to read it, it will be here."

★   ★   ★

Tankar now lived in a small apartment near the Patriarch's home. He had a job in a lab, officially building a tracer but in truth building the instrument of his revenge. The real job was not going well, and he was struggling with the notion of doing harm. The Pilgrims' religion remained a mystery to him, and he doubted that would change. Aside from the faith issue, his hosts were kind and attentive to his needs. He became fast friends with his lab colleagues; aside from their severe clothing and religion, they loved life.

Anaena's letter stayed on the table where the Patriarch had left it for a long time. Eventually, he tired of looking at it, put it in his pocket, and burned it without opening it. On one occasion he had been called to the main door but, when the sentry told him a young redhead was waiting, he turned on his heel.

Slowly his wounded pride healed. He tried to block his last few days with the Stellarans from his mind. Despite moments of recall that caused him to grind his teeth, he started to forget. Little by little Anaena's face vanished from his memory. All he saw was a blank empty frame beneath a halo of red hair. At times, he would feel a painful sense of missing her, a gap that occasionally kept him awake at night, his eyes staring at the night sky. Then the feeling would pass. And one day, at the six-month mark of his time with Pilgrims, he tried, in a fit of rage, to bring to mind her face so as to hate it with all his might, but another face appeared, a calm and gentle face with big brown eyes and a mouth still in the blush of youth.

Iolia! He had kept his distance at first, troubled by her questions and by her open admiration for him as an earthling and as a soldier. His heart felt raw, and he had studiously avoided any contact with females among the Pilgrims. That was easy as Pilgrim girls were reserved and nothing like the crude if openly friendly Stellaran girls. Love affairs were out of the question in this strict society.

Iolia. He thought tenderly of her, as if she were a fragile and untouchable thing. Often in the evening he would sit on a bench in the park near his home, and she would join him, followed by her fan club of young children. He rarely spoke of battles, not wanting them to hear stories involving blood and guts. But he did tell tales of the Earth-to-Rigel round trip race or the pomp of court life while cautioning the kids about the vague evil that underlay the luxury. He led the children to think of the Empire planets as he described the cities, the animals, the human and non-human peoples he had seen. Once he made them laugh with the anecdote of the time he had been tasked with carrying a political-police dignitary on his little scout vessel.

"You guys need to understand that our vessels are not as new generation as your city-states. Entering or even leaving hyperspace is no fun. We, the Stellar Guards, were used to it, but this man wasn't. He wasn't a very nice man, and when I saw the face he made after the first dive, I got an idea. With the help of the chief mechanic and the crew, I rigged up an egg-shaker type machine. It involved a slight malfunction of the hyperspace apparatus. So we pretended to dive in and out of hyperspace five times per minute for a full 15 minutes. For safety reasons, we couldn't have gone on any longer. None of us looked great when we stopped, but the police passenger? He was a total wreck. The funniest part was that once we resumed normal flight and the guy caught his breath, he thanked us, and I received a medal when we landed!"

Some evenings Iolia came on her own. At those times, they spoke of the sea, mountains, lakes and trees. She never tired of hearing about them. As a soldier used to noticing and remembering detail, he was good at description.

Bit by bit, just as his suffering began to ebb, so did his lust for revenge. He was half-heartedly seeking a way to harm the Stellarans without making the Pilgrims collateral damage. An aura of peace and quiet reigned within the compound, and it gradually transformed him. He never would have thought such serenity possible and had no desire to fight it. After the inhuman trials of his youth, after the never-ending fights of his teenage years, after the tense stopover with the contemptuous Stellarans, he allowed peace and joy to draw him into the world of the Pilgrims.

Of course, he knew that peace would come to an end. Being peaceful was not his natural state, but he refused to contemplate the future. He knew it was not possible to spend the rest of his days in the compound fiddling around in the lab. Sometimes he wished things might be different, especially during the evenings he spent with Iolia at his side. He was not arrogant enough to believe she loved him in a meaningful way. Hers was an unspoken teenage crush, without fear or complaint, on Tankar the righter of wrongs, rather than the real Tankar. He did not love her either. He felt tenderness, friendship, a touch of desire. He felt something when an arched movement tightened her gray dress over her young breasts. Yet he knew that when she was no longer in his life, she would leave a hard-to-fill void.

She was not as sparkly as Anaena, or as provocative as Orena; she also lacked their sophisticated and outspoken intelligence. With Iolia, the future would be like a neat landscape of green prairies, bubbling fountains, and cool shade. Sometimes he was tempted, but then there was the image of a different destiny, a landscape of rugged rock above abysses wracked with winds, the wild storms of his life. And wistfully, but no longer painfully, he imagined what life with Anaena might have been like.

One day, he left the lab early after a quiet day. The tracer had been ready for a while, and nobody else knew that the misshapen assembly of wires, transistors, crystals and dials was anything other than a failed attempt. Even his colleagues remained in the dark as he had told them that a much less advanced but more attractive model was operating in a room on the *Tilsin*. He had started work on another project: creating a communicator that might penetrate hyperspace ad infinitum. He lacked the theoretical knowledge to complete it, but he kept trying, using pencil and paper rather than hands-on experimentation.

He'd spent the day thinking and had come to the decision that he no longer needed to exact revenge. Were the *Tilsin* to come within range of an Empire planet, he might ask to disembark. Any human world would work. He felt no loyalty to the Empire now that he had considered it in light of his experience with the Stellarans and the Pilgrims. That loyalty no longer meant anything to him. His warrior faith was dead, diminished by his conversations with Orena, turned to dust by his conversations with Holonas. Only his code of honor remained, and he clung to it with all his strength. And the code told him he needed to confess.

He met the Patriarch in his apartment, and they went to his monastic office. Tankar wasted no time beating around the bush and simply outlined what his aim had been when he requested asylum. The older man listened quietly. "I thought as much."

"And you didn't do anything about it?"

"Nothing at all. There is no room for hatred in this enclave where God watches us at all times. I knew your hate would disappear on its own."

"You took quite a risk."

Holonas smiled. "Not with you, Tankar. You don't really know yourself. If I had thought you were dangerous I would not have granted you asylum."

"But the convention...?"

"It allows us to grant you asylum, Tankar, but it does not oblige us to do so. God commanded us to be good, but he did not say stupid. Oh, we might have tried to save you from yourself in other ways. Go in peace, my son. I wish that all men were like you, despite your shortcomings."

Tankar's thoughts were in turmoil. The Patriarch's moral courage was beyond him. Tankar had braced himself for his confession, trying to postpone the moment he expected to be sent away.

In spite of his admission, the Patriarch had spoken kindly to him, as if to a child charged with a misdemeanor. His relief was tainted with shame and resentment. That he, the man nicknamed Tankar the Devil, might be judged as harmless mortified him.

He did not realize that the Patriarch had no doubts whatsoever about his bravery or energy but did doubt Tankar's capacity to hate.

Looking closely at himself for the first time ever, Tankar understood that he was not made to hate. Even in the throes of battle, he'd always maintained respect mixed with regret for the deaths of his enemies. His violent streak had, at times, in the heat of the moment, led him to undertake horrific acts of violence without regret. But he never would have been able to join the Popol, the political police. He recalled the underground torture cell that he had almost been forced to guard. Later that day, he had spent a long time standing under the shower trying to wash away the dirt that covered him by association with such dreadful people.

Iolia walked toward him, looking lovely in her monastic dress. She sat.

"I need to tell you something, Iolia. Lord knows I would prefer you never know these things, but I must tell you." Her eyes rounded in surprise. For the second time in one day, he confessed. At the end he could not look her in the eye, and fully expected her to walk away.

"That cannot be true, Tankar." She spoke without hesitation.

"But it is!"

"No. There is no evil in you. What you did is your evil Empire's doing, not your own. You would never have killed innocent victims along with your enemies."

He laughed sadly. "Innocents. Alas, even some of them have bled on my hands."

"Your hands, yes; your conscience, no. Everything you have said about the Empire proves that you were simply an instrument for others, for those in charge. What could you have done other than carry out orders? You were locked into a routine that never gave you time to think."

"You don't think I'm a monster?"

"There are few men as worthy as you, Tankar, even in our compound. The man who has not considered taking revenge would not be human. What matters is that you never followed through. That takes real courage." He refrained from suggesting he had given up out of weariness.

Sometime later, the Patriarch called for him. "Why not stay on with us?" The old man was blunt. "Our physicists tell me how clever you are. You know a great deal, and you are a fast learner. You are well versed in the art of war, and that could prove invaluable if, God help us, the Mpfifis attack. Would you like to work with us, maybe start a family?"

"I don't share your faith."

"That does not matter just so long as you do not actively oppose our religion. I pray that your eyes will open one day."

He thought for a moment. "I don't think so. I'm not made for such a quiet life."

"It is hardly quiet all the time; occasionally, we visit a planet. Do you think we are like clams, hiding in our shells? We need adventure and renewal like everyone else; we are explorers and mapmakers for all God's planets that our city-state visits. Stellarans have their own teams, but we do half the work."

"I'll think about it."

"One last thing. Iolia is in love with you."

Tankar shook his head. "No. She admires the person she thinks I am. She'll get over it when she's a bit older."

"How old do you think she is?"

"Sixteen, maybe seventeen."

"She just turned 22. She looks younger than she is. Believe me, she is in love. She is not as beautiful as Anaena, but her heart is pure, and she is trustworthy. The question is, do you love her?"

"I don't know. Maybe. Sometimes I think I do. But I'm not really sure what love is. If it's a mash-up of desire, the need to be loyal or, at times, to do harm, then that is what I felt for… someone else. Is that love? If that's true love, then I'm not in love with Iolia."

"There are many paths to true love, Tankar. There is no hurry. Take the time you need to know your own heart."

CHAPTER FIVE

The Stopover

The *Tilsin* orbited the fourth planet of an unfamiliar sun. The planet appeared uninhabited. From a distance of ten thousand kilometers, as close as the traveling city-state starship could approach, it looked much like Earth. Tankar studied it from the Pilgrims' observatory with Iolia at his side. He had not yet reached a decision, but the Pilgrims' community accepted as a given that the two young people were engaged and would marry soon. Sometimes the thought bothered him, as if he had said too much. But, at other times, it gave him great happiness.

"The *Tilsin* will be orbiting for a long time," the Patriarch had told him. "We need raw materials, water, metal, hydrogen. As soon as the explorers return, much of the population will set up camp and mine for necessities. Would you like to be our advance man, Tankar?"

"How would I know? What would I be doing?"

"On the first flight, you would fly low, take pictures, and secure soil samples, mainly from the atmosphere. Once we establish that none of the microorganisms would be harmful or resistant to our pan-vaccines, you will disembark and, without taking any needless risks, make sure there are no dangerous animals."

"I'll do it."

Iolia asked, "Can I come with you? There are three seats on the vessel."

"Too dangerous. Maybe later."

"You always say that. Do you think I am a coward?"

He smiled kindly. "No, Iolia."

"I can pilot a vessel."

"I don't doubt that, but these are the rules set down by your own people. The Stellarans always send a big crew. Look over there." He pointed to the images of the planet. "Lovely, isn't it?"

The spinning planet was majestic behind stripes of misty cloud. In between the openings, blue and green zones could be seen. "I'll be there shortly. I'll come back very soon, so you won't have to wait too long. Now I need to go."

She walked him to the entrance of the lock area. The vessel was ready, and a technician gave Tankar the final instructions. "Breathable atmosphere, somewhat rich in oxygen. High probability of plant life. Don't land, not this time."

"See you tomorrow, Iolia."

"I shall be listening."

"Don't do that. I might not call for a while. You'd fret for nothing."

"Okay. I will pray for you, Tankar."

He kissed her forehead and stooped to enter the craft. He had piloted Stellaran launches when he was setting up revenge and escape plans. The tiny vessel was designed as a shuttle between city-states and planets and had no hyperspace equipment, but it was powerful and easy to use.

He locked the doors, checked the waterproofing as well as each individual piece of equipment. Guards did not joke about that kind of thing, and his life had been saved more than once by last-minute detailed effort.

"If I'd been this thorough on my last departure from Earth I wouldn't be here now," he thought out loud without knowing whether or not he regretted that oversight.

When everything was shipshape, he nose-dived toward the spinning planet below him. His radar revealed another object zooming in the same direction at top speed. It had to be the Stellaran explorers.

My work will be redundant, he thought. *But the Pilgrims will have their independence, even though I'm sure that the Patriarch and the Teknor will review both our reports.*

He lowered gear to enter the atmosphere so he would not end up a meteor. As a result, he lost sight of the fast-moving Stellaran vessel.

He zigzagged a kilometer above land for a long time, allowing the vessel's camera to film the widest possible surface. The planet was beautiful and the landscape varied. He saw vast oceans, mountain chains, large continents and many islands. A dense, deep-green forest covered swathes of terrain, broken here and there by savannah, brush, lakes and swamps. A long river snaked lazily through the mountain ranges. He spiraled downward, to see herds of animals, swift and graceful as they loped through the tall grasses. Nothing suggested the presence of any of his two-legged counterparts. No villages, no roads, no sown fields. All the radio frequencies emitted silence save for the rumble of a faraway storm.

If there's any intelligent life here, it's stuck in the Stone Age, he thought.

The external temperature was 32 degrees centigrade. He methodically collected atmosphere and soil samples. From the distant mountains a smoke cloud rose to the sky: a volcanic eruption. Maintaining his distance, he watched as each explosion produced enormous volcanic bombs. Something rocket-shaped approached, and he recognized a Stellaran vessel. It circled the crater much too closely.

They're nuts! They'll be forced to crash!

An even more violent explosion littered the sky with debris.

When the smoke cloud dissipated, the vessel had disappeared. *Goddamn idiots! Now I have to go.*

He did not for a second anticipate any joy at the steep price the hated Stellarans might pay, but another pilot, a comrade, was in danger.

He approached as speedily as prudence allowed, estimating the distance separating the ground and the crater. The volcano's slopes, furrowed by shreds of lava, curved downward into a maze where the vessel might have fallen. At last he spotted a stack of twisted metal in the path of molten rock and magma from the volcano.

Shit, they're in trouble. I need to move.

The volcanic eruption was losing potency, but a westward bar of gloomy descending black clouds promised a storm on the way. Tankar found a landing point, a narrow platform between two ravines. Landing required a great deal of effort but Tankar, one of the Guards' top pilots, managed it on his second try.

He yanked on the light planet-specific spacesuit engineered to protect him from bacteria or poisonous plants. Along with provisions, he packed two fulgurator-pistols, four grenades, and a first aid kit.

The ground he stepped onto was burning hot and trembling. He descended into a ravine through an avalanche of ash and cinders. Sensing immediate danger, he ducked. He would never have managed to climb out of the ravine without his ice ax. A chaotic collection of rocks awaited him on the rim at the other side. He walked around it and finally reached the right-hand side of the wreck that had been eviscerated by rocks.

Tankar did not look for the cause of the accident. Any survivors would require immediate medical attention, and the volcano was ready to erupt again at any moment. He entered the ship through a gap between two disjointed panels and almost immediately slipped on viscous liquid, swearing as he tumbled to the surface. A crushed male figure lay in a piteous state far beyond all help. Tankar picked his way around the corpse to see that the nose of the vessel had fared better. The distorted, unhinged command-post door was in his way, but he could hear cries and rapid breathing on the other side.

He grabbed a section of the door and pulled. It twisted, groaned and gave way. Armed with a discarded molecular saw, Tankar whittled out a tunnel for himself. A blood-soaked human form fell into his arms. Gently, Tankar laid the man on the ground and poked his nose into the opening. A quick, first look told him there were no survivors, but he pulled out his first aid kit and lit a lamp.

"Anaena!" It was indeed Anaena, covered in blood, a long scar across her forehead. He checked for broken limbs and assessed the depth of her wound. He injected a stimulant and disinfected the wounded area.

A dull groan shook him to his core. The volcano, perhaps? But nothing was raining down on him, and he remembered the brewing storm.

Softly, he said. "Anaena?"

"Who is it?"

"It's me, Tankar. We need to get out of here. The volcano's going to blow again at any moment."

She tried to sit up but fell back with a moan. "I can't."

"That's not true. Nothing's broken, and we have to get out of here right now. Courage, please. My launch is nearby."

"The others?"

"Gone. Stand up."

He helped her stand, and they made their way through the opening in the fuselage. The sky was inky black, and the first raindrops pelted the hot ground. Tankar held her by the waist, almost carrying her. Anaena groaned with each step, but she clenched her teeth and bravely continued. They could not see the far side of the ravine as the rain pounded down. Tankar's spacesuit protected him, but Anaena was drenched. Rivulets of rainwater flowed around their feet; the wet ash turned it all into a thick bog. Over the torrential sound of the rain, he thought he heard the first hints of an avalanche.

He sat on the ravine's edge and placed the young woman on his knees. Holding her with one hand, his ice ax in the other, he sledded through the mud. They made it down, but they had to climb out on the far side. He swept the walls with his hololight and saw that where the cooling lava flow had sealed the ashes, it had created footholds. He sheltered Anaena as best he could under an overhang and paddled through the mud to the other side.

"I'm going for some rope; I'll be right back. Don't move." He did not know if she heard him.

He angled his hololight upward. The rain shone through the cone of light, but he could not see his vessel. He stumbled several times on the way up the other side, but finally reached what remained of the platform. An entire chunk of the overhang collapsed under the weight of his craft, which was now, no doubt, covered in debris.

"Shit!" he swore furiously. He wasted no time feeling sorry for himself and retraced his steps to find the young woman rolled into a little ball. "The launch is gone. I'm afraid we're shipwrecked, Anaena."

She moved ever so slightly, and he listened to her labored breathing. He put the lamp on top of a small rock and gave her a second injection. After a moment, she sat up, wearily ran her hand over her forehead, and then saw the blood, dark under the light. Flashes of lightning still rumbled, even though the deluge had pretty much ended. She looked down at her splayed fingers. "Tankar, Tankar, am I disfigured?"

He burst out laughing. "No, there's nothing there the *Tilsin*'s surgeons can't put right. That is, if we make it back, which I doubt."

"Your vessel?"

"The landing platform collapsed under the weight of the rainwater. No idea where the devil the launch has got to. It'll be useless in any case. Come, let's move on, we're much too close to the volcano."

"Can't we wait for daybreak?" she pleaded.

"No." His tone left no room for argument. "The lava flow's moving toward the wreckage of your starship. It'll reach us before dawn."

"I'm so weak. Do you think we'll get out of here alive?"

"I hope so. You need to help. Please try to eat something." He handed her a package from his provisions. "Here's some food."

"And you?"

"My spacesuit has hung on till now, and I've not had contact with indigenous bacteria that would put us in jeopardy. I'd like to stay in this bubble as long as possible. In a few hours, the air supply will run out. After that, I'll try my luck with the pan-vaccine. Eat, drink this, and I'll be back soon."

He followed the ravine and explored for a few hundred meters below. Then he widened his search to include the rim of another ravine. Tankar climbed that one, hoping to spot the wreckage and secure weapons and provisions, but an enormous mudslide blocked his passage, and he realized that his vessel was now buried underneath and completely inaccessible.

He doubled back and found Anaena standing in her wet clothing, ready to go. They made their way along the floor of the ravine. The hololight illuminated the ground under their feet and the base of the ravine walls. The top was still black despite slivers of reluctant light. A slight mist rose from the hot, wet ground. The path was bumpy, littered with crumbled rock. The steep incline helped rather than hurt, and they managed to descend one kilometer.

The volcano continued to make threatening noises. Though they had moved out of the worst hit area, from time to time a small yet violent burning pellet smashed onto the ash with a whistle. Instinctively, Anaena clutched Tankar's arm and ducked her head. He did not make a sound. Nature's bombing campaign was paltry compared to others he had been through. Finally the ravine broadened, the walls grew shallower, and the incline more gentle. They still encountered scattered lava flow, the remnants of earlier eruptions. Anaena was close to collapsing with exhaustion, so Tankar decided to stop right there. It was a relatively safe place. He spotted a natural cavity left by a gas bubble. The hole was big enough to hold both survivors.

"Climb down. I think I saw some bushes; I'll try to start a fire."

Sparse dry vegetation sprouted from cracks in the lava, and dead tree trunks dotted the surface around the cave. The wind rustled through their white branches with mournful snapping sounds. He returned to the grotto with an armful of twigs and palms. He lit a fire with his fulgurator, and soon it began to crackle and shine light through the darkness, bathing the little cave in a reddish glow.

"Take off your wet clothes so we can dry them. I won't look."

He sat at the entrance gazing into the distance. He had seen no fauna and doubted any animals would approach the erupting volcano, but the fire might lure them. Keeping the fulgurator handy, he waited, listened, but heard only the sounds of the young woman changing her clothes.

"How did you get shot down? Who was your idiot pilot?"

"Me."

He chuckled with contempt.

"I can pilot as well as you can," she snapped.

"How many were on board?"

"Five. But the others all agreed to fly over the volcano," she insisted. "I didn't kill them, if that's what you're suggesting."

"What were you doing atop the crater? Catching a show?"

"We're free! But I was planning to collect debris and gas samples. Those can help identify the deep crust."

"Ah." He did not speak. In his view, the act of folly had transformed into a dangerous mission. She had scored a point.

"Why did you leave, Tankar?" she asked abruptly.

"You're not surprised that I did, are you?"

"Hand me some wood, but don't turn around. Yes, it did surprise me. It surprised everyone."

"It was about the blueprints."

"I didn't have them stolen."

"I don't believe you."

"Why would I take them? You'd promised to hand them over."

"To stop me from doing just that. To prove that I'm nothing more than an untrustworthy planetary."

"It's very likely we'll never make it back to the *Tilsin*, Tankar. Why would I lie now? I didn't take the blueprints. I found out they were gone when the Patriarch told my uncle."

"Then where are they?" Tankar demanded.

"I don't know," Anaena sighed. "Maybe some advantist took them. The next Teknor election isn't scheduled until two years from now, but the timing can be brought forward if a petition gets enough signatures to charge the Teknor with tyranny, or if a candidate brings something really useful, like a tracer, for instance. You wouldn't be able to prove that the tracer was built from your blueprints."

"Oh, yes, I would!" he insisted.

"Hmmm. Maybe the people who stole the blueprints built one. It could be operational without the Teknor suspecting it. Can you imagine the outcome if this or that person were one day to warn of the approach of a city-state? Most of my countrymen wouldn't give a damn that the information had been stolen."

"That may well be. But it's too late for me in any case."

There might have been one or more tracers in operation. There was at least one, his own. He thought it highly likely that others might be out there. Despite Anaena's protests to the contrary, there might be one in the command post itself.

"It's not too late, Tankar."

He remained still then spoke slowly. "Yes...it is. I'm probably going to marry Iolia."

"Do you think that bothers me? That's not at all what I had in mind." Despite her bravado, her voice sounded off. "You can turn around now. I'm dry."

"Sleep now, you need the rest."

He collected some sand, tucked the provisions bag under her head, and then resumed his spot at the entrance.

"Tankar?"

"Yes. Go to sleep!"

"I'm too tired. Do you think we'll get out of here?"

"It all depends on the *Tilsin*'s rescue actions. If the Guards were in charge, they'd comb this entire place rather than leave one comrade behind."

"We would also do that."

"All right. Even then, the odds of our getting out are slim. We should be okay if the beasts aren't too beastly and a rescue team comes fairly soon. We also need the bacteria not to be harmful and to see if we can find something to eat. A lot of ifs there."

"Tan will do his utmost."

"That I believe. But if you're not going to sleep, at least be quiet. I need to think."

Tankar was still pacing around the fire when daylight broke outside the cave. The weather was fine and the air fresh. He ambled up a cone-shaped heap of lava. The volcano was still smoking, but the plume wavered in the wind. An occasional explosion launched a pellet in the air, sketching dark freckles against the pale sky. The first rays of an unfamiliar sun scanned the sierra and pinpointed the shadows in the valley.

Below his observation point, lava was flowing and vanishing under the forest floor. He could just make out birdlike flying creatures in the half-light. They were too far away for him to get a good look, but he heard their piercing cries. The cluster of massive trees seemed dark and impenetrable. Much farther away he spied the barren mound of an extinct volcano with a spout at its center. He could not fully make it out, but he knew that was where they needed to go to set up an SOS.

CHAPTER SIX

On the Planet with no Name

Tankar returned to the cave and gently shook Anaena. She mumbled, curled into herself and went back to sleep. He watched her lying on her hard bed of sand, her clothes in tatters, her red hair in tangles and her face streaked with dry blood. This Anaena bore no resemblance to the proud young woman he had met on the *Tilsin*.

War and dangerous adventures are not for most women, he thought. He shook her more forcefully this time. She struggled to open her eyes. "Oh, yes, right. We're shipwrecked," she recalled. "I forgot."

"Let me look at your wound." He gently pushed aside the hairs stuck to her forehead. "This is better. No sign of infection. Your biogenol works really well."

She noticed a change in Tankar. "You've taken off your helmet?"

"No air left, so I removed it about the time you fell asleep. We're going to trek over to that mountain." He pointed. "We must, at all costs, set up a signal if we want to have a chance of getting out of here, and we can't do that on the volcano. When was your crew due to return to the *Tilsin*?"

"Today at noon."

"I'm not due back until tonight. They may worry about the lack of communication, but we can't count on any rescue mission setting off before nightfall."

"Tan will dispatch every launch we have."

"Anaena, a planet's a very big thing, even this one that's smaller than Earth. I'm going to take the lead carrying the bag of provisions and the first aid kit. You know how to use a fulgurator? Here you go. I wish I had a hunting rifle just in case we come across any potentially edible fauna."

They walked down the gently declining slope of the volcano and cut through the brush. In a short time they found themselves at the entrance to the forest. The trees were very tall, their smooth trunks a poisonous shade of green. Secondary vegetation grew in thickets and vines.

Tankar stopped to consider their next move. "I don't like this. Anybody could be hiding in there, and we know nothing about the animal life of this planet. I don't need to remind you that our own lives will depend on our being cautious every second."

He belted his fulgurator and grasped the molecular saw before moving forward. In the distance, under the shade of the trees, they heard a shattering cry followed by bloodcurdling cackles. Tankar hesitated, debating whether to continue through the trees or pick a different entry point to the forest. He shrugged. His fulgurator was potent enough to deter a Cretaceous tyrannosaurus. He raised the saw and set it to section molecular mass. Branches tumbled to the ground. Once they had penetrated beyond the outer circle, the vegetation in the forest grew sparser, smaller trees were smothered by shadows. The temperature grew hotter and became increasingly intolerable as the sun rose. Drops of water slid off the foliage, and the soil under their feet grew soft and spongy. To their right, a swamp gleamed in the half-light.

Tankar used his compass. There were no landmarks to guide them. At times the trees seemed like columns propping up the temple of some unknown deity, a humid and ferocious god. He and Anaena slithered around the tree trunks enveloped in disgusting, slimy moss. Tankar always led, shielded by his waterproof clothing, although the pines and brush he'd walked through had shredded the suit some time ago. Already a rash had begun to spread across one of Anaena's arms, so he used a knife to scrape the tree trunks to prevent her having contact with the mosses.

They arrived at the site of a massacre. The burned skeleton of a decimated tree rose at the center of a clearing where the earth was covered in grasslike vegetation that had for some years escaped the darkness but now showed signs of frantic trampling. A long body lay in pieces in a pool of pinkish blood. The quadruped must have been 10 meters high with a sinewy body elongated by a slender tail. The short protruding head was split and revealed two sharp antennae. The skull had been smashed. Part of the animal's intestines and its front legs had been eaten.

"Not a mammal, not a reptile," Anaena observed.

"I can't imagine this animal is a friendly one, but whatever killed it was even more terrifying."

"Tankar, do you see footprints anywhere?"

He kneeled. The prints were about a half meter long, shaped like a star with four points: one forward, two oblique, and a short one at the back. At the end of each point an enormous claw had left its mark.

"This thing must weigh several tons. Judging from the distance between steps, it must be several meters high. Also, look up at those broken branches. Looks like a biped, maybe one of those carnivorous dinosaurs from long ago on Earth. On terra firma there really can be only two types of predator: lion or tyrannosaurus. Or it could be a pack-style animal such as wolves," Tankar concluded.

"I didn't know you were a zoologist," Anaena mocked.

"This isn't my first wild planet," he replied, then paused. "Of course, we'd better include a third type of predator: man. If it's still in the area, I'd rather not meet it. I wonder how it survives in this dense forest?"

They found the answer not long after. A new belt of brush allowed light to filter through the tree trunks, indicating the forest was giving way. They emerged into a reddish-brown savannah broken up by groves of trees and bushes.

"From my initial perspective, I'd thought we'd see only trees until we reached the extinct volcano. I was wrong. This is much better...or perhaps much worse."

"I prefer this plain," Anaena replied. "At least you can see the enemy coming at you."

"He can see us as well and set his ambush in motion," Tankar countered. "From now on, we need to be even more cautious."

The volcanic cone was too far away for them to expect to reach it in daylight. They proceeded cautiously, wasting some time crossing a brook by using a tree trunk as a bridge. The water teemed with carnivorous, ferocious fishlike beings. The many skeletons they spotted at the ford's basin bore witness to the fishes' voracious appetite.

At midday the two trekkers stopped at the crest of a hill. Up until then they had spotted only small animals except for one herd of enormous creatures a long distance away to their left. They ate their concentrates sparingly and drank water from the stream that they sterilized first. Anaena had grown feverish and weary, and this worried Tankar. Her head wound was healing well, but he feared possible infection from some other source.

They had not reached their goal by nightfall. Tankar stopped near a ravine and sought shelter but found none, so he built one, interlacing the branches of five intertwined trees. He hesitated to light a fire. In the end, he stacked a large number of twigs and

branches at the entrance to the shelter that he could set alight
with his fulgurator if need arose. He made a bed for Anaena but
lay down first, asking her to wake him as soon as night fell. He
quickly fell sound asleep.

When she shook him awake, the night was black. Neither of
the two moons had risen yet.

"You shouldn't have let me sleep so long!" Tankar scolded.

"You needed to sleep. I kept watch."

Nothing had happened, after all, and he had to admit she had
been brave if not skilled. He asked her how she was feeling.

"Light-headed. I think I'm still feverish."

He took her pulse at the wrist. He put his other hand on
her forehead. He whistled. "Feverish? You're at least at 39
degrees!" He fumbled through his first aid kit and pulled out a
box of syringes. "The label says this should work for you. Give
me your arm."

"I'll do it myself."

"Don't you trust me?" He handed her the syringe.

"I want to see exactly what it is. General antitoxin C-126.
That's all right, then. I was concerned it might be Z-3."

"The last-chance hoorah drug? We're not at that point. Try to
sleep; you'll feel better in the morning."

He kept watch by the enclosure's opening, his hololight in
hand, his fulgurator at the ready. A pearly light from the east
filtered through as the silver moon rose from behind the hills. He
stared at the moon for a long time while maintaining his vigilance,
noting that its face was marked by shadows different from those
he knew from the Moon back home. Above the horizon he saw
a second, smaller moon chase the first. That satellite was a reddish
hue and very far away. The landscape, lit by both sources, was
clearly visible: staggered plains, shadowed valleys, slopes and
brush that shone in the moonlight like one big wave. A sound

came from behind him as Anaena emerged from the shelter. "My fever has gone down."

Tankar did not reply. He was both troubled and happy to have her at his side. She remained silent for a while. Finally she said, "It's so beautiful."

"Yes, but I'd enjoy it more if my launch were nearby, or if I had a few Guard colleagues at my side."

"May I ask you something?"

"Okay...no!" He rose, gripping the fulgurator tightly in his fist. "Go back inside!"

"What is it? What have you seen?"

"Over there. Behind the trees."

She squinted out into the night. In the paltry light of the two moons, shadows shifted and moved. There was no doubt something stirred about three hundred meters away. One of the trees trembled as if hit by an enormous bulk.

"Tankar?"

"Yes?"

"What is it?"

"How the hell should I know? Is your fulgurator ready? Be brave. If something attacks, please let me shoot first."

"I'll try."

"Stay here on your own, then. I'm going to hide behind that rock. If the thing comes at me, fire. If it comes for you, don't shoot unless I shout *Fire!* I'll try to get it from the flank."

He disappeared into the tall grasses. She waited, but nothing moved in the distance. She could not see Tankar, but she was sure he was glued to the rock in order to display a single shadow. She focused on the grove. That's when the beast appeared.

Several meters high, it resembled a kangaroo. She remembered what Tankar had said: *On terra firma there really can be only two types of predator: lion or tyrannosaurus.*

The animal closed in taking long strides. It moved without haste but with deliberate speed. The animal's movements quickly ate up the space between itself and her. She saw a fierce-looking head, a thick neck and a long tail that slapped the grasses rhythmically like a pendulum. Frozen in terror but determined to defend herself, Anaea noticed strange hyper-details such as the reflection of the two moons off the creature's skin, its paws, now in light, now in the dark. At times the monster would lean forward to sniff the ground. Then it stood to its full six-meter height, its head swiveling from left to right. The moonlight shone on its sharp white fangs. Then the head stopped swinging and the thing looked straight at the enclosure. The animal bounded, its size increasing with each jump as it closed the distance in a rush. Clutching her weapon, the young woman waited to shoot, expecting to be crushed under tons of live flesh.

"Ana, come to me! Now!"

She froze for what seemed like forever before her brain conveyed the message to her legs. She raced to join Tankar behind the rock and felt the earth shudder under the monster's weight. The beast saw her, emitted a terrifying scream, and then stopped abruptly. A slender blue beam crossed the sky and settled on the beast as it poised to leap forward. The beast's fall crushed the trees that created their shelter. Trunks collapsed, and the monster's tail slapped the air over and over again, sending clumps of soil and broken branches flying. Finally, all movement stopped.

Tankar stood at Anaena's side. "Not too frightened?"

"No," she lied.

"Well, I was scared for you," he admitted "If I hadn't shot he would have killed you. If I had taken a shot he would have crushed you in the fall. We'll be safer on the mountain tomorrow night."

They leaned against the rock and waited for dawn. When daylight broke, they were able to examine the beast's cadaver. "A tyranossauroid. But a hot-blooded one, which means it can move more swiftly, and it has a larger brain, yet I reduced the monster to dust in a stream of ions. It was unlucky to come across the third type of predator: man. The bad news for us is our bag is under its carcass. Do you remember where I left it?"

"That tree over there." She pointed.

Tankar leaned in. The trunk had shattered about a half meter from the ground and created a corridor where he spotted the bag, still intact. He used a branch to snag it and pull it to him. "That was lucky!"

He used the molecular saw to extract the beast's two largest fangs. He handed them to Anaena. "A souvenir."

She shook her head sadly. "Keep them, Tankar. I'm not entitled; they belong to Iolia."

He offered them to her once again. "I'm not giving them to a woman. I'm giving them to a comrade-in-arms."

Anaena didn't understand her sadness at that remark. After all, what did this arrogant planetary mean to her? He wasn't one of her people. When the *Tilsin* rescued him, she'd felt the same way about him as the other Stellarans had: why add another useless refugee to their ranks?

She had followed the Teknor's orders with disgust. She was to gain his trust and get him talking with a view to discovering if the Empire had tracers. As she had done so, she had become aware that Tankar was human like herself, like other planetary types. He had shown himself to be a fearsome, mysterious, harsh and tragically solitary man. Out of human kindness, she had asked him to her home; he might well have tried to take advantage of her, but he did not. He also had spared her life at a time when even the Teknor could not have prevented the punishment she had earned for intervening in a duel.

She remembered the night of the conjunction. Tankar had

been so kind, so generous, so well-intentioned. When they danced, she had felt his muscular arms around her. She had gone home that night, her feelings all tangled. For the first time ever, she wondered if she had not been caught in her own trap and fallen in love.

Fall in love with a planetary! It had happened to Orena's mother, but that case was not a good example. The planetary had not assimilated and, in the end, he had silently, secretly slipped away during a stopover on a human world. As a mixed-race woman, Orena had suffered the consequences and never gained full acceptance. Anaena was disgusted at the notion that her children...whoa! Had she come that far already? Tankar was too much of a man to abandon her, even if he was a planetary....

And then that idiotic burglary. She had searched relentlessly but never discovered who had done it. Orena? Why? For her advantists? If those guys had the plans, they would have used them immediately and to their advantage. Anaena decided the thief – or thieves – might have come from a small gang of malcontents playing out a pointless plot. The Teknor had worked ceaselessly to find out what had happened, but the blueprints had vanished without a trace. They might well be on the *Frank* with the thieves.

And so, Tankar had sought asylum with the Pilgrims. At first she had awaited his inevitable return, but he never showed up. She had written him but received no reply. Then people told her he was spending time with Iolia, that sorry-looking nobody in a gray dress, and she had begun to worry. Tankar's affair with Orena or with any other Stellaran woman did not bother her. She knew them and knew how much more interesting she was. Those women would get bored quickly with this strong foreigner, but Iolia was a different story altogether.

Anaena considered the young Pilgrim pale and lacking attractive features, but she knew the girl had qualities that would appeal to a man untethered, in turmoil. She was patient, kind, maternal even. Ana had tried to visit Tankar, but he had refused to see her. Now Anaena had him all to herself, and she knew their moment had come and gone. If he had promised himself to Iolia, he would never leave her. And Anaena was fairly sure he had made a commitment.

If we get out of here alive and he marries Iolia, I will have to go to another city-state. It would be too painful to know that Tankar is behind only a few sheets of metal, but I can't get to him.

She watched him. He was unshaven with a three-days shadow, torn clothes and messy hair. She could see him in the half-light of the pink horizon. He was both massive and slim. She wanted to run to him, to snuggle up against him, to confess her love and to tell him nothing else mattered. Instead, she spoke in a clear and neutral voice. "When do we leave here?"

"Right now."

It took them a long time to cross the entire plain only to arrive at a chaotic terrain covered in ravines and shattered blocks of stone. They would have to cross it to reach the extinct volcano. Tankar was ever more cautious. Anything might be lurking behind those rocks, but initially they saw only small, tame herbivores. Still, they nearly died.

Tankar had remained behind to tighten the straps of his bag. Anaena took a few steps alone and stopped to examine an interesting section of land, a few square meters peppered with foot-high cones. The cones, all the same size and the same shade of pale brown as the clay beneath, were truncated with a circular opening at the top. She kicked one, and found it to be as hard as metal. It rang hollow.

"Don't touch those!" Tankar's yell came too late. By kicking the cone she had busted the thin shell. Buzzing loudly, garbed in a flutter of see-through wings, an insect shot straight up. The other

cones began to vomit out distended shapes flying too quickly
to be seen clearly. Anaena ran to Tankar and suddenly felt her
shoulder burn. She squashed the thing that stung her. Tankar
leaped to her side with his fulgurator at its highest setting. His
hand frantically swept the air. In the blueish hue of the new
day's light, little red stars danced.

"Let me see your shoulder! Now!"

He yanked at her shirt, which she pulled over her breast.
A red mark had spread quickly within an inflamed, swollen
circle on her tender skin. He pulled out an antitoxin syringe and
injected her.

"Damn, I hope this works. You played a dangerous game!"

"Tankar!" Ana warned.

He turned around. As the insects emerged from a giant nest
hidden behind an enormous boulder, they blackened the sky.
Tankar handed Anaena the second fulgurator.

"Keep watch on the right. I'll take the left."

For several long minutes, they fought off the droves of the
winged enemy. One stung Tankar and two more struck Anaena.

When the insects gave up the fight, Tankar saw there were
only two anti-poison syringes left in the first aid kit. He pricked
her with both and, his back turned, pretended to inject himself.

"What demon possessed you? Don't they teach you anything
on the *Tilsin*?" he demanded furiously. "We have similar things
on Earth. We call them hornets, and a few stings will kill a
person as easily as a bullet. Didn't you know not to touch
anything you've not seen before?"

Her body ached all over. And all she could think was that he
had picked a really lousy time for the health and safety lecture.

"Let's go," he ordered. "We need to keep going while we
still can. Heaven knows if we'll even be able to move in a
few minutes."

He stopped and collected one dead insect that was not fully burned. It was about four centimeters long with four wings, eight legs and a barbed pin jutting out from a pointy stomach.

Anaena spoke as if to explain her actions. "We've never seen anything that looks like this."

"And we've never seen anything on the *Tilsin* that looks like a snake, but anything can happen in a new world." He bit his lips as, all of a sudden, a sharp pain caused him to cry out. "Run!"

They aimed for the slope of the dormant volcano, now within their line of sight. Anaena was surprised to find herself sometimes in the lead. Tankar, in agony, was struggling, hunched forward as he moved. *But he was stung only once*, she thought. She looked closely and saw that his face was red and bathed in sweat.

"What's wrong?"

"It's nothing, Anaena. Keep moving."

He was in agony all over. Through a reddish fog, he could see the young woman walking ahead of him. His own legs were slack and slow to respond because he could not feel the ground. His head buzzed, he was dizzy, and he suspected his death was imminent. He stopped and crumpled to the ground. With a shout, Anaena tried to pick him up.

"It's over for me, I think." He spoke with difficulty. "Take the bag. Climb onto the volcano, light a fire as a signal. Maybe they...."

"I'm not leaving you alone."

"Maybe I'll feel better later. I'll catch up with you. Leave the red fulgurator with me." He knew it was low on ammunition.

"Tankar, this is all my fault."

"It's nothing." He spoke softly. "Comes with the job...." His head rolled onto his chest, and he stopped moving.

She hesitated for a time in a whirlwind of anguish and guilt. She had killed him through sheer stupidity. In desperation, she rifled through the first aid kit and blanched at the sight of the empty antivenom compartment: all three doses were gone.

He gave me all three, she realized. Deeply shaken, she looked at him. His staccato breathing came heavily. *What could she do?* she asked herself. What could she do? She rummaged through the bag again and found some stimulol.

She injected Tankar with two doses and huddled next to him in despair. She wondered what effect the insect poison might have and looked at her own body for clues. There was phantom pain in all of her muscles that made her move awkwardly and out of synch. Did the insects carry a poison that attacked the whole nervous system?

Far away, she saw an unusual dark stain in the sky near the horizon that glittered for a moment as it moved in the sunlight. A launch? A rescue vehicle? She stripped off her clothing and waved it at the sky. Whatever it was continued moving in the same direction and disappeared behind the mountaintops.

They didn't see me.

She waited, but Tankar did not move at all. She fashioned a roof from pieces of her clothing and branches to shield them from the sun. The day slipped away. Tankar was not worse, but he had not regained consciousness. His pulse alternated between fast and slow while his mouth moved at times but emitted only unintelligible mumbles. She built a low wall around Tankar by rolling some large stones together, after checking nothing lay under them. She considered adding flat stones on top, but superstition got the better of her. It would have looked too much like a tomb.

The sun set in the west, and that brought cooler air. She collected dry wood and arranged a circle of small fires. She heard a very soft sound. Tankar was speaking haltingly. She felt a burst of joy. He was getting better! But then despair took hold again. He was delirious.

His mumblings were audible. "No, don't kill him.... I will never.... I could never do that, sergeant.... I can't jump that far.... Where are you, Mommy? ...I didn't know how hard it was to kill a man who's looking at you.... The sole survivor is just a cat.... Come here, kitty.... We are poised for the greatest glory of the Empire.... Iolia, Iolia, I'm not worthy of you.... I have blood on my hands, Iolia.... It's blood on my hands.... Red, red like Anaena's hair.... Iolia, she stole my blueprints.... I love her...but there's blood on her head.... Where are you Anaena? ...I gave you the syringes...."

She touched his burning-hot forehead. "I'm here, Tankar, I'm right here with you."

He shook his head. "Don't stay. Climb the mountain, send signals. No, don't, they might come and bomb everything. The Empire! ...I killed everything.... They're here but their faces are gone...."

He shuddered and tried to stand but fell heavily to the ground. She wrung her hands, powerless to help him.

He sank into a torpid state. Night fell, and she thought back to the previous evening as a sort of paradise lost. At that time, Tankar stood tall and strong as both her shield and her source of hope. Cold and sick with exhaustion and worry she put her clothing back on and forced herself to eat.

The early part of the night remained calm. She and Tankar were on high ground next to rich savannah sparsely dotted with tufts of grass and shrubs that would have no appeal for herbivores and, by extension, carnivores. But after the two moons rose, she heard the sounds of predators. The noise filtered through the darkness as it grew closer. She sat up, one fulgurator in her fist, the other on her belt.

With a sound of rustling branches, an animal burst through the shrubbery. She had time to see a graceful shape moving in agile bounds.

The prey, she thought. *The hunters will follow soon.*

They came shortly after, appearing as fast-moving, shallow shadows, their movement a combination of crawling and running. She counted 20, all of which ignored her. She sat down with a sigh of relief and struggled to stay awake. She wondered if she should not just take a stimulol but opted instead to save the drug for Tankar and began to pace back and forth in the humid evening.

The screeching started up again, not far away. The prey must have escaped, so the hunters were returning to the form they'd spotted earlier. Anaena started a fire with the fulgurator.

The beasts stopped at a respectful distance, and she got a good look at them. They were about two meters long, low on their paws, rocket-shaped, covered in black fur with thick tails. Their round heads ended in a slender muzzle similar to those of a species of crocodile on Earth, split in half by a mouth with long reptilian fangs.

The leader, also the largest of the pack, slowly approached Anaena, and she stood ready to shoot. Revealing its white throat, the animal stopped a few meters from the flames and howled for a long time. From a distance, sounds echoed in response. The beast howled again, and Anaena shot. No sooner had the beast fallen to the ground than the others jumped in and devoured it in an orgy of claws and jaws. To hold them off, she shot twice again and hit two of the others, but reinforcements, hot on the heels of the first arrivals, poured in from the bushes. Before she knew it, more than a hundred animals had formed a circle around her. Their fangs shone in the reddish reflections, and their tails slapped the ground as they gained courage. The pack teased her by moving backward, forward, and sideways, taking little jumps. As long as the flames clearly burned, she was relatively safe. After that.... The irony was that the animals' victory might prove short-lived as the proteins in her and Tankar's bodies would likely kill them anyway.

She picked bits from her meager supply of firewood – silently scolding herself for not collecting more – and fueled the dying fire with a big branch. Sparks flew as the fire crackled and grew. The beast closest to pouncing held off. She could have shot at them until she ran out of ammunition but opted not to. What would happen if she did not kill them all? And what would happen the next day, if there were to be a next day? She would still have a chance to kill them when the wood ran out. If she could just hang on until dawn, the beasts might well be nocturnal as she and Tankar had spotted only herbivores during daylight.

She thought long and hard and eventually came up with an idea. The bushes were dry, and she might be able to chase the enemy away with fire. She picked up a brand and threw it, but it didn't go far enough before dying out. But, with a second try, she rejoiced as she saw the fire crawl the length of a tuft of grass and then snake its way up the branches. Very soon the fire blazed like a torch, but her success almost caused her downfall.

Caught between the two blazes, the beasts chose the smaller one, and 10 or so animals rushed to attack. She killed several of them, but two bounded over the hearth at the entrance to the enclosure. She stepped back, stumbled on the stone wall, and fell. One of the beasts jumped over her head, just missing her, and landed in the flames before fleeing, howling. She stood right back up and shot the other one.

Little by little, her stock of flammables dwindled, and dawn still lay many hours away. Save for a miracle, she was out of luck. Even more painful than the thought of her own imminent demise was the knowledge that she had failed to protect Tankar.

Two of the fires had dimmed to collections of embers, and soon the beasts would breach the protective circle. White dust built up to cover the firebrands; the fires no longer roared. The impatient animals approached and, in a gesture of defiance, lay down right next to the embers as if enjoying the warmth. One animal yawned, opening the big gash of its black mouth in stages.

"Anaena, the grenades!"

She jumped at the sound of Tankar's voice and turned around. He was leaning against the stone wall. Why had she not thought of the grenades? She had seen them at the bottom of their bag!

"Come here," he urged. "Throw one into the pack. I'm not strong enough. As soon as you're done, flatten your body against the wall."

She took the item and weighed it in her hand, yanked off the pin and threw it, then buried herself in Tankar's arms. The violence of the explosion surprised her as sods of dirt and pebbles flew around their heads. Something landed with a thud at her feet, a handful of flesh stuck to a clump of fur. She bounded upright.

The beasts fled in a rout. The ground where the grenade had landed lay covered in mangled black shapes, some of which still moved a little. She took a second grenade and threw it as far as she could. This time she simply squatted and watched the purple flame. Tankar gently pulled her back.

"You idiot, do you want the shrapnel to kill you?" As if to make the young man's point, a metal fragment ricocheted, making a whining sound before bouncing off into the distance.

"They're leaving!" She danced to celebrate her victory and Tankar's return to life. Then she crumpled onto a large boulder and burst into loud sobs. She wept violently but briefly and soon turned her attention back to her companion.

"How do you feel?"

"Weak," he admitted. "Aside from that, I'm fine, just a bit of cramping in my legs. What about you?"

"Me? I feel great! Oh, Tankar…if you had died…and you gave me all the serum, as well. Why did you do that?"

"When you're in the Guards and a comrade is wounded, he comes first. In jeopardy such as this, a woman is like an injured person."

"Noble of you," she acknowledged, annoyed, "but you know I've already explored several planets, even if I did mess up last night. Do you think your little Iolia—" She sounded hurt.

"She's not my Iolia, and I have no doubt about your abilities. I'm very grateful to you for defending me, even though it was risky. Iolia would have done the same thing, perhaps less enthusiastically. Help me stand, I'm hungry."

"Here's what's left of the provisions. Don't worry about me, I've eaten. What are we going to do when we run out of food, Tankar?"

"Well, we can try the local meat dishes, or fruit, if we find any. Not sure what the outcome will be."

"When I think of all the analytics stuff on our launch vessel… I think I spotted one flying low far away. I signaled, but they didn't see me."

"They'll come back, I'm sure. The sooner we set up a flare or something like it on this mountain, the better. Help me walk, please."

He took a few baby steps, leaning on her, then stopped, exhausted. "You go on ahead."

"I can't leave you alone!"

"I won't be in much danger in daylight. I'll follow you in stages. I don't know what kind of nasty poison those insects secreted, but I feel as if I've lost half my blood." He turned and asked, "Where are the weapons?"

She handed him the fulgurators, which he examined in the light of the dying fire. He made a face. "One still has two charges, the other has six. We really need help, or I'm going to have to craft a bow and arrows."

They set out together at first light. Walking was painful for Tankar but, to his surprise and delight, the exhaustion seemed to ebb rather than increase as they made tracks. He did, however, send Anaena ahead. He did not catch up to her until the afternoon. The slopes on the old volcano were gentle, but they were covered in boulders and brush.

They set up camp for the night in a cave-like shelter within an eroded boulder. Its roof was a slab of hardened lava. Here and there they saw shiny debris of glassy volcanic rock. "Well, I have plenty of time to make arrows if we don't get rescued soon enough," he joked. "Once night falls, light a fire."

They had already gathered a big stack of brush and small trees. The flames danced gaily into the night.

"I'm feeling positive now, Anaena. I remember telling the Patriarch that I'd start exploring directly beneath the position of the *Tilsin*. That means that the surface to be combed is fairly small, and your sighting of a launch suggests that they're surveilling close to where we are."

Anaena asked quietly, "Are you in love with Iolia?"

Tankar paused. "I don't know. I think so."

"Have you pledged yourself to her?" Anaena persisted.

"No, why?"

"Nothing, just curious. What about Orena?"

"I don't think I ever loved her, but I needed someone…a friend. I amused her, and she gave me moral support. We made our peace."

They didn't speak for a while. "I'll stand watch first," Tankar announced. "Get some sleep."

"No," Anaena refused. "It's my turn. Besides, I'm not as exhausted as you are."

"I'll call you as soon as I feel weary." He sat down, his back against a boulder. Suddenly a flash of light took him by surprise. It scrolled down from the sky and swept across the slope, then settled on him. "Anaena! The launch! Look! They're here!"

She was by his side within seconds. She jumped into his arms on impulse and kissed him passionately. He pulled away gently. A small black launch landed on the platform. "It's your buddies, the Pilgrims," she murmured.

The door opened and a petite figure hopped out and ran toward them, face lit by the fire. Iolia raced to Tankar.

"I prayed and prayed we would find you. I was just about to return to camp when I spotted your fire." Tears rolled down Iolia's face, and she looked ready to faint. She continued, "I have looked and looked for you. I couldn't find a trace of wreckage."

"The eruption must have swallowed up the crash site," Tankar explained.

"How did two expedition vehicles have accidents at the exact same place?"

He gave her the short version.

Iolia turned to Anaena, her eyes flashing with fury. "So he almost died because of you?"

"Iolia, she's the one who saved my life," Tankar intervened.

"Right. And how many times did you save hers?"

He stood between the two women. He had no intention of losing either woman's friendship.

"Let's not start this. It'll only cause us to fight. Take Anaena on board your ship, drop her at the camp and come back for me."

"No, you first. She can wait."

"This is a dangerous place for a young woman."

"You've barely gotten over being ill," Iolia objected.

"All right," Tankar sighed. "I'm familiar with this type of vessel. If we sit snugly it can carry all three of us especially if the camp is not too far."

"Three hundred kilometers."

"Let's go."

"We're not going anywhere until she and I set things straight," Iolia declared. She turned to Anaena. "Thank you for helping Tankar. That said, I want you to know that he will be marrying me. Soon."

Anaena turned to Tankar. "You told me you hadn't pledged yourself to her...."

"I haven't officially, Ana, but...." He was too embarrassed to speak further.

The Stellaran filled the silence. "Tankar was convinced that I'd stolen the tracer blueprints, so he came to you by default. Now that he knows he was wrong, everything changes. Get it? He doesn't love you." She tossed her tangled red hair. "He told me so."

Iolia moaned like a wounded animal. "Is that true, Tankar? You don't love me?"

"Enough," he roared. "No, I said nothing of the kind to Anaena. I did tell her we were going to get married."

"You didn't sound happy about it," she reminded him. "You said it was too late to...."

"May the Devil toss you both into space! I refuse to let you fight over me. Does my opinion matter in all of this? Maybe I love you both or maybe neither one of you. I'm not sure. I'm exhausted, and if this continues there will nothing left for you two to fight over." He slipped to the ground.

"Please forgive me, Tankar," Iolia begged. "Come. Let me help you into the launch."

Supported by both women, he tumbled into the vessel and immediately fell asleep.

He woke up stretched out on a bed. The curved pale green plastic arc of the ceiling looked like metal. Curious, he sat up halfway in the large tent and, through the open flap, saw trees, a slope, a clear space, and monitors at work. Men passed in front of the opening without stopping. Tankar dressed and went outside where he realized it was still early in the day as the sun was barely rising over the eastern hills.

"Did I sleep for only a short time? I feel so rested."

A man approached and Tankar realized he was a medic from the *Tilsin*. "How are you feeling? You were asleep for three days."

"Three days!"

"You were worn out, but we did help you out with hypnosis. Sleep was what you needed most."

"Anaena?"

"She's not awake yet."

Still feeling weak, he took a seat on a tree trunk. Aside from the doctor, the only people he could see were dressed in standard severe Pilgrim clothing. *So even on the planet surface the people remained in voluntary separation, he wondered. If so, why was the doctor here? The Menians had plenty of competent doctors of their own.*

The man seemed to guess his thoughts. "I'm here at the request of the Teknor and the Patriarch, but I'm not here to treat you; my colleagues took good care of you. I'm here to find out how you are. Tan Ekator wants to see you as soon as possible."

"Where is he?"

"At our camp, about two hundred kilometers from here, near the volcano."

The doctor left, and Tankar lost himself in his thoughts. He was troubled and did not know what to do. The future looked complicated. Did he love Anaena? Iolia? Or, as he'd said at the shelter, did he love them both? He didn't know. During his long stay in the Pilgrim compound, the redheaded Stellaran had slowly faded from his memory, or so he'd thought. But the past few days in her company, facing a perilous unknown world together, had shown him he'd not forgotten her at all. And yet, there was Iolia.

Guards were not encouraged to think introspectively. While he had done some soul-searching since taking shelter among the Pilgrims, what he really wanted remained unclear. Part of him wished for a quiet life with Iolia that would, of course, be broken up by adventures. He knew she would be a dependable, fresh and tender companion.

And yet, the other part of him, the part his former Guard comrades had nicknamed Tankar the Devil, leaned toward Anaena. Life with her would be an eternal battleground; clashes of will every day, but what a life it would be! Still in the habit of making quick, irreversible decisions, he suffered and blamed both women.

The ideal would be to have Anaena for the rough times and Iolia for the peaceful times, but he knew that was a self-serving fantasy. His mind focused on practical matters.

What would he do on his return to the *Tilsin*? He could, of course, stay on with the Pilgrims. In that case, he would have to marry Iolia as he had more or less sworn to do. Or he could return to his small apartment, which Anaena told him was still his. His anger over the blueprint business had subsided. After his sojourn among the Pilgrims, he would be welcome once again. If worse came to worst, he could redraft the blueprints and hand them directly to the Teknor.

But had he ever really been accepted? During the conjunction, maybe. On the other hand, were he to marry Anaena.... He had made no decision by the time the woman in question appeared. Aside from a faint scar on her forehead, she bore no traces of the hardships they had shared. She was once again herself: the Teknor's niece, the anti-Mpfifi boss. She came to him smiling, and he rose to greet her.

"So, Tankar, how are you?"

"Good, how about you?"

"Perfect. I'm even ready to begin all over again."

Her boasting annoyed him. "So...ready to start kicking the nests...?" he teased.

"How many times are you going to remind me about that?"

"I didn't mean to hurt your feelings, Ana. Everybody makes mistakes; the key is not to make the same one twice."

She smiled again, looking reassured. "It was my first mistake on a planet."

"It's tricky to make the same mistake twice. Enough. You're returning to camp, I imagine?"

"Yes. And so will you."

"I haven't made up my mind about that."

Anaena scoffed. "Oh, come on! This self-imposed exile is ridiculous. I promise you nobody on our end will bother you again; I'll make sure of it. And I want you by my side at all times."

"As to the first part of your plan, I can defend myself. As to the second, I haven't made up my mind about that either."

"We need you," she insisted. "Tan wants to put you in charge of defense."

"Would I have to leave the compound to do that?" he asked.

"Our men will struggle to take orders from a Pilgrim," she replied impatiently.

"I'm not a Pilgrim. And I suspect they'd struggle even more with orders from a planetary."

"You won't be a planetary once you hand over the blueprints!"

"Don't you already have them?" he demanded sarcastically.

"I told you we didn't steal the blueprints! I said that when I thought we were staring death in the face and had no reason to lie. For the last time, I'm telling you that we didn't take them." Her voice dropped as she turned red with fury.

"So be it. But none of that means I have to leave the compound. I feel more comfortable there than I do among your people, Ana. Your society is alien to me."

"And the society of half monks isn't alien? Tankar of the Guards with the Pilgrims, ha! Just say out loud you're not in love with me."

"I don't know. I did love you, the evening of the conjunction. But so much has happened since...."

"Yes. The thing in the gray dress happened. Too-perfect-to-be-real Iolia. The filthy little Pilgrim. Tankar the hero seduced by a girl who knows only her prayers!"

"Shut up!" he hissed. "You're in no position to judge her. Don't forget she saved our lives."

"From a comfortable seat on a launch."

"After 30 hours of uninterrupted searching. Thirty hours with no sleep, almost going blind, hunting through bushes, mountains and clearings."

"I would've done the same thing! And I watched over you when the beasts surrounded us."

"I know that!"

"You saved me twice," she said in a gentler tone. "I know that, and I'll never forget it. Don't you see that all of this has created unbreakable bonds between us? Imagine all the things we could accomplish together. The war against the Mpfifis will heat up, and you can provide invaluable assistance. You might become Teknor in a few years. The city-states will have to co-operate closely among themselves, and we'll need a leader who's a man of resolve and of skill, one who is used to giving orders. You could be that man, Tankar. You could command all of the People of the Stars."

"Have you ever asked yourself if I might want such a thing?" He also spoke quietly. "I don't hold you all in contempt by any means.

But I'm a planetary. I love space, but I was born on the Earth, not among the stars. Sometimes I need to feel earth under my feet, the sky over my head, the wind, the clouds, the grass between my toes."

"I didn't know you could be so lyrical," she sneered. "What do you have under your feet right now? No grass, of course, since the Pilgrims razed it all to land their craft, but it is earth. What would stop you from coming here when the mood took you? There are a lot of planets out there."

"What do you see in me, Ana?" He paused and waited for an answer that didn't come. "A man as he really is? An image that you created of someone larger than life? I was trained to be a soldier, but I'm no strategic mastermind. Do you see me as someone who can achieve your dream of power? What am I to you, really? A possible life partner? Or a tool to gain power for yourself? I'm sick and tired of all this back and forth. Give us the tracers, Tankar. Train the militias, Tankar. Use me as your pedestal, Tankar. I've had enough."

"We rescued you!"

"When I was falling through space, yes. But that's not really how it was. You picked me up as a means to an end. The only people who have asked absolutely nothing of me are the Pilgrims who haven't even tried to convert me."

"Oh, no, no, no. They're far more subtle than that. Let's marry him off to one of our girls, and after that…."

"Stop it! I really don't want to fight with you. Let me think. But know that if I come back to you, I won't come as a tool. Not for you. Not for anyone."

Anaena's tone turned cold. "Got it. Go back to your little imbecile. You may be right, after all. I'd really like to see what happens when a planetary mates with a Pilgrim girl."

He grabbed her arm. "You don't even know what you're saying. If you were a man…."

"Let go of me!" Her eyes sparkled and narrowed with malice. "Your girlfriend's here. Go to her."

She escaped his grip and walked to Iolia, blocking her path. Tankar froze. He knew they briefly exchanged words before he heard a dry slap. Anaena turned on her heel and strode off toward a waiting copter. He ran to Iolia who stood in a daze massaging her reddened cheek.

"Why did she do that, Tankar?"

"It's nothing, Iolia, nothing at all." He took her in his arms, feeling her young body under the rough gray tunic, and a wave of tenderness overtook him. "Will you marry me, Iolia?"

She trembled. "Yes, Tankar," she whispered.

PART THREE

CHAPTER ONE

The Mpfifis

Tankar pushed aside the worksheet covered in equations. He had completed the theoretical part of the task, and soon he would be able to begin construction of the hyperspace communicator. The lab was quiet after hours, his co-workers having long since returned to their homes. He was weary but happy.

I wasn't made to be a soldier, he thought for the umpteenth time. *Mathematical research, the struggle to conquer the unknown....*

Much had happened since the stopover on the virgin planet. He had not seen Anaena since. The day after their return he had a short, stormy meeting with the Teknor.

"I don't approve of what my niece has done," Tan said. "But I don't approve of your conduct either. What do you want?"

"Nothing," Tankar calmly replied. "To live quietly until the day you can drop me on Earth or some other human planet."

"Will Iolia go with you?"

"She will."

The Teknor shook his head. "I expected better from you, Tankar. I thought you'd help us against the enemy, an enemy that won't spare any planet, human or other."

"I was about to do exactly that when someone stole my

blueprints. Somebody here has them. Find the plans. Find the thief. Then I'll settle the score with him in one of your parks. After that, you and I can talk in a more meaningful way."

"Your stubbornness puts everybody in danger, including Iolia," the Teknor pointed out.

"I don't agree, but, if you're right, we'll take the risk."

"What if we were to just leave you here?"

"You can't," Tankar smiled. "The Pilgrims brought me into their fold. You're tied to me in the same way you're tied to them. They won't let you abandon me."

Tan waved his arms in frustration. It was useless. He walked away.

Tankar and Iolia were married even before the mining camps had been set up. The Pilgrim-style ceremony was short and simple. Since that day, the Pilgrims considered him one of their own even though he had not adopted their faith.

He stood, put away his notes and glanced at the tracer. Nothing. He filled his pen with ink, packed a roll of paper, and was about to head out when the needle wavered slightly. He reset the external antennae and searched for the source. Far away in hyperspace, something was moving.

A city-state? Or might it be the Others? he wondered. Should he alert the Patriarch? The Teknor? Whoever had stolen the plans could warn Tan. Tankar hadn't yet told Holonas the tracer was operational. His colleagues in the lab thought the machine was the preliminary result of Tankar's research into hyperspatial communications. And that was exactly the way he wanted it....

The needle abruptly swerved, then reset at zero. In any event, they were wandering in hyperspace a long way from the danger zone. Contact was lost. They were not at risk. He waited in the lab for another hour anyway and then went home.

Iolia was already asleep, so he gently slid into bed next to her.

She tucked herself into his arms and hugged him without waking. He lay staring into the darkness, and thought about getting up, calling the Patriarch, before exhaustion overtook him. Little by little, numbness overcame him. He was tired of his long vigils and was in bed, warm and happy. *I've been married for three months now*, he thought, *three months of happiness.*

The sound of a thud woke him, and his warrior instinct kicked in. Another, lighter thud followed, and then came an explosion that caused the hull and the metal partitions to vibrate. The sirens wailed, and Iolia bolted upright. She lit a lamp. "Four bells," she said. She was shaken to her core. "Major incident or...."

Overcome by guilt, he finished her thought. "Or the Mpfifis...."

He threw on his clothes and listened to the communicator. "Attention, all. The Mpfifis have attacked. All males, grab your weapons now. Do not waste a second in joining your sections."

Tankar furiously ripped off the security seals on the weapons chest and took two fulgurators, a short-nosed rifle and his ammunition belt. A very pale Iolia armed herself as well. "I'll go to the hospital; that's where I belong."

"I'm off to Section 4." He kissed her passionately. "Be careful, Io. Whatever happens, thank you for making me so happy, and remember that I love you. Take no unnecessary risks!"

As he headed out the door she called after him, "Until later, my love!"

"Don't worry," he assured her. "I've been here before."

Tankar took a last look at the slender figure in her white nurse's smock and left. Pilgrims raced through the streets as he swiftly made his way to military HQ where his section waited. The enormous room swarmed with armed men coming and going in the usual chaos that was war. He managed to reach the captain.

"Tankar Holroy, Section 4. Where's the attack?"

"Five Points, look at the map. Immediately join Sections 6, 7, and 8 at Point 3."

Out of habit, Tankar saluted and clicked his heels. Despite the urgency of the moment, the Pilgrim smiled.

Tankar's entire section had come together: a hundred men holding two fulgurators each and 10 machine guns. They headed straight out of the Pilgrim enclave and raced through deserted streets toward Point 3 on Bridge 4, Sector 2. A Stellaran wearing an officer's armband stopped them before they got there.

"Destination?"

"Point 3."

"Too late. Our lines have been breached. The fighting is in Park 15. Go. Now!"

The soldiers split into two groups before diving into the gravity slide and connecting with another section. Tankar could not help but think of the Pilgrims' refuge. *Luckily, none of the combat points is near the compound!*

All of a sudden his thoughts turned to Anaena, and he imagined her with Tan at the command post trying to direct the troops. He felt a pang of regret; his rightful place should have been there, at their side.

As the soldiers approached the battlefield, they could hear the dull sounds of explosions, the whistling of fulgurators, the bursts of machine-gun fire, and another choppy sound that Tankar did not recognize but surmised was produced by the Others' weapons. At the Park 15 checkpoint, Tankar and another section commander, a skinny brunette, walked toward an officer. "You, Scott, take the left flank and meet up with Sections 122, 123 and 127. They badly need reinforcements. As for you...."

"Holroy."

"Ah, the planetary. Well, this is our chance to see how the Empire's Stellar Guards fare in battle. You go right with your

Pilgrims and support Sections 80 and 87. They're in pretty bad shape too. You'll need to stay with them for two hours."

"Enemy position?"

The officer pointed to a map that displayed a pencil drawing in a crescent shape. "Last I heard, about 10 minutes ago, they were here."

"Classic," Tankar mumbled. "Can't we use the roof sprinklers to flood them?"

"No…. Ah, wait, that might be an idea. We could make holes in the…. Now, you get going. I'm going to run that idea past the Teknor."

Tankar shrugged and turned to face his men. "Let's go. Do nothing foolish. Simply do as I taught you during drill. Everything will be okay."

They entered the park through a small secondary gate and plunged directly into the battle. The air was thick with smoke, bushes were in flames between the two lines, and bullets whistled above their heads before scoring the metal flooring.

"Forward! Camouflage yourselves behind the small trees. You, machine gunners, deploy in one line. One fulgurator in the right hand, one in the left."

The men progressed with Tankar in the lead. He looked back occasionally to ensure that they were following him. Then they heard the harsh sound of ammunition almost on top of them. "Get on your stomachs! Crawl! Supply team, let's move."

Tankar found himself nose-to-nose with a man moving toward the rear. "Where are you going?"

"I wanted to see if reinforcements were on their way."

"We got here as fast as we could. Take me to the lines."

"What's left of them? Sure."

In the dry bed of a small stream the remainder of Sections 80 and 87 tried to contain the enemy.

"Who's in charge here?"

A man crawled to Tankar. "Me. Ballart, Section deputy chief."

"Okay. Section Chief Holroy. I'm taking over. How many of you are there?"

"About 50."

"Down from two hundred?"

"No. Four hundred. We also had Sections 76 and 40. Be careful!"

A lethal hissing sound whizzed over their heads and crashed about 10 meters from them. A short flame, a cloud of dirt and smoke rose toward the high ceiling.

"At least there's a limit to the firepower they can use," the deputy chief grumbled.

Tankar was not listening, instead barking orders into his microphone. "Fulgurator number one, sweep those bushes, then decamp immediately. Machine guns? Get ready to fire."

The hedges burned furiously, collapsing to the ground in heaps of ashes. Tankar glanced over the bank of the dry stream and got a view of the far side of the small park where alien shapes flooded through the gates and dropped to the ground.

"Machine guns two and four, concentrate your fire on that gate! Stop them bringing in reinforcements! Damn it! This should've been done a long time ago. Where the hell are your machine guns?"

"We didn't have them, sir."

"You were sent into battle empty-handed?"

"We had rifles, grenades and lightweight fulgurators. We had to hold out until reinforcements arrived."

"Your sections don't have machine guns as SOP?"

"Yes, but we didn't have time to go to the storerooms to pick them up."

Tankar choked with rage. Weapons outside the Pilgrims'

compound were kept in storage? "Of all the asinine things I've ever heard. No surprise, then, that the Others almost always triumph. Pay attention: they're about to attack again!"

The Mpfifis leaped toward the Pilgrims under cover of mortar fire that sent shells raining down like hail.

"Aside from machine guns three and four and a couple of rifles, nobody fires," he ordered. "Wait until you see their eyeballs."

The stoic, disciplined Pilgrims did not flinch as the projectiles poured in among their ranks. A shell landed in the stream just 50 meters from Tankar and, once again, he heard the terrified screams of men being blown to bits. The enemy line inched forward; for the first time, he saw the enemy with his own eyes. Bigger than humans, they ran with a supple grace while their weapons spat out a deluge of bullets and incendiary tracers. They started at 40 meters away, closed to 30, then 20.

"Fire!"

The eight concealed machine guns, the fulgurators and the rifles joined the action. Tankar stood and fired as though he were at target practice, seemingly invulnerable. The enemy assault wave retreated leaving countless dead and wounded in its wake.

"Cease fire! Swap places! Quickly!"

A machine gunner passed by Tankar's side followed by six men covered in sweat and dirt. One of the men was a Stellaran. Tankar could not remember who had been with that team and who might now be missing. He buzzed the four deputy section chiefs.

"Malpas here. Two killed. One lightly wounded."

"Turan here. Three killed. Two gravely wounded."

"Rau here. No men down."

"Smith here. One dead, no wounded."

The enemy onslaught resumed, stronger and more precise than before.

"No reason to wait this time since they know what to expect. As soon as they get up, fire at will, but don't waste a single bullet."

They repelled the attack again, but this time suffered great losses of their own. The sirens had first sounded only one hour before, at least according to his digital timepiece.

The battle raged for two more hours. The left flank split, so the enemy now attacked them from that direction. Tankar thought to retreat a moment before he received the order to do just that. They'd been asked to fight for two hours; they had held out for almost three.

He and his men took to the street single file, dodging well-timed salvos that led to another handful of fatalities. Tankar latched on to a captain. "How's it going on the other fronts?"

The man pulled Tankar aside. "Things are bad. We're being sunk at Points 1, 2 and 5. Only you and 4 held them off. The enemy has managed to infiltrate pretty much everywhere."

"What's the Teknor up to?"

"I don't know. I haven't received new orders from him for an hour. I'm afraid we've been cut off."

"What's in this sector?"

"Dwellings. Empty. The noncombatants have been evacuated into the central parks."

"Then what the hell are we doing here?" demanded a frustrated Tankar.

"We're defending the city, planetary," the captain righteously replied.

"That's not the way to win this thing! We need to launch a counter-attack. Take the fight to them!"

"Easier said than done," the captain retorted.

"We can give it a try. Let's head back...."

"No. We have to stay here. Teknor's orders."

"But that's idiotic! As soon as the Others break through

our lines, as they well may have done already, they'll spread throughout the city and the situation will be hopeless! We won't be able to stop them!"

The captain gave him a weary look. "What can I do?"

"You can come with me and bring your men."

A violent explosion sent both men crashing to the ground. About 20 meters from them, the jagged partition broke open and released a flood of Mpfifis.

"Too late, planetary!"

But Tankar was not there. He had turned a large machine gun on to the advancing enemy with the help of a handful of Pilgrims and launched heavy machine-gun fire. Ignoring the bullets and mortars whizzing past him, he aimed and fired at the seething mass running through the street.

"Let's go! Forward!"

He ran and threw two grenades that cleared a passage. He threw a third into the breach, jumping ahead of it to find himself and 30 others with two machine guns on a deserted street. He slipped into an empty apartment and tried to reach central command without success.

"No reason to get killed for nothing. There must be second lines somewhere." They found them at the next intersection. From there he got through to the Teknor. "Holroy here. If this position is blocked, we lose. Give me a free hand and two hundred men, and we'll attempt a counter-attack."

"What do you plan to do?" the Teknor asked.

"You'll find out."

"Then...no."

"Listen, Tan. I don't give a damn about your city, but my wife is treating your wounded in one of your hospitals. I don't want to be burned alive by aliens. I don't have time to lay out my plans for you."

A different voice broke in: Anaena. "What do you want, Tankar?"

"To save you in spite of yourselves, but I need two hundred men and a free hand."

Silence. "Fine. Take them but not from where you are. Select from the reserves at the command post. Release your men to the officer in charge."

He raced through the streets, ran into reinforcements, vaulted onto automated walkways, and climbed stairs. The gravity slides were too slow.

Anaena was waiting. "The men are here, the best ones we could find. I won't deny that you're probably our last hope, Tankar. Why didn't you accept Tan's offer?"

He laughed bitterly. "I've done far worse since. But this isn't the time to look back. How's the battle progressing?"

"I'll show you."

A thick red line on the command post wall tracked the enemy's progress through the web of bridges. Tankar breathed a sigh of relief. The Pilgrims' compound was secure.

"Where's their city-state?"

"Glued to ours. What do you want to do?"

"Invade it!"

"With only two hundred men?"

"Just enough to distract the enemy while others climb along the hull to plant explosives. My plan is to cut off the tunnels that connect them to us. After that, the *Tilsin* will move into hyperspace while the atomic bomb on their hull goes off."

"Crazy enough to work," Anaena acknowledged, "and we don't really have an alternative. I'll authorize this, but you must take a thousand men."

"That's either too few or too many," Tankar refused. "Two hundred will be enough. We'll exit via one of the airlocks in the Pilgrims' enclave and proceed under the *Tilsin*. I need someone I can trust to command the diversion team."

"Me?"

"Will you know what to do?"

"As well as any other Stellaran. But the Teknor needs to be in the loop. He's the only one who can authorize a lightweight atomic bomb."

As they crossed the Pilgrim compound, Tankar took two minutes to try to reach Iolia, but nobody could find her, so he left a message. They went through the airlock in their magnetic boots and walked along the underside of the *Tilsin*. Even without reference points their walk proceeded normally until they reached the edge and had their first impression of staring into a bottomless chasm of gleaming stars.

The crushed upper deck of the Mpfifi city was the source of the five access tunnels anchored to the hull of the *Tilsin*. "Anaena, first blow up two tunnels. There may well be airlocks at each end, but the explosions will draw the enemy's attention. Try to penetrate the enemy city, but don't go too far no matter how curious you are about the inside. Make sure the other three bridges blow up 10 minutes later, and then dive through the gaps back onto the *Tilsin*." He paused before adding, "I'll find you there. See you later…or goodbye, I can't be sure which."

He set the rockets on his suit and shot up to the hull of the enemy city-state followed by six men hauling the bomb on a hydraulic sled. He had time to see the fireworks before the hull's curve obstructed his view.

"Stop." He signaled to the other men. They had to avoid passing in front of an observation post, or they'd have been spotted.

A light briefly shone on the *Tilsin* followed by a second blast, and Tankar knew the first two bridges had been blown. He smiled at the image of Anaena and her men rushing through the breaches into the Mpfifi ship especially since rushing while wearing a spacesuit really was not possible! Chasing away the image, he looked for the best spot to deposit the bomb. With no knowledge of the layout of the enemy ship, one spot was as good as any other. Five minutes elapsed. The men attached the device to the hull, and Tankar activated the delayed-action apparatus that, in 10 minutes, would set off the hydronuclear reaction.

"Get going," he ordered his men. "Warn our comrades on the way. I'll be there soon."

As he carefully adjusted the equipment, he abruptly sensed someone near him and swore. "I told you to get out of here!"

Recoiling from a hard hit to his helmet, Tankar turned and saw an enormous Mpfifi in a spacesuit looming over him. Straightening quickly, he almost lost his magnetic boots. The enemy was a good 30 centimeters taller than he but did not appear to be armed. He must have been a mechanic inspecting the hull. The Mpfifi was poised to attack again, but Tankar ducked, grabbed the Mpfifi by its legs and heaved it off the hull. As the creature drifted through space, Tankar recalled his own fall and felt sorry for him. Then something tapped the soles of his boots.

The other tunnels are exploding! The Tilsin *is about to dive into hyperspace!*

He ran awkwardly taking long, slippery strides. The city-state was still there, and he saw two wide gaps that seemed simultaneously close by and far away as the last human shapes rushed in. He knew that he did not have enough time to descend the usual way. Using all the power of his rockets, he shot forward. Straight ahead of him he saw a long shape strike the *Tilsin*'s prow in an explosion of light. Then he dove headfirst inside one of the openings. Using retro-rockets built into his spacesuit he attempted to slow down, but his helmet slammed into the ground, and he fainted. He woke up in an apartment he did not recognize surrounded by Anaena and two doctors.

"So?" he asked.

"You won, Tankar. Right now we're decimating the last pockets of resistance."

He fell back against a pillow with a sigh. "Then I can go home now. Congratulations, Ana. You've got guts, which I've always known. Can't we be friends? Although you'll find out what I did...." He stifled his next words and struggled to get to his feet. "I'm going back home to sleep. Iolia must be impatient to see me."

The look on Anaena's face made him blanch. "She... she didn't...?"

"The enemy's final torpedo, Tankar," she said softly. "It slammed into the middle of the hospital where she was working. She didn't have time to suffer...or even to know...."

★   ★   ★

He awoke from his deep sleep with a violent headache and a dry mouth. He gazed at the ceiling not understanding where he was. Then he remembered, and he wished he was dead.

He was in his former apartment where Pei's paintings still lay rolled up just as he'd left them. Just as he'd found....

The room reeked of alcohol. He started to get up when the sound of breaking glass told him a bottle had crashed to the floor adding to a pile of glass shards. The motion aggravated his headache, and he felt as if his brain were being tossed around and ricocheting off his skull.

Eight days! I've been here eight whole days.... He stood, carefully putting his feet on the ground and sidestepping the shattered glass on his way to the tiny kitchen where he drank several glasses of cold water. He sat at the table, head in hands, and remained there immobile, incapable of weeping.

Eight days! Eight days already....

He remembered, as if it were a dream, making his way through the city's streets surrounded by Anaena and other Stellarans, cheered on by men and the women, unable to understand why. He had gone into the compound and walked, like a blind man, to the apartment he had shared with his wife. His pajamas still lay crumpled on the unmade bed next to Iolia's neatly folded nightgown. Then, finally, he understood.

He remained alone for several hours, pacing the three small rooms, trying to forget, struggling to convince himself none of it was true. Everything in the apartment bore Iolia's imprint. He cherished the final moments when he could still hope that she had just gone away for a little while, that she would be back soon and smile at him. Then, suddenly, he had given in to the grief, collapsed onto the bed and clutched the nightgown that still smelled of her.

Afterward, he calmly sorted through the items he wanted to keep to remember her and set aside those he would give to her family just as he would have done for a fallen comrade-in-arms. Then he'd left the apartment forever. He could no longer stand the idea of living alone in rooms Iolia had so indelibly marked.

He wanted to see where she had died. The torpedo had slipped through a hallway after penetrating the hull. Instead of exploding immediately, it decimated a ward with 30 wounded, two doctors and five nurses, one of whom had been Iolia. They found nothing of the victims, nothing identifiable.

Finally, he had paid his respects to Holonas, also shattered by grief. Tankar left the compound rather than attend the funeral ceremony. He had returned to his former apartment. Ever since, he had been drinking nonstop, passing out, trying to forget that he was, in part, responsible for his wife's death.

The doorbell rang. He ignored it, wishing the visitor would leave him alone to grieve.... Insistently, the doorbell rang again.

He opened the door, and Anaena entered. She looked at him with pity and put one gentle hand on his shoulder.

"Don't do this, Tankar."

"Do what?"

"Let yourself go like this. It's not worthy of a man like you."

He stared at her, brimming with hatred. "You mean Tankar, Lieutenant of the Stellar Guard, don't you? Tankar, the hero? Tankar, the savior? Drunk for eight days straight."

He stood close to her so she could smell the alcohol on his breath, waves of it coming off his body. "When the hell will you leave me alone and let me be a man like any other? When will you let me howl in rage, anguish and shame in my own little corner? I don't give a damn what is or isn't worthy of me." Turning his back on her, he shouted, "Get out!"

"I don't know what to say, Tankar. I understand your pain...."

"Oh, no you don't! You understand nothing! You can't...I killed her." Turning back to her he whispered, "I killed her."

"Don't say such a thing." Anaena shook her head.

"You don't know!" He began pacing in little circles, waving his arms as he talked. "I had a working tracer in my lab. And I knew something was pursuing us just a few hours before the attack. We could've been ready for them! I said nothing because I hated you Stellarans so very much, and because I was convinced that, having stolen my blueprints, you were capable of building at least one tracer and, by keeping watch over it, capable of defending yourselves.

"I dumped my responsibilities onto you without making sure that you had them...the tracers. And that's how I killed Iolia, just as surely as if I'd come back that night and strangled her with my bare hands."

"You...you had a tracer?" Anaena stuttered in shock.

"And you don't have one, do you? You told me over and over,

and I never believed you. I didn't believe you because, when I first arrived on the *Tilsin*, you all made me a pariah, untouchable. After that –" he shrugged, "– it was too late. I simply couldn't believe anything you told me. You killed her too."

Anaena was pale. "Five thousand dead. Five thousand in addition to Iolia." She shook her head again. "We paid a steep price for our prejudice, and you? You paid a steep price for your pride."

"True, that. We made a fine mess, you and I. And you ignore the deaths of the Others. An entire city-state. How many were they, forty thousand?"

"Them? I don't count them."

"But you see, I simply can't hate them. I hate myself and you. That the enemy kills us? That's normal. But out of sheer stupidity you and I...that's what I can't forgive."

"You'll forget, Tankar. Man forgets in order to go on living."

"Forget her? Do you know that, aside from my mother, Iolia is the only person ever to show me kindness? For three months I was happy, Anaena. You never can comprehend my happiness."

"Oh, yes, I think I can since I know what three months of heartbreak can be."

He acted as if he had not heard her. "I'd never known such peace of mind, such lively friendship, such warmth. When I came home from the lab in the evening, she was at the door waiting for me, every night except that last one when I came home too late to see her give me one last smile. Can you understand that I loved her? Aside from a handful of comrades among the Guard – and that's a very different thing – I'd never loved any other person.

"When I fought in the park trying to stop an enemy you couldn't contain, I wasn't fighting for this city; I wasn't fighting for the Empire; I wasn't even fighting for humanity as a whole. I fought only for Iolia, for her alone. She was the one person who cared about me and, just as she needed me, I needed her." He stopped pacing and stared at nothing, seeing no one. "I betrayed her. I failed to protect her. I killed her."

Tankar turned to face Anaena again. "For the rest? I don't give a damn. Get the hell out of here and let me drink. When I'm drunk I sleep, and when I sleep, I forget."

"And do you think Iolia would approve?"

He stood, unmoving, as if she had struck him, still gripping the bottle in one hand.

Anaena continued. "She saw the man in you. She saw beyond the soldier, and she did that far better than I did; I admit it. Better than any of us."

"Yes. And I killed her."

"You didn't kill her, Tankar. We're all guilty, me first of all. If only I'd been able to see beyond my stupid prejudice.... If only I'd befriended you from the start, then that wall of mistrust never would have been built. But...." She hesitated before admitting, "But I suffered so much to see you with that woman!" She paused before whispering, "That's the truth."

"Orena?" Tankar was stunned. "But she never mattered to me. She was like a rope thrown to a drowning man."

"I think I fell in love with you the day I met you," Anaena confessed. "Don't worry, I'm not going to bore you with my feelings. You preferred Iolia to me, and you were right to do so. She was a far better person than I am, and I will always regret having slapped and insulted her back there on that vile planet. If it makes you feel even a little bit better, you're not the only one suffering right now, although I know our sufferings aren't comparable."

He remained silent for a long time then placed one arm

around her shoulders. "I'm not sure if I'll ever be able to love you, Anaena."

"I'm not asking you for anything except the chance to weep with you, to mourn Iolia and to mourn what might have been."

CHAPTER TWO

Return to Earth

"Here." Tankar tossed a batch of papers in front of the Teknor. "It'll be easy for your technicians to build as many tracers as they want with these plans."

Tan stood and approached the earthling. "We treated you badly, and we've paid dearly for it. I should've...well, what's the point of trying to rewrite the past? Could I have done things differently?" He paused. "The *Tilsin* tragedy was written when Kilos II forced the technicians into exile, sowing a seed of hatred that has grown ever since. You were its victim, and now we've suffered too."

Tankar shrugged. "What does it matter? However it started, what happened, happened. Iolia died. It was my fault and yours. I don't give a damn what happens to the People of the Stars. I give you these plans in memory of Iolia and out of respect and affection for the Pilgrims."

"Is there anything we can do for you?"

"Yes. Take me back to Earth."

The Teknor frowned. "That could be risky for the *Tilsin*."

"Not now that you have the tracers. You can leave me in space within reach of the planet surface."

"I've been hoping that you might come back to live among us, Tankar." Tan's voice was tinged with regret. "We need men of your stature to contain the Mpfifis. And Anaena...."

"I won't be bought! Not with offers of a woman or laurels or power," Tankar snarled.

"Anaena will mourn," the Teknor replied calmly before adding, "Do you really think so little of me that I would barter for my niece?"

"Now you understand that we'll never see eye-to-eye. It's better that I return to my people."

"All right. I'll see you again before you go."

A short time later, Tankar was on his way. Earth orbited under his craft, an Earth that he recognized through gaps in the cloud cover. Tankar had made radio contact a few minutes before and had been given his landing orders. In three hours he would set foot on his native soil, and yet the prospect left him cold.

"You will be back, Tankar," Holonas had said when Tankar came to bid him farewell. "You have become more of a Stellaran than you know, and you will find that you are leaving too much of yourself here to abandon us forever.

"You have matured, as well. If I understand the lessons I have learned from history, you are not going to like what you're going to find on Earth any better than you like what you are leaving behind here, especially given what you have learned since you have been with us."

Tan also warned him, "You'll be back, Tankar. You'll find the Empire on its knees, and nothing will be as it was when you left. And, when you return, you'll find a transformed *Tilsin*; nobody on this vessel will forget that you saved our lives."

And Anaena had said, "You'll be back, Tankar. You'll come back because I love you."

He did not think so. However he might find Earth changed, it was still his home, his world, his civilization. In time, he would forget. It had been only two months since Iolia had died, and already he could think of her without going mad. The pain would

diminish but never vanish, the emptiness never would be filled...
but he had so much to accomplish on Earth.

He reminded himself of the information he had picked up
on the com stream from the stations on Earth. He still did not
understand the exact circumstances of the collapse, but the Empire
had, indeed, fallen. He learned that the council now governing
the planet sent out frequent calls to the last of the Imperial Force
asking them to cease hostilities and join the reconstruction efforts.

The astroport instructed him to land. He gently glided over
the European continent appalled at the devastation below. Br'lin,
Lyon, Marsei lay in ruins. At last he saw Imperia straddling the
strait between Europe and Africa. The intercontinental bridges
had collapsed, and few ships sailed the waters. On the south bank
where the imperial palace had stood so arrogantly lay only an
enormous crater. The massive expanse of concrete that used to
buzz with the activity of countless cruisers and scouts lay virtually
empty. Heaps of rusted metal sat where the control tower used
to stand. A much smaller tower, only a hundred meters tall, now
displayed the directional antennae.

Tankar felt a stab to his heart when he spotted the *Scorpion*, his
torpedo, pretty much still intact except for a dent in the chassis.
He would have recognized that vessel among a thousand others.
None except the *Scorpion* had such a long slim prow and two
retractable turrets just near the midship. *Good old* Scorpion*! Came
out of it still in one piece! Who commands her now? One of my old
comrades?* he wondered.

Ignoring the signals from the control tower, he landed the
launch right next to the *Scorpion* and jumped to the ground. He
ran across the cracked concrete and touched the sun-kissed steel
with his cheek.

"Hey, you! What were you thinking? We might've shot you,
you know," a familiar voice greeted him as a car with four men

in it parked next to him. "Tankar Holroy! They told me it was you, but I didn't believe it! Where've you been all this time? You were listed as MIA." Per Erickson smiled at him from behind the windshield.

Tankar smiled in return. "I'll tell you all about it."

"Have you come to surrender?"

"Surrender? Maybe. I really don't know what's going on here."

"Get in. I'll explain."

"Who's commanding the *Scorpion*?"

"Me. But we don't go much of anywhere these days. Other things to do. You do know the Empire's finished, right? The people have seized power, and the Council is in charge. There's no more nobility."

"And you're in the army?"

"I never was a big fan of the old order. I even was suspected of being a traitor quite recently. I surrendered pretty much immediately. You?"

"I did far worse," Tankar lied. "I never delivered the orders to the 7th Fleet." He pulled the envelope still bearing the imperial seal from a jacket pocket.

"See? They're right here."

"That's wonderful! You'll be welcomed with open arms. Had the 7th Fleet arrived everything would have turned out differently." Erickson paused. "I wouldn't have pegged you as a rebel, though."

"Do you remember Hekor?"

"He was your friend, wasn't he?" the man remembered and nodded. "I understand."

"So who's in charge now?" Tankar asked.

"There's Jon Simak, Louis Lantier, Herman Schwabe. I don't think you know the others."

Tankar grimaced. Three former generals, known throughout

the Empire for their corruption and ruthless ambition. "I thought the people—"

"The Council governs in the name of the people," Erickson cut him off and jabbed his friend in the ribs. "Later today you'll be interrogated about your adventures. For now…have you had lunch? No? Okay, come on."

The mess was in a cabin thrown together made of forged planks and sheet metal. The food was copious but tasteless.

"Tell me what you've been up to," Erickson demanded, "Although I'm not supposed to talk to you about it…."

Erickson leaned forward so as not to be overheard. "We former Stellar Guards need to stick together. You might know things that are dangerous for you to talk about. I'll tell you which ones."

"Oh, I don't think I've got much to worry about. After I received my orders, I took the Fomalhaut route and, when I was beyond communications range, I changed course. I flew to the edge of the Empire and landed on a human planet."

"One of the first colonies? How are things out there?" Erickson wondered.

"Not bad. I was well received even though I blew up my ship. One of their starships brought me back and dropped me off about two million kilometers from Earth in one of their launches."

"Are they powerful?"

"At its peak, the Empire could've crushed them; now, we'd do well to leave them alone. They're part of a confederation of more than a hundred planets and have some non-human allies as well."

The deception came easily to him; he had carefully constructed the story during his final week on the *Tilsin*. "I'll fill in the details to the investigative services. Tell me how things are here."

"About as good as they can be. I'll talk to you about it in greater detail when we have more time this evening at my place. While you wait for an apartment of your own, you'll stay with me! You can't refuse; former Guards must stick together."

"Why didn't the investigators meet me when I landed? In the days of the Empire...."

"Probably too busy. You're my responsibility for now. I have to take you over to them in an hour."

The friends talked about this and that: the rebellion, which comrades had died – most of them – and which ones had survived.

The interrogation was slow and meticulous. He did not know any of the men who grilled him. He told his story and provided details about the world where he had supposedly hidden out. He even showed them a few photos of various worlds the *Tilsin* had visited, provided by the Teknor.

"And they entrusted one of their ships to you?" The question stank of suspicion.

Tankar smiled. "A small interplanetary scout that could travel a few billion kilometers but lacked a hyperspatial device."

"Which one do they use?"

"Not sure. Different from ours, I believe, but they never let me get close to the machine room or the cockpit. They did, however, show off their weaponry, arms much like the ones we have...or had. I'll provide a written report."

"What was their policy toward us?"

"Wait and see. They were aware of the Empire and hated it. They also learned of its downfall, which is when I found out and asked to be brought home."

"Good. While you wait for an assignment, remain available to us. You'll be paid your lieutenant's salary." Tankar stood, prepared to leave, but froze upon hearing, "But if you've lied to us, you'll be sorry."

"I failed to deliver the imperial orders! What more do you want from me?" he demanded furiously.

"We know," one of the interrogators sneered, his hand on the folder containing the orders, its self-destruct seal untouched. "You may go."

Erikson's apartment was small but comfortable. Seated in a leather chair, glass in hand, Tankar relaxed until a question from his host took him aback. "Okay, old buddy, now that we can't be overheard, tell me the truth. Where were you?"

"But...I told you," Tankar insisted.

Erickson grinned. "Yeah, right. You hated the general for sending Hekor to his death, but the Empire itself was the only thing you lived for. You? Not transmit an order? You're joking! Were you in prison? Nothing to be ashamed of there. Who sent you? The Martians?"

"The Martians? Have we sunk that low?"

"Yup. Mars is independent, and so is Venus. The Empire, or I should say the People's Commonwealth, is down to Earth and the Moon. We've had no news from planets in other systems. Unless, of course, you can give us some."

"I've told you the truth! I swear."

"Fine. Not important." Erickson shrugged, then got serious. "But I'm going to tell you the truth. Of course, you know nothing about any conspiracy. I'm gonna try and fill you in even though I don't know all the details. Bel Caron led the rebellion against Ktius VII."

"The historian? The Emperor's cousin?"

"That's the guy. Now you can see why we struggled to arrest the conspirators! Bel Caron himself was a member of the Emperor's private council!"

"But he was such a gentle dreamer."

"Not a dreamer, not gentle." Erickson grimaced. "Anyway.

As you know the rebellion broke out and, from the beginning, it took off in ways nobody could've predicted. Twenty days after you left, without the support of the 7th fleet, the Emperor surrendered, but most of the cities were in ruins, most of the factories destroyed, and famine and epidemics decimated the population." He stared sadly at Tankar. "Do you know how many people live on Earth now, at least as far as we can tell? One billion, five hundred million...."

"One and a half billion instead of...?"

"Seven billion, yes. But that's the least of it. The first few months were full of hope. Caron surrounded himself with honest, energetic men and began to put what was left of the Empire back together. For the first time in centuries, the people enjoyed new freedoms, small ones but real. Faith re-established itself, and the rebellion might have given rise to many good things if the generals' coup had failed.

"But it succeeded. They assassinated Caron and his ministers and took their place. You know their worth as well as I do. Freedom suppressed again, militia everywhere, Mars and Venus have seceded, and we disemboweled Titan with an A-bomb, the last one in our arsenal, I believe. That's the world you've rejoined, Tankar."

"What about you?"

"Me? I'd surrendered before the end of the revolt, as I told you. The Caron government asked me to stay available while they did a background check. Eventually the generals called on me to join them. I'm a fleet admiral, Tankar! Some kind of fleet, though. Two torpedoes, one of which is your *Scorpion* that serves as my flagship. We also have five scouts and a limping old cruiser.

"Our crews are filled with dirty, undisciplined, technically illiterate people. There are a few acceptable survivors. The competent technicians who weren't executed by the Empire have been killed by our current dictators. Only three or four of us in the entire world remain familiar with hypertron theory." Erickson got up to refill his own glass and offered Tankar another round. Tankar thanked him and declined. "The Great Twilight has fallen on our beloved Earth, Tankar. Will she ever rise again?

"You should've stayed where you were, believe me. But it wouldn't be such a big deal without the constant snitching, the stupid executions, the endless petty tyranny. If I'd been alone when you landed I would've asked you to take me back with you. But I was with Betus, whose sole job is to keep an eye on me. I was able to fill you in some in the mess hall only because we sat in the one area where the hidden mikes don't work."

Tankar recalled Holonas's words, *If I understand what I learned from history....*

He asked his friend, "What do you think might happen to me?"

"Oh, if you don't oppose them, everything'll be fine. They're desperately in need of technicians. You're a traitor to the previous regime since, for whatever reason, you didn't deliver the orders to the 7th Fleet. So, like me, you'll get any job you want with restricted liberty if you hide your real feelings and obey without hesitation. That'd make three of us: you, me, and Jan Malvert. Maybe someday we'll be able to escape...?"

You'll be back, Tankar. Maybe that prediction had been accurate. But he needed to see for himself before he decided. He would see what the generals had to offer. In any case, the *Tilsin* would not be at the rendezvous point for another six months.

Meanwhile, he would report for duty.

* * *

"Damn it! Not that way! I've shown you 10 times already!"

Tankar yanked the key out of the hands of the new recruit

and unscrewed two nuts. The heavy fulgurator's cylinder head dropped into his left hand.

"That wasn't so hard, was it?"

"Sorry, Captain."

Tankar looked at the young man, skinny, clumsy, and half-starved. *And they want me to turn these pathetic specimens into astronauts.*

The sun pelted down on the cracked concrete, and a revolting smell of stagnating weapons' oil seeped out from below the training-center hangar. More than five months had passed. His stay on the *Tilsin* seemed like a dream. He did his best to think about it as little as possible since those thoughts brought back the grief, muted yet still present. Where were they now? Surely headed toward Earth unless the Mpfifis.... No, that enemy had not yet broken through into this part of the galaxy, and the *Tilsin* now was able to fight them off.

Tankar glanced at the time and saw it was just noon. "Take a break," he ordered. "We recommence training at 2 p.m."

The men saluted and left flanked by two officers. He watched them go, feeling both disgust and sympathy. It was not their fault they were such mediocre candidates. One cannot train an astronaut simply by calling up any old twenty-year-old. They were willing, enthusiastic even, but they lacked the most basic knowledge of mechanics, and they were in terrible physical shape.

Tankar shrugged, remembering that, under the Empire, at least people got enough to eat. He had not been much more at liberty then than he was now. He wondered if there had been any happy, hopeful times under Caron's brief governance. Had it been worth the deaths of billions of people? The conspirators had wrongly believed that, other than the members of the old regime and those who had profited from it, everybody else yearned for freedom. Many probably just wanted to turn society upside down, to debase the high and mighty and to raise up the poor and humble.

Why did it matter to him? He had wanted to return to Earth to renew ties to a past he discovered no longer existed. In this new society, he was like a fossil, a relic from long gone and forgotten days of glory. If only Bel Caron had succeeded...Tankar would have fully devoted himself to any ethical enterprise. He would not have been able to support the Empire again; he knew that, because his stay among the Stellarans had changed him too profoundly, upsetting old ideas and values. He had become an eternal outsider, a sort of hybrid who still carried within him shreds of outdated ethical codes that had prevented him from fully integrating into Stellaran society. And yet, on the other hand, he no longer could live with those same codes without questioning whether the authority giving orders had the right to give them.

But he needed to make up his mind soon. Within 10 days the *Tilsin* would slip behind the Moon and wait for him for 48 hours after which he would no longer have a choice. The *Tilsin* would leave and never return carrying with it Tan, Holonas, Anaena, Petersen, his friends, his enemies, and the memory of Iolia.

He smiled to himself. *And I mustn't forget Pei's paintings!*

Escape would not be easy. Erickson would probably help, and Malvert too, but all three of them remained suspect and under constant surveillance. Since his return, Tankar had managed only one short flight on the *Scorpion* accompanied by two 'guests' who wore Guard uniforms that failed to mask their stiff political police affiliation. The launch from the *Tilsin* was out of operation because its motors were being 'studied', and now, too slow and lacking weaponry, it wouldn't survive 10 seconds against a scout in spite of the fact that the scouts also were in deplorable condition. Tankar's only hope was the *Scorpion*, but it required four people to operate.

Tankar left camp on foot. The only person allowed transportation off base was Erickson given his standing as Admiral of the Fleet. In order to get to the canteen, Tankar had to cross a poor neighborhood largely destroyed in the recent bombings. He preferred the canteen to the sinister mess hall where any overheard conversation could lead to execution or assassination. He refused to frequent the trendy restaurants preferred by the new regime profiteers. Crowds shuffled along around him. The men were in tattered clothes, the women indifferent to their appearance, children silent with the pain of hunger. His uniform earned him some hateful looks, but most of the passersby could muster nothing more than apathy, the despair over the revolution that had been stolen from them still too potent for anyone to re-engage with the idea of rebellion. Tankar thought of Erickson's cynical words, "The Great Twilight has fallen on our beloved Earth, Tankar. Will she ever rise again?"

What was Tankar doing in this world in the midst of its death throes? What had he achieved since his sabotaged starship had sent him careening into space? Had he really tried to gain the acceptance, the respect, of the Stellarans? No. He'd sulked and paid back their stupid prejudice with his own stupid stubbornness. As a result, he had indirectly caused Iolia's death. From the perspective of the Stellar Guard's ethical standards, his actions had been inexcusable. The only times that he could recall without misery or shame were those he'd spent with Anaena on the unnamed planet. Anaena, the woman who loved him....

He had loved her too, passionately, for a time, before Iolia's kindness won him over. Perhaps if there had not been the scene with the Pilgrims, or if Anaena's insults had not provoked his pride, he might never have married Iolia. He, himself, did not regret the marriage as he had been happy for the first time in his life. *But could it have lasted?* he wondered. In the depths of his soul, he doubted it. Maybe the way that things turned out was for the best. Maybe there had been mercy in the Mpfifis' final torpedo.

It was the screaming that brought him back into the here and now. Two soldiers in a tavern doorway pulled a young woman toward the street. She resisted, but two other soldiers inside the bar pushed her out. The tavern owner looked pale and silently wrung his hands.

Tankar approached. "What's going on here?"

One of the soldiers stood up straight and insolently stood to attention. "Nothing, Captain. A whore who refuses to go to bed with us four."

"Let go of her. Orders are very clear: no disturbances in town."

"But, Captain...."

"Leave her alone! And stand properly!"

"Yes, Captain."

The woman stood up and shook her long black hair away from her face. Tankar glanced at her and saw a young woman, pretty enough, but with skin badly marred by rosacea. Where had he seen her before? Some bar, most likely.

"What's your unit?"

"Third infantry, Captain."

"Good. You'll present my respects to your colonel, and you'll ask him on my behalf to stick each of you with eight days in jail. Here's my card."

He scribbled a few words on the card and handed it to the soldier, who saluted and walked away.

"Holroy, watch it!" The shout prompted him instinctively to lower his head and duck. He heard the rustle of the bullet, spun around and shot the soldier who stood there with his gun still smoking. The man fell to the sidewalk, and his companions rushed away as fast as they could.

"Who warned me?" he demanded.

"I did," said the young woman.

"You know my name?"

"Who doesn't know the former champion of the stellar race?"

"Come with me," he offered.

"Where?" she asked warily.

"To my place first, and then to lunch."

"I'm a singer, nothing else."

Tankar blushed. "I don't ask people to pay for my assistance, miss. But if you have a mirror, take a look at yourself; you may see you could benefit from freshening up."

The young woman grimaced. "I'm sorry. I misunderstood. In that case, I'd actually prefer to use my own room. Would you like to wait here or come with me? That is…if you still wish to buy me lunch."

He followed her into the tavern and crossed a big room, dark and low-ceilinged, empty at that time of day. The manager, an older fat man, approached. "Thank you, Captain, for rescuing Elda from those brutes."

"Your daughter?"

"No, a friend of my daughter. She's a wonderful singer and works hard at it. She could make really good money if she chose to, given the fat bastards who come slumming to this joint." The man came closer to Tankar and whispered, "If anyone bothers you, I know a guy who could, for a small price…."

"No, thanks."

"At your service," the man said with a bow, quickly vanishing into the gloomy tavern.

The young woman asked Tankar to take a seat in a small room and slipped into her own saying, "Ten minutes, I'll be back."

He waited and admired a chromo of the battle of Anatares III on a wall.

"Here I am!"

Tankar turned and looked at her. Speechless, he stood and bowed deeply before her. "Countess Iria! It's you!" The young woman had transformed. Her golden-hued skin was clear, her hair a reddish blond.

In an anxious voice she pleaded, "You won't betray me, will you, Holroy? You and the kindly tavern owner are the only two people who know my true identity."

"Have no fear. But he...."

"Once upon a time, I did the same favor for his daughter that you just did for me. He's never forgotten, and he'd die before giving me up."

"Countess Iria...!"

"Yes," she smiled sadly. "The Inaccessible Dream. The Stellar Guards used to call me that; you may have called me that yourself. During those god-awful days I became all too accessible, but not by choice."

"Aren't you concerned about people recognizing you when you go out?"

"I present the real me to you now for only a few moments. Some quick-dye hair color, a little makeup on my face, and I'll be the woman you saw earlier. Pretty enough for a singer in a shady bar, but not pretty enough to be worth kidnapping."

"And yet, those soldiers...."

She shrugged. "Things happen. It was only the second occasion." She took charge. "We're wasting time here. I'll get ready quickly...it's just that I wanted to know if you'd remember me."

"You haven't changed," he assured her.

"I was 20 then, and I'm two hundred now." She paused before returning to her room to ask, "Do you really want to go to a restaurant? Uncle David can make us a very nice meal here."

"As you wish," Tankar conceded.

Served in a tiny windowless room, the meal was the best Tankar had had in a long time, the best he had had since leaving the *Tilsin*. The meats were delicious and beautifully prepared, the fruits fresh and the vegetables perfect. He expressed surprise.

"Oh, it's not that unusual. Uncle David's tavern appeals both to the dregs of society and to those who claim to be the new elite. They're no better than the ones who came before, of course. Our new noble class has money, and Uncle David has no reservations about taking some of it off their hands."

"Uncle David?"

"That's what he likes me to call him," she explained. "I won't talk about his past, or even his present, but toward me he is always a gentleman. I 'saved his little Thesa from shame' is the way he puts it. He took me in after...."

"It must've been terrible."

"Yes. In just a few months I fell from the height of society to the dregs. My family was murdered, and all of my friends killed or disappeared...."

"How did Caron permit it?"

"I'm not talking about the first revolution. That time my family suffered losses, of course, as did many others, but it was all tolerable. Caron was a cousin of mine, and he looked after us. We were one of the few noble families that commoners didn't despise. The bad things, the very bad things came later. After the degenerates you currently work for came to power."

Both sympathetic and exasperated, Tankar demanded, "What do you want me to do? To restore the Empire all by myself? When I returned from my mission almost six months ago, I found things as they are now. I knew nothing about anything. They offered me the training job. What should I have done? Pulled out one of those fulgurators I no longer own and get myself killed? I don't intend to serve these people until I die, Countess."

With a dismissive gesture she sighed, "Oh, spare me the old title. Now I'm just Elda the singer. In the end, out of sheer exhaustion, I'll probably end up marrying some commoner I can train to bathe regularly, and we'll produce a litter of little slaves for the regime." A tear rolled down her cheek. "I don't have much choice either."

Suddenly, she spoke with passion. "Oh, if I could leave! Emigrate! Somewhere among the planets there must be a place that's not as horrid as this one. But commercial travel is forbidden, and my yacht, the *Diamond*, languishes somewhere disemboweled. I'll never again have the joy of piloting, that's over. You at least, now and again…."

"Yeah. With two cops on my tail all the time…but I had forgotten you have a pilot's license."

"I even won the Earth-Pluto round-trip race, women's division." Responding to the look on his face she added, "Oh, I know you annoying male chauvinist Guard types look on that race as second-rate."

Tankar thought out loud. "So, you're a trained pilot? Do you know how to keep watch on hypertrons?"

"I've never done it…. But why do you want to know? Tell me."

"Don't get your hopes up. A foolish idea, perhaps…."

Iria stood up and gripped his arms hard. "You want to leave? You want to steal a starship? Don't leave without me, Holroy. I'll do anything, I'll clean the bridges, I—"

He smiled reassuringly. "Nothing like that. The only thing I need to know is if you can track hypertrons. The *Scorpion* could leave at any point except for one small thing. The automatic adjustment system has been removed and the special police have it under lock and key, so we'd need four people on board: a pilot, a navigator, someone to take charge of the artillery, and the fourth on the hypertrons so as to manually compensate for any deviations. Would you be able to do that?"

"If I remember correctly, in the old days there was always a mechanic in that post. It's not difficult. One just needs to turn a wheel until the red alarm lights go off."

Tankar nodded. "No, it's not difficult but it requires cold-blooded focus. If the deviation widens until the axes cross, you know what'll happen."

"I'm ready to take that risk!"

"Yes, you are, but are we ready to take the risk? I'd need to test your reflexes and your response times, but you won't be allowed into the camp, so I can't." Tankar made the decision. "I'll speak to the others and let you know." He stood up. "Can I entrust Uncle David with a message to you?"

"You'll come back to see me, right?"

Tankar quickly shook his head. "No. Bad idea to draw attention to the tavern."

"Don't you think the corpse of that soldier will attract attention?"

"No. Every day we need to kill one or more of them for murder, mutiny, that kind of thing."

"Then just tell Uncle David that you're confirming our appointment."

"If everything goes according to plan, you'll see me in the big room while you're singing. As soon as you finish, quickly exit through the side door. I'll be waiting for you."

★   ★   ★

Tankar leaned over the man he had just shot and saw the average face of any anonymous soldier. This one had suffered the misfortune of being in the wrong place at the wrong time. Rain pounded down on the astroport's runway concealing the minimal illumination.

"Let's go, come on! Let's get out of here!" He and Countess

Iria left the body in the guardhouse and raced through the downpour, wading through the puddles created by holes in the decaying concrete. Slowly a shadowy figure emerged from the darkness in the gleam of a lighthouse stationed at the far end of the tarmac.

"Who goes there?" whispered a voice.

"Tankar!"

"Move fast. Malvert just told me they've changed the times of the relief rotation, so we've got just 15 minutes."

"Damn it! Come on."

A brief glint from a hololight revealed a gaping hole in the side of the ship directly above a metal ladder. "Everyone on board!" The lock snapped shut with a click that sounded loud enough to echo as far as the city.

"Iria, follow me," Tankar ordered.

"This is my first visit to a warship," the countess whispered as she quickly scanned the interior.

"This is your post," he explained. "See this row of eight red lights? They're off now. Six of them control spatial alignment and two control temporal alignment. They're laid out in four groups, each with a steering wheel. If a red light comes on, steer to the right. Same on the left until the red lights go off. Whenever a lamp flashes you'll hear a whistle sound for about five seconds. If it takes you longer than that, pull this red lever –" he pointed, "– all the way back. That'll short-circuit the hypertrons if the alignment isn't out of whack."

"And what if more than one lamp comes on at the same time?" she worried.

"Two at the most. Do your best. Don't get scared; five seconds is a lot longer than you think!" he encouraged her.

"It's very unusual for a misalignment to take place on two levels. When the hypertrons start working again, you'll see a green light. From then on you can't take your eyes off the red lamps. Buckle in tightly, because if you need to switch off everything, the ride'll get bumpy. Do you understand? Repeat everything I just said....

"Fine.... See you later...and good luck!"

"Good luck to all of us, Holroy," Iria called after him.

Tankar entered the cockpit, familiar from the countless times he'd piloted the ship. Erickson sat in the navigator's seat. Malvert had disappeared, locking himself into the weaponry control turret. Erickson asked, "Do you think she'll hold?"

"My *Scorpion*? Of course! We're good to go," Tankar insisted cheerfully. "Let's do a run-through of the checklist. Piloting circuits?"

"Clear."

"Vision circuit?"

"Clear."

"Artillery circuit?"

"Clear."

"Gravitons?"

"On charge."

"Hypertrons?"

"On charge. Neutral. Aligned."

"Inertrons?"

The men heard the grinding sound of motors. Tankar turned on the night screen and saw four trucks zooming toward the *Scorpion* and men running toward the cruiser just a hundred meters away.

"Screw the checklist, Tankar! Lift off, lift off now!" Erickson called.

"Don't panic, we've got plenty of time." Over the intercom he announced, "We're taking off!"

The *Scorpion* slowly lifted off and gained altitude, its nose tilted toward the cloud-covered sky. Grenades exploded where the ship had been parked moments before. Tankar pressed hard on the joystick, but the inertrons, which were in bad shape, barely compensated; the acceleration shoved the crew down onto their seats. The intercom groaned.

"Hang on tight, Iria. As soon as we exit the atmosphere, I'll activate the hypertrons and it'll be over."

"I'll hang on," she returned.

"Have you calculated the jump factor, Eriks?"

"Two A.L.s."

"That's enough. Altitude? My altimeter seems to be out of whack."

"Forty kilometers. The cruiser's taking off," Erickson warned.

"Zap down those chemicals, Malvert. Show them the *Scorpion* still has sting in its tail. Altitude?"

"Fifty."

"I'll move us into hyperspace when we get to a hundred," Tankar confirmed.

"That could be dangerous!"

"Can't turn back now. Where's the torpedo?"

"Not there yet...oh, yes it is!" On the rear screen a flower of fire erupted, piercing the night.

"We'll need more than one to knock out a cruiser," Tankar noted, "but the first one'll slow them down. Altitude?"

"Eighty-two."

He shook his head. "I thought we were higher. The *Scorpion*'s lost some of her luster. But the hull must be red, if I can believe the thermal indicators. Let me know when we hit a hundred."

"We're there!" Erickson announced.

"Look sharp, Iria, I'm activating the hypertrons—" Suddenly, he turned to Erickson. "You son of a bitch! You blocked the altimeter so I wouldn't see we'd hit 110!"

"We had plenty of time," his friend countered. "And it really isn't a good idea to enter hyper fewer than two hundred kilometers from a planet!"

Tankar cooled off. "Okay. Fine. We have about seven seconds till jump. Get ready...three...two...one...zero." The familiar nausea hit them all. "Let's hope their crew of new recruits won't be able to follow us," he sighed.

"I inspected the cruiser myself this afternoon," Erickson chuckled. "They're going to have a hard time getting their tracer to work." He and Tankar shared a grin. "What route should I calculate, Tankar?"

"Two A.L. One hundred eighty degrees."

"What? You want to go back to Earth? Why? Let's head straight for the world you lived on."

"I have a rendezvous behind the Moon. I never lived on a planet; I apologize for feeding you all a pack of lies. If I'd told you the truth, you'd never have believed me." The look on Erickson's face forced him to explain further. "We're going to meet up with a vessel belonging to the People of the Stars. After that, we'll decide what to do. If you don't want to stay with them, they'll drop you off on the world of your choosing."

"The People of the Stars?"

"They're descendants of the scientists who fled during Kilos II."

"And you came back to Earth to spy on us for them?" Erickson accused.

"No. They don't give a damn about Earth. It's far more complicated. I'll tell you all about it later, but you can be sure I haven't betrayed you."

★　★　★

"Tankar, you're back! Who are these men?"

"Friends who helped me without knowing anything about you all."

"And is the person here a woman friend?"

Tankar smirked. "Calm down, Ana! I'll explain. Right now, we have more urgent matters to attend to. Tan, can we take the *Scorpion* instead of the launch? She's slightly bigger."

"We can try." The Teknor nodded. "It should work."

"I'd really like to keep her. She's a good ship, and she might be useful, since she's armed." Turning to Erickson, Malvert and Iria, he waved and said, "See you all later."

★   ★   ★

"So that's it," Tankar finished telling his story to the Teknor and Anaena. "I can't live on Earth anymore, and I don't think I can live here with you. What's left? A former Empire planet? An external world? I'd feel like a stranger everywhere. When I was with you, I had the hope of going home. Of course, I knew there'd be changes, but I never could've imagined what I found."

"You'll adapt more easily to life on the *Tilsin*, now that that false hope has died," Tan said.

"Perhaps," Tankar conceded. "I don't think you can understand how difficult that would be for me. You see things so differently from me. For example: for you all it's normal to move from one city-state to another. Oh, I know the cultures remain the same, but that's the key. To me, each of your different cities would represent an entirely new world, and I lack the communal spirit that makes you so adaptable. I'd end up having issues with dialects that I didn't fully grasp, old jokes that I simply wouldn't get, like what do you mean when you talk about Jona the Great's spacesuit? What does the Teknor's blow mean? And too many other idioms...."

"You're so impatient, Tankar," Anaena said. "You lived among us for only a few months. Everything's changed since then! We've come to understand that planetary civilizations have many qualities that we'd do well to adopt. It was a hard lesson to learn…much harder for you, of course."

"I won't forget that anytime soon," Tankar grimaced. "All right. I'll try in good faith to adapt. What about my crewmates?"

"Whatever they want," the Teknor promised. "They may remain with us, or we can drop them off on a planet of their choosing." He paused to give Tankar a look, then added, "For you, it might be better if they stayed."

Tankar nodded. "You may be right. I'm exhausted. May I go?"

"I'll take you there," Anaena quickly offered.

Tankar barely recognized his little apartment. Pei's paintings had been framed and new furniture brought in. For a moment, he felt like he was coming home.

"I knew you'd be back, Tankar." Anaena broke into his thoughts. "I would've picked you up myself on an armed launch if you hadn't found a way to escape. Does this décor suit?"

"Yes, thank you, Ana." He studied her. "You know, I really don't deserve all this effort. I'm nothing more than a pig-headed ass who made himself and others unhappy."

"It's not like we were much better! Make an effort, Tankar… please. I'll help you, you'll see. This time you'll make it work."

"Everything around me has gone to pieces. The Empire, the Guards, my self-esteem, my self-confidence. Don't cling to a living corpse, Ana. Any of the lesser *Tilsin* men will be a better choice for you."

"I don't believe you. Let's talk about something else. We put your friends in neighboring apartments. Who are they?"

"The men are friends from the Stellar Guard. The woman is a former aristocrat who was slightly less dreadful than the others."

"She's very beautiful," Anaena observed.

"Yes. The young officers used to call her 'the Inaccessible

Dream'; she was very proud of that. Her family was very wealthy, so none of us could've hoped to marry her, but she's not mean-spirited, just…vain. She did have the courage to pilot her yacht in space." He smiled. "I danced with her once…."

"You're not in love with her, are you?"

He laughed. "Me? I don't love anybody, including myself."

"Yes," Ana said sadly. "I know."

"I'll get over it someday, I suppose. Goodnight, Ana, and thank you." He waited until she had crossed the threshold to close the door behind her.

CHAPTER THREE

A Face in the Abyss

The cosmos unfurled its frigid splendor across the screens of the Teknor's private command post. Tankar paced back and forth in his small apartment, glancing occasionally at the communications screen to see Tan, comfortably ensconced in a low-slung chair, glass in hand, and Anaena, elbows on the gleaming polished wood of the Teknor's desk where she sat.

"What's the point of living when everything around you has gone to hell?" Tankar demanded. "Okay, yes, my life in the Guards may have lacked meaning. Certainly the life I lived was based on a series of lies:

"Fight bravely, be loyal to your superiors, worship the Emperor, and all will go well for you in this world and in the next.

"But above all don't ask questions. Accept the life that has been given to you: kill, pillage, rape if need be. A thousand commoners are worth less than one Stellar Guard. A thousand soldiers are worth less than one Stellar Guard."

He continued reciting the Guards' mantra by heart in a tone so sarcastic it almost certainly would have cost him his life during the Empire.

"You have lovely toys to play with and powerful, speedy starships that can rip out the insides of a planet. Enjoy yourself as you follow the Emperor's orders.

"Leave it to others to answer the tough questions; leave it to your

commanders to devise battle plans until you become a commander...or lay
down your life in battle; leave it to priests to debate the last rites.

"Do you not have the Emperor, a descendant of the divine, who will
never fail you?

"That was my life," he went on. "I knew that not everything
was perfect in the Empire, that best of all possible worlds," he
sneered, "but it wasn't up to me to try to change it!" His tone
turned defensive. "Then the rebellion happened, my starship was
sabotaged, and I found myself adrift in space.

"I wasn't afraid to die; in fact, now I'm sure that it would've
been better for me to have perished the way I should've: as a
Guard! Instead, you rescued me. You fed me and gave me freedom
within your wandering world.

"And then you humiliated me. In your eyes I was just a
planetary dog, barely worth holding in reserve on the off chance
that I might have an interesting secret. I don't blame you for that;
how could you have done anything else?

"To tell you the truth, when I look back on the pitiful beliefs
that served as the foundation of my life and conduct, I have to
admit that you were right to treat me the way you did. I deserved
the contempt that any civilized person feels for a barbarian, but
that contempt proved to me that your society was as unjust and as
cruel as the Empire, since it never even crossed your minds that
my being a barbarian wasn't my fault! Also, it never occurred to
you how dangerous it might be to humiliate a barbarian if you
don't kill him right away. Finally, you never considered that a
barbarian might suffer."

Tankar, knowing that one or both of his listeners would object,
raised his hand to stop them. "I know, I know. After a while, you
changed your mind about me...a little. A few of you even began
to see me as a human being like yourselves. Orena was the first. In
the beginning, I merely amused her. Now I regret how I treated

her. I used her like I would've a commoner girl in the Empire."

Anaena broke in. "She didn't deserve any better! She was the one who took your blueprints!"

"What?" Tankar stopped pacing.

"After we built the tracers, we used the notes you'd left in the lab to develop hyperspatial communicators. We were pretty damn surprised to connect with the *Frank* and to realize they had them as well."

"But...but why did she do it?"

"She suffered from a profound fear of the Mpfifis," the Teknor calmly explained.

Anaena jumped back in. "She was convinced you'd never hand over the blueprints, so she just took them to benefit all the People of the Stars and, I'm sure, to bolster the advantist cause," she added with a sneer. "She also probably hoped to turn you against me." Barely above a whisper she sighed, "She certainly scored on that count."

"So it's her fault that…. Well the past is past." Tankar resumed pacing. "As you know, the theft of the plans reinforced my belief that we had nothing in common. But even that might not have mattered, if you hadn't destroyed my faith, my reason to live, without giving me anything to replace it.

"Oh, nobody engaged in full-on anti-Empire propaganda," he acknowledged with a wave of his arms. "You just said you hated it, and I understood that. But your conversations? Your books? Your way of life? They all served to destroy my faith in the Empire. If a civilization as powerful as yours could develop on such radically different premises from those on Earth...that proved the Emperor was not the divinity he claimed to be." He stopped pacing and looked at the screen. "And then I met Iolia."

His voice softened. "Her people behaved so much more kindly to me than you did, and they were honest with me too. They offered me their faith because they sensed the emptiness in my soul. But it was either too soon or too late: too soon, because the Empire was still imprinted in me; too late, because of the damage you'd already done."

He glared first at the Teknor, then at Anaena. "I hated you. God, I hated you. I truly hated you, Anaena. And then, when circumstances turned us into brothers-in-arms on the unnamed planet, I still might have loved you and saved myself." He resumed pacing. "But I remained certain that you were the one who'd plotted to steal my plans, and then your treatment of Iolia repelled me. So I married Iolia, Iolia the sweet, the gentle, hoping to find with her both respite and love. You know, of course, what happened as the result of my stubbornness, my arrogance, and your prejudice.

"So here I am, once again, returned from Earth where, like a spoiled brat, I sought refuge. You seemed so happy to see me again; you've even encouraged me to assimilate this time. Okay. I'm willing. After all, what other options do I have? Do you really believe I'll have more success if I understand you better?" He stopped pacing again and stared directly at Tan Ekator. "What is it that you believe in, Teknor? What is it that keeps you going?"

"We believe in mankind, Tankar," the Teknor replied softly, put down his glass then shook his head. "Let me rephrase: we believe in intelligence, because there are non-human races that look different from us and yet are human, at least as I understand it. We believe in the type of man you haven't yet become despite your powerful mind, your muscles and your bravery because, in some respects, you're still a child. I don't doubt your manly qualities, Tankar, but they're not enough to make a man. To be able to stare death in the face serves no purpose.

"Most of us Stellarans don't believe in anything else," the Teknor admitted. "We don't deny what we don't know. There may be a God, but, if he exists, he's very different from the deity that appointed the emperors of Earth. After all, Earth is little more than a miserable planet orbiting a tiny star in a medium-sized galaxy.

"He's not the Pilgrims' God who made those people a promise. Call God the unknowable, if you like. Maybe it's reassuring to think that the universe isn't a void, that there's a transcendent being, a creator. I myself am not drawn to that idea; in my opinion, if God doesn't care what happens to human beings, he might as well not exist.

"We know that life sprung up on millions of planets, out of the mud of marshes, from the dirty warmth of early waters. There's no proof that life is part of an established plan; rather that it inevitably resulted from some physiochemical process.

"The abundance of life throughout the cosmos, even on the many worlds where life once thrived only to die out, seems to me proof that life has only one purpose: to propagate itself. Life has a curious quality, a stubborn determination to fight savagely against entropy, to fight to continue even under the worst conditions, to perpetuate itself even where there's no hope.

"Then, as life developed and grew more complex, it evolved a conscience; in time, intelligence followed. The cosmos granted itself a vain witness and a futile judge.

"Our footprint on the cosmos is still tiny; a few planets ravaged by our wars, other tiny worlds added by our efforts, but life is still in its infancy.

"It's only existed in this corner of the universe for the last thousand years. On our mother planet, intelligence is barely a million years old as the first modern humans appeared only forty thousand years ago. Among all the races we've encountered, we know of only two that predate us: the H'rtulus at fifty thousand years, and the Kilitis at sixty thousand. Both have suffered through such hard times that, even now, they're only at our level of development.

"Other species have disappeared, crushed by a blow of the universe – a star going nova or some other cataclysm. We ourselves have crossed the threshold where we could vanish, Tankar, although it's hard to imagine a catastrophe spanning one hundred thousand light-years. Soon we'll venture into new galaxies; in fact, two of our city-state starships already are exploring the Andromeda Nebula.

"We don't think of ourselves as achieving victory over the cosmos. After all, we're little more than fragile insects that die off from disease or senility, but, if we have time, we'll beat those enemies too. We'll spread out, in partnership with allied races, throughout the universe.

"Why will we do all this? Our human will. Intelligent life has no goal in any metaphysical sense. Intelligence sets its own goals, for itself. We'll conquer the universe because we want to, or simply for the fun of it!

"But all of this is just one piece of the puzzle, Tankar, and not the most important piece. The most important piece will fall into place when intelligence conquers itself." The Teknor explained, "What I mean by that is that the more intelligent a being is, the more he sees the absurdity of evil, and the harder he fights against it.

"I know there are species – the Mpfifis, for example – who appear to be both intelligent and evil. I say appear because they're either ill or idiots despite their material success. One has to be either crazy or stupid to use one's talents, one's abilities, to destroy rather than to create, unless one is too confused to know the difference.

"The first goal that mankind set for itself was to extend its consciousness as widely as possible. The second was to perfect that consciousness, to make it as constructive as possible. We're well on our way toward the first goal. But if human beings can't see it through, other species surely will. Unfortunately, we're quite far behind on reaching the second goal," Tan Ekator admitted, "although we Stellarans have advanced further than the Empire. Here on the *Tilsin* you yourself have seen we've still got a long way to go."

The Teknor continued, talking more to himself than to his listeners. "I don't know what motivates any one man. What I do know is that any sane person gets more pleasure from creating than from destroying. It's through creation that man really can blossom, both individually and as a species.

"It isn't easy to think that humanity's big adventure is a collective one, or that a species can achieve immortality in a way that one man cannot. Being alive myself, I want life to continue. I could even project that desire into a belief in personal immortality, but I don't because I think doing that would be lying to myself."

He returned his attention to Tankar. "I sometimes envy people like the Pilgrims who can so easily, so convincingly, lie to themselves. I certainly can't fault you your own barbarian faith, your belief in some sort of a warrior Valhalla, because you sincerely believed it at the time. But you no longer can hold on to that belief, and it's terrifying when you find yourself face-to-face with a blind and deaf universe. We've all of us been afraid, but to be a man is to stare the reality of the abyss in the face, even if it's troubling…even if it's horrifying. Can you do that?"

Tankar wondered, "But if the universe is meaningless how do you fight despair?"

"By committing yourself to give it meaning."

"And what do you do when your faith falters?" Tankar persisted. "There must be times when it fails you."

The Teknor stood and walked toward a screen. The *Tilsin* was stationary in space some distance from a gas nebula that appeared to be expanding its fiery, feathered cloud against a background of stars. The cosmos itself extended in every direction, a black abyss that the stars vainly tried to illuminate.

"What do I do?" the Teknor replied. "I face the universe and, with no illusions whatsoever, I spit in its face."

Anaena interrupted. "Tankar, we're about to emerge. Are you coming?"

"Where?"

"Tan's place. He's spotted a supernova, and we're going to pull in near to it so the astronomers can study it. You don't see one of those very often."

"I'll be there in 10."

Anaena's face disappeared from the screen. Tankar fell back onto his sofa and picked up his glass. Since his return to the *Tilsin*, he'd been drinking a lot without getting drunk.

He had wandered through the past three months as if in a dream, alone most of the time. He performed his military instruction then hid in his apartment to read, meditate, drink and sleep. At first he had spent time with his friends from Earth. Both Erickson and Malvert were taking well to the *Tilsin*. After a stormy start, Iria now found herself at home. The shock of the revolution seemed to have cut her off from her roots, and Tankar almost envied her.

I have to admit the Stellarans have changed since I cleared the path.

Anaena tried anything and everything to keep him occupied, but her very presence reminded him of the past he was trying to escape. They had both suffered. He strangely enjoyed the pain as a sort of punishment for a wrong he only half remembered. Tan would meet him and try to pull him out of his melancholy, but the Teknor always ended the meetings disappointed.

Tan discussed this with his niece. "He'll heal someday, Anaena.

For now, he can't stop blaming himself for Iolia's death, or the deaths of the other Stellarans who died in the Mpfifi attack. I understand, because I feel the same way; the difference is that we all feel the guilt, so it's lighter for being shared."

A deeply unhappy Anaena started to ask, "Do you think...."

"That he will love you one day? You're the only one he's ever loved, Ana. He felt tenderness and affection for his wife, but I don't think he truly loved her. Because he knows or guesses that, he feels even greater remorse. He'll forget, and you're both still so young, you have the future ahead of you."

"I wish I could believe that!"

"Little Ana marrying a planetary," Tan Ekator mused. "That'll be something on the *Tilsin*." Tan grinned.

"But what can I do? He's so miserable."

"Do nothing," her uncle urged. "Either he'll heal on his own, or he never will...but you should remain hopeful."

After brooding over what had felt like a classroom lecture from the Teknor, Tankar got up and ran a hand through his crew cut. He should check out the supernova. At one time he would have been intrigued to observe such a rare cosmic event.

"We waited for you," the Teknor said.

He gave an order and the screens of the gray monitors opened to reveal an enormous disk of fire. It stared at them, suspended above the abyss. Its hair floated in the cosmic wind, and a strong forehead dominated shadowed eyes as a kind of bushy beard waved on the screen.

"What is it? What...?" Anaena stammered and clung to Tankar.

"The supernova." The Teknor spoke calmly. "But I wasn't expecting this."

He tweaked the settings and the face expanded and moved as if to smack the *Tilsin*. It also lost definition, and then it was over. All that remained was bubbling gas where a star once had been.

The communicator screen lit up, and they saw Holonas looking radiant. "It's the sign, Tan! The sign! I have lived to see that God has forgiven mankind!"

Tan hesitated. Should he tell the old man the truth? The Pilgrims were good astronomers. They would figure it out. "Did you try to magnify the picture, Holonas?"

"Do you think we're children, Tan? Of course I know it's a supernova. But tell me: how likely was it that, from a distance, it would take on the appearance of a superhuman at exactly the instant we could see it? It's the sign we were hoping for! Praise the Lord." The screen went blank.

The Teknor spoke softly. "And so the Pilgrimage has ended. Our friends will turn back into humans like us. I doubt that they'll be any happier once their elation dies down. I fear that this well may be the beginning of their real tragedy."

Tankar turned away to hide his tears. Iolia would have been so happy. And because of his own.... He bit his lip and left the room.

EPILOGUE

Tankar slipped into the airlock wearing his spacesuit. No one had seen him. The buzzing of the pumps gradually ebbed, and the airlock was free. He opened the external door and stepped out onto the hull, which shone in the light of the now-distant supernova that no longer looked like a person. Now it looked more like a fraying ball of yarn.

He sat down on a sort of railing that ran the full length of the metal hull into infinity; it was one of 52 such barriers. In about an hour, the *Tilsin* would plunge into hyperspace, and everything below the railing would vanish. Everything above, including Tankar himself minus his feet, would remain in normal space. *It'll take no time at all*, he thought.

He had considered leaping into the void, but his earlier experience of plummeting through space changed his mind. No point in prolonging the agony. Now he had just an hour – nope, 59 minutes – to consider eternity.

He was infinitely weary, his energy drained. The Guards might well consider suicide the worst form of disgrace other than treason, but where were the Guards? And what did honor mean? He saw no future for himself, and he didn't wish to be an exile for the rest of his life, always dreaming of a bygone world. If only Iolia had not died…if only he had not killed her.

Anaena would cry. She loved him, but she would have no trouble finding a better man in one of the city-states. *She'll forget me*, he thought bitterly.

He had no choice. He was finished, a tool that had outlived its purpose. The Empire and the Guards were dead, his faith in tatters, and he could not shed the weight of knowing he had killed the woman he loved. The best thing for him was to disappear.

He regretted nothing. With the exception of Iolia, his conscience was clear. He was no more at fault than the *Scorpion* was. He had been an instrument crafted in a way the Stellarans would never understand. In service to the Empire, his hands had slaughtered other humans, but he felt no responsibility, no blame. And then there were times when he felt nauseous realizing that the Empire had used him – and the other Guards – as little more than executioners.

He looked up and, as astronauts often did, he thought the *Tilsin* was rocking back and forth and that he was swinging upside down. The cold stars shone, and he had a moment of real regret for the worlds he never would see. Then again, he could spend his life crisscrossing the cosmos and still see only a tiny part of the universe.

In any event, the universe was too big for mankind. He thought of Tan's cynical views and the despair behind them. Was the Teknor right? Was the universe simply an enormous blind machine through which men traveled to quench their thirst for certainty?

Maybe the Pilgrims had the answer. They believed in a God other than the one he had been taught to worship and fear. A benevolent God who did not abandon creation even in punishment. Would there be anything left of him after his death? Would he be with Iolia again somewhere beyond space and time? He would have liked to believe so, but, in these last few minutes, he could not. Tan probably was right that humanity's wanderlust had no purpose, that only a race can expect to be immortal.

The human race! Something lived in him, the same something

that lived in early men, that lived even before them, that lived in the early warm seas, something passed to him…something perfect. But he refused to pass it on. The connection forged through the circle of life would be broken forever. The universe had crushed him, so he would snatch victory from the jaws of defeat and, voluntarily, extinguish his contribution to the future.

He checked the time: 10 more minutes.

"Tankar?" Anaena interrupted his musings. "What the hell are you doing? Are you nuts? We're about to dive!"

Aggravated, he turned and saw Anaena standing in front of him, her anxious face within the transparent helmet she wore clearly illuminated by the supernova.

"Quick! I didn't have time to tell anyone I was looking for you. At last, I saw you through the scope. I'm so happy to have found you!"

"Leave me alone, Ana. You can still save yourself."

"Come Tankar, I beg you. I love you," she pleaded, "Please, come…."

"Leave me. I'll never be anything other than a pariah. Let me disappear." When she said nothing, he continued, "I don't deserve you."

"You're a coward!" She stood so close to him that he feared her magnetic soles might lose their grip on the hull, so he put his hands on her shoulders to protect her.

"You may be right, Ana. You probably are, and that's why I don't want to live anymore."

"Fine." She shrugged. "So I'm in love with a coward. Well, that's just too damn bad. But I'd take hell, the sky, nothingness, anything would be better than living without you. I'm staying here." She reached out to him. "Sit down and hold me close to you…."

He grabbed her and began to walk her toward the airlock. She pulled away from him and drew a fulgurator from the pocket of her spacesuit. She pointed it at him. "Oh, no you don't! No way you're putting me back in the airlock!"

"Don't be stupid, Ana! You've got your whole life ahead of you!"

"Without you, I don't care." She maintained her distance and her grip on the fulgurator. "We still have a few minutes, so think. Did you ever really try to adapt to life on the *Tilsin*? No. Baby Tankar broke his toys because they weren't exactly what he wanted. You're so sure you're a pariah on the *Tilsin*? I call bullshit! One of these days you'll make me believe that we're right that planetaries…." She paused.

"You can't forgive yourself for Iolia – do you think I can forgive myself?" she resumed. "You know we could've been happy together. Our children could've become part of a new generation of Stellarans who'd know nothing of prejudice because we're going to have to join forces with the planetaries to fight off the Others.

"In any event, I'm staying right here on this hull. Now you'll have my death as well as Iolia's on your conscience."

Tankar stared at her. She had tied her lustrous red hair into a thick bun at the nape of her neck so that she might fit into one of the transparent helmets. "Our children playing the game of the universe?" he mused aloud. "What if the universe isn't playing a game? What if it's the dumb blind beast the Teknor thinks it is?" In a swift flick of his wrist he wrangled the fulgurator from Anaena's hand. Then he embraced her and jumped into the airlock and put her back on her feet.

Propping herself up against the metal wall, Anaena trembled with nervous tension, still unable to believe that she had won, that she had saved him from himself. He did not lock the door right away, instead giving a lingering look at the constellations above them.

"What are you doing? Close the damn thing!"

Tankar lowered the handle, and, as the heavy door pivoted shut, he turned to the woman he loved and smiled. "I just wanted to take one last look into the abyss."

FLAME TREE PRESS
FICTION WITHOUT FRONTIERS
Award-Winning Authors & Original Voices

Flame Tree Press is the trade fiction imprint of Flame Tree Publishing, focusing on excellent writing in horror and the supernatural, crime and mystery, science fiction and fantasy. Our aim is to explore beyond the boundaries of the everyday, with tales from both award-winning authors and original voices.

•

You may also enjoy:
American Dreams by Kenneth Bromberg
Second Lives by P.D. Cacek
Vulcan's Forge by Robert Mitchell Evans
The Widening Gyre by Michael R. Johnston
The Blood-Dimmed Tide by Michael R. Johnston
Kosmos by Adrian Laing
The Sky Woman by J.D. Moyer
The Guardian by J.D. Moyer
The Goblets Immortal by Beth Overmyer
A Killing Fire by Faye Snowden
The Bad Neighbor by David Tallerman
A Savage Generation by David Tallerman
Ten Thousand Thunders by Brian Trent
Two Lives: Tales of Life, Love & Crime by A Yi

Horror titles available include:
Snowball by Gregory Bastianelli
Thirteen Days by Sunset Beach by Ramsey Campbell
The Influence by Ramsey Campbell
The Wise Friend by Ramsey Campbell
The Haunting of Henderson Close by Catherine Cavendish
The Garden of Bewitchment by Catherine Cavendish
Boy in the Box by Marc E. Fitch
Black Wings by Megan Hart
Will Haunt You by Brian Kirk
We Are Monsters by Brian Kirk
Hearthstone Cottage by Frazer Lee
Those Who Came Before by J.H. Moncrieff
Stoker's Wilde by Steven Hopstaken & Melissa Prusi
They Kill by Tim Waggoner
The Forever House by Tim Waggoner

•

Join our mailing list for free short stories, new release details, news about our authors and special promotions:

flametreepress.com